REASONABLE DOUBT

THE DOUBT SERIES - BOOK ONE

JASMINE CASSIDY

STORIES & DAYDREAMS, LLC

Formatted with Vellum

To all the versions of myself. We did it.

AUTHOR NOTE

This book contains themes of sexual harassment, violent situations including gun and knife use and physical assault, as well as the mention of suicide and sexual assault not on the page.

This book contains sexual content and is not suitable for young readers.

REASONABLE DOUBT *(noun)* -

a doubt that arises or remains upon fair and thorough
consideration of the evidence or lack thereof.

CHAPTER 1

NAOMI

I stood in the tiny open plan kitchen the great city of Crestwood graciously kept stocked with stale granola bars and burnt coffee beans.

It had been less than an hour since I downed four shots of espresso at miraculous speed, but the coffee had done nothing to chase away the constant pressure behind my eyes, and I had too much to do not to be alert. If I were thinking logically, I would have told myself that getting another cup was ridiculous, but since I had gotten very little sleep in the last couple of days, weeks, months, or years, my voice of reason was long gone.

Chucking my empty paper cup from the much nicer shop around the corner of our twenty-story downtown building, I checked my phone. I had maybe thirty minutes before the head district attorney and my boss, John Coleman, would be ready to go to our last hearing before the biggest case of my career began.

I picked up the lukewarm pot, only to put it back down when I found the cup dispenser empty. Rummaging through the cabinets with no luck, I stared daggers at the trashcan where I had foolishly discarded my perfectly fine one.

"You alright, Naomi?" Dorian strolled past me to the large white refrigerator that creaked as he opened its shabby door.

"Fine," I murmured, rummaging through the snack basket to look busy before I made a clean getaway.

Dorian Keates was tall and lanky, that skinny strong that

basketball players achieved, with a high yellow skin tone that turned red before brown in the sun. He was a nice enough guy, but we had barely said two words to each other when I was prosecuting battery and domestic dispute charges for the four years I had been in the office before I'd gotten my promotion.

Now, six months had passed since Coleman had asked me to replace Dorian as the second chair in the Drayman case, and it felt like I saw him everywhere.

Even though he wasn't working with Coleman anymore, Dorian had been nothing but kind to me whenever we bumped into each other, so I accepted that the uneasy feeling was probably one-sided but still didn't like to linger longer than I needed to around him.

Dorian smiled as he pulled out two canned coffee drinks with his name scrawled on the side and extended one out to me. I smiled politely, but didn't accept. Unperturbed, he set the can down on the counter beside the snack trays. "Come on, I know you don't want to drink that old coffee, and I don't think Regina remembered to order fresh cups, anyway."

I smiled, picturing our receptionist tapping her pen to the beat of whatever James Brown song she had playing just loud enough that you couldn't hear it unless you were at her desk. Last holiday season, I had bought her wireless earbuds, but she told me she didn't like things in her ears and, besides, she was bringing a little groove to everyone's day.

Dorian's smile got bigger at the sight of mine and, being that this was the longest interaction we'd had, I noticed for the first time that he wasn't a bad looking guy. His brown eyes were playful, making him look younger than his thirty-eight years, and he had a symmetry to his face that gave his sharp features a soft touch.

"Thanks." I took the drink as my phone buzzed, gave a quick wave of it as a goodbye and rushed back to my desk. I glossed over the 'How are you?' message from my dad as I sat down and promised myself I would respond later. Right now, I wanted to go over our case file one more time.

Last night, we learned that the defendant, Ronan Drayman, had switched lawyers for the fourth time, and I was determined to prevent another delay of our trial date.

It had already been three years since the suspected murder of his wife, Candace, and while we didn't have a body, her long disappearance and the nonstop news coverage about the missing socialite was enough for Coleman to get the indictment last year.

Drayman was extremely rich and just as entitled, so his arrest made the front page and garnered weekly updates the city ate up, but he had avoided a trial until now. His new representation was the Charles and Charles firm—a flashy legal team that I'm sure promised him further delays or even a quick dismissal. I had heard plenty about the father/son team Langston and Malcolm and knew they were the worst kind of defense attorneys.

Grandstanding press conferences, dramatic showboating in the courtroom and million dollar retainers, the duo only took on cases that kept the cameras on them. Langston had at least built the company from the ground up, making it what it was today, but Malcolm Charles had been born with a diamond-encrusted spoon in his mouth and fell into the family business ten years ago after floating through the best schools in the world, including my alma mater. Every time I saw his face in the news, I was grateful he was five years older than me and I had missed having to share any classes with the man.

Unfortunately, I still knew all about his playboy exploits. Regina loved to fill me in on any recent drama within the lawyer community, no matter how many times I told her I didn't care, and she especially loved Malcolm Charles. He had a different woman on his arm every month, and with the amount of photos she shoved in my face of him attending galas and award ceremonies, I doubted Malcolm was much more than a pretty face who smiled at the camera while the people under him did the real work.

I had never been up against such a powerhouse law firm before, but for all their bravado and showmanship, I had spent every waking moment and even some barely conscious ones of the past six months going over this case and there was nothing they could throw at us that Coleman and I couldn't handle.

We had already successfully suppressed the proceedings, with no press being allowed in the courtroom and no vital information about the case being disclosed to the public until after closing arguments. Langston and Malcolm would have to keep their theatrics to the courthouse steps.

"Naomi, have you seen this article?!" Regina was already pushing a picture of the man I was soon going to see toward me before I could respond. "Malcolm Charles is in Mahogany magazine!!" she whisper screamed. My heart involuntarily skipped a beat at the image. He was attractive; I'll give him that.

Malcolm stood with his hands in his pockets, filling one side of the magazine page, wearing head-to-toe black, with a ruby red tie accented by the same color cufflinks. His smooth dark skin made the slight beard connecting to his perfectly tailored fade look slicked on like butter. I took the magazine to stop Regina from suffocating me with it and scanned the page.

Malcolm Charles Will Get You Out of Trouble...And into Some, too.

I rolled my eyes at the title and didn't read further, looking up at Regina instead. She was wearing her usual light blue cardigan that she kept in the office because it was always on the brink of freezing, no matter the weather outside, over a simple black dress that went to her ankles.

She had never volunteered her age in all the time I'd known her, but Regina had that classy regalness that only Black women over a certain age could portray after they stopped giving a fuck about what other people thought.

When it was clear I wouldn't play along, she snatched the magazine back from me and pointed to a passage in the multi-page article. "The thirty-five-year-old eligible bachelor spends his days arguing for the powerful elite and his nights rubbing elbows with the affluent. He fits right in, having grown up as both..." I focused back on my computer, but Regina wasn't having it, only speaking louder. "It says here he's never been in love!" She dropped her voice a couple of octaves and then continued. "'While I've been honored to know many gorgeous and talented women, I still haven't found that magic yet.'"

I started typing with more force than needed. Of course, Malcolm Charles was in a fashion magazine talking about stuff that didn't matter while I was losing sleep and stressing over my career. "Regina, the man keeps criminals out of prison. I don't care about his love life," I groaned.

Winning this case would bring justice to Candace Drayman and prove to Coleman that he hadn't made a mistake in asking me to come on board. This was my ticket to handling bigger cases on my own and a major step toward my goal of becoming the first Black female Head District Attorney in Crestwood. My mother had been a prosecutor for fifteen years before she became a judge, and I was going to make her proud. The work was worth it.

"You're too young to be this grumpy," Regina said as I stood to pack up my heavy bag. "I'm not grumpy. I just have principles." Regina side-eyed me and tucked the folded magazine under her arm. "Mmhmm, well, I can sacrifice some principles for someone as fine as Malcolm Charles. I'm not too old to show him a little something." I huffed a small laugh and looked around to see if anyone was listening in on our highly inappropriate conversation, but everyone was doing actual work like I should have been.

Regina must have noticed my demeanor change because she leaned in and whispered, "You tell him I said hi and that he can come by the office anytime. I'll take *any* affidavit." She fanned herself with the magazine as she walked away, leaving me with my mouth open.

I quickly shut it as I glimpsed Coleman heading my way, his stout stature framed in a brown suit that matched his skin tone and patches of his short hair that hadn't completely grayed yet. He clasped his hands together when he got to me and smiled. "You ready for this, Ms. Vine?" He asked, his assured voice honed from hours in the courtroom. "Absolutely, sir!" I said, matching his energy. His wry smile blocked out any other thoughts of that smug attorney we were going to beat.

Coleman and I had discussed potential arguments Langston and Malcolm might have for a delay during our drive over, and I was confident they would not get the outcome they wanted.

The judge had granted three postponements already for Drayman's past attorneys so that they could fully acquaint themselves with the case material, but there had to be a line, and we would make sure this was it.

"Chime in at anytime in there, Naomi. You know this case, and we're in this thing together." Butterflies fluttered in my stomach, and I couldn't tell if they were from fear or anticipation as I nodded my head.

We walked through the open, thick wooden door into the

judge's chambers, and I readied to meet our opposition. Langston Charles sat on a small leather couch against the merit-lined wall, silently engrossed in a thin black leather folder in his hands. But it was the standing figure, all dark and too handsome in a deep blue bespoke suit, that caught my attention.

Malcolm turned from the judge's desk and took me in for only a moment before approaching my boss. "Mr. Coleman, great to see you again," Malcolm said as he extended his hand. Coleman took it, but the handshake was brief.

"Mr. Charles," my boss returned. Malcolm again glanced my way and gave a smirk, but otherwise discarded my presence as if I were a piece of lint on his fancy suit. He turned back to the judge's desk, and my fingernails dug into my palms as I ignored the warmth of my cheeks.

Langston, who hadn't seemed to notice or care that we had entered, finally stood and patted Coleman on the back. "John! Lovely to see you. Let's see if you can actually make it to court this time," he mused.

Coleman's lips thinned into a straight line, and his brow knit tightly, but he said nothing. I knew Langston and Coleman were around the same age and had heard about their many bouts in court, with Coleman being on the losing end most of the time.

"Oh, lighten up John, it's a joke." Langston turned his twinkling eyes to me, his smile wide as he extended his hand. I noticed a large Whitmore class ring on his middle finger. "I see you've got some new blood in that office of yours! It's a pleasure, Ms. Vine."

I nodded with a polite smile and dropped his hand, not wanting to betray Coleman with anything further and still feeling the sting from Malcolm's disregard. I looked over at the rude man and sucked in a breath when I realized he was staring directly at me. Startled by his intense gaze, I turned back to Langston and broke the connection.

"Mr. Charles, I wouldn't doubt that we'll see you in court, and I suggest you get your opening statement in order." I said cooly. Langston only chuckled. "Oh, I like you, Ms. Vine. Looking forward to it." Langston glanced at his son, and I caught the subtle nod he gave him. I followed Langston's gaze to see Malcolm's stern frown before he turned his back on all of us.

Judge Lee came in from a side door in the back of the office behind his desk, taking everyone's focus. "Perfect, everyone's here. Let's get started. I have a trial coming back from recess in thirty minutes." Langston stepped forward. "Well, it's quite simple, Your Honor. My client has just retained my counsel, and we will need sufficient time to review the files to construct a case." Coleman spoke before the judge could respond. "Your client has had plenty of time to find a defense. He's been through firm after firm and has postponed these proceedings long enough."

Malcolm stepped up next, just as calm as his father appeared, his eyes fixed on the judge. "Your Honor, Charles and Charles weren't involved then, so I can't speak to the actions of other attorneys, but this is a delicate case, and our client has just disclosed his alibi, something the prosecution doesn't yet have." Langston tapped his black folder, directing his practiced smile at Coleman.

Drayman claimed to be home alone after Katherine had gone out for a late night walk. It was one of the main reasons the prosecution could indict him. Coleman's expression went blank, but I noticed his mouth twitching. I was talking before I realized what I was doing.

"Your Honor, the defense is attempting to prolong this case under the guise of a nonexistent alibi that appeared out of thin air." I moved in closer to the judge's desk as I spoke, bringing me next to Malcolm. He was much taller than I was and made his height apparent as he looked down at me with that same blasé smirk.

"Apologies, I wasn't aware Ms. Vine was a psychic and already knows not to take Mr. Drayman's alibi seriously without looking at a single shred of evidence." Malcolm cocked his head to the side, continuing to analyze me as he spoke. "Perhaps the prosecution doesn't need the extra time after all? What a bold stance to take during your first murder trial."

I struggled to keep my focus on the judge as heat inched up my body. Embarrassment pricked at my skin like tiny needles, but I would not let it show, and Coleman was giving me the space to handle the argument.

"Not psychic, Your Honor, just smart enough to know when an attorney is grasping at straws because they're afraid of going to trial." I turned to look up at Malcolm, our eyes meeting. "And while this is my first murder trial, Mr. Charles, I advise you not to underestimate my abilities. Perhaps if you focused more on the case rather than being in magazines, you would know that your client already submitted an alibi."

Malcolm's smirk turned into a full-blown smile. I focused on making my point but felt an odd shiver run up my spine. "Didn't know you were a fan." I scoffed, forgetting where I was for a second. "Hardly. Everything I know about you has been against my will." I waited for his rebuttal, but all Malcolm did was stare down at me with the same bright eyes his father had. Although Malcolm's looked...hungrier. Like a predator savoring the moment right before it took its prey.

Judge Lee chimed in, breaking the quiet. "How long have you had this new alibi?" His tone suggested he did not like to be played with, which made Malcolm's smile finally falter, but he still didn't seem fazed.

"Your Honor, we just took this case last night, and we received the information when we met with our client right before this meeting. While Mr. Drayman gave a statement about his whereabouts the night of his wife's disappearance, it was the same night as the incident, and he was obviously not thinking straight. Now, he realizes his honest mistake and would like to set the record straight. With witnesses."

While Malcolm spoke, Langston handed both the judge and Coleman paperwork from his black folder. Judge Lee was quiet as he looked over the document, and I peered at Coleman's to see what nonsense they were trying to pull. Drayman now claimed he was at one of his establishments, a gentleman's club called Marlow's, with five people listed for confirmation. Coleman huffed out an irritated sigh. "Your Honor, their client is simply buying an alibi because he knows his old one won't stick. This is laughable!"

The judge looked at the Charles men with a vexed expression and then eyed my boss and I almost sympathetically. "I don't like surprises, gentlemen, and you will find that this won't work in the future, but I will allow this new alibi."

"Your Honor—" Judge Lee put up a hand to stop me from continuing. "The prosecution will receive one extra day before trial; detectives can contact these new witnesses, and you may raise the discarded alibi during cross-examination."

I worked not to slump my shoulders at the defeat and nodded once to the judge. "This trial starts Friday, everyone. Close my office door when you leave, please." As he said it, Judge Lee was standing and heading for the same side door he had entered from.

"Thank you, Your Honor," Langston smiled, and Coleman's expression was heading towards a grimace. I didn't even glance at Malcolm, knowing that the smile that made me a little light-headed earlier would probably make me want to smack it off his face right now. They knew the judge would probably be on our side and wouldn't readily grant any significant extra time, something we might need now that Drayman had a shiny new alibi. We had a day and a half to investigate this, while the defense probably had already been through all the other case files with their dozens of associates.

I'd be the first to admit that I wasn't the best at losing, which is why I was fine heading straight for the door, but found my path blocked by an annoying giant. Malcolm waited patiently until I met his eyes to speak.

"Nice to have met you, Ms. Vine." Thankfully the smile wasn't there, but that smirk was, and it wasn't lost on me I now garnered a goodbye when I apparently wasn't worth an introduction.

"See you in court," I responded curtly, maneuvering past him and continuing out the door with Coleman close behind. The defense could worry about shutting it, since they weren't worried about time.

CHAPTER 2

MALCOLM

Naomi Vine. The headshot I found on the Crestwood County website didn't do her nearly enough justice. She was stunning. She was also one of those stuck-up Black women who turned their noses up at anything remotely fun. Boarding school and my mother's many failed setups afforded me the ease to spot her type a mile away.

Still, there was something about Naomi that kept her on my mind as my father and I walked to the elevators. Maybe it was the way she inserted herself into the argument instead of staying quiet and letting John talk, like I figured she would do, since this was her first case in the spotlight.

Or maybe it was the genuine disdain on her face when she called me out about the article. It wasn't my fault I was the most eligible bachelor in Crestwood. Well... not entirely, anyway. Women were fun and plentiful in this city, so why limit myself? I was also very good at my job, and my firm was coming back into the good graces of the public eye thanks to my influence over the last ten years.

"We have a meeting with Ronan at three." As always, Langston's voice threatened to impinge on my good mood. I hated having to play nice with my father, but it was a necessary evil until I could oust him from the company for good. "I'm aware," I said as we stepped into the elevator. "The only thing they had was the loose alibi, and I know John can see the writing on the wall," my father added.

The doors opened to the garage, and I walked out, fully intending to head to my car and let Langston continue to babble on his own. From a young age, I realized my father loved nothing more than the sound of his own voice. "That Naomi, though..." Her name from his mouth halted my steps, and I turned to see his slightly dazed look, as he was no doubt thinking of the woman in question. "...She might be fun."

I couldn't tolerate talking to him for very long, but he had somehow gotten on my last nerve in record time. "Worry about shoring up those convenient new witnesses you and Ronan cooked up, instead of daydreaming of a woman half your age." I turned again as Langston's laugh bounced off the garage walls. "Whatever you say, son."

The meeting with Ronan was short by my design. The judge's acceptance of his new alibi pleased him; and although I disregarded his feelings, a happy Ronan was easier to manage.

I didn't even want this case. Bottom-feeders like Drayman were the exact opposite direction I was trying to steer my firm, but if Langston had his way, his kind would be our only clientele.

What was important was that we were back in the limelight where Charles and Charles belonged, and I was going to make sure we stayed there for the right reasons. It didn't hurt that Drayman was paying a premium for our services, well over what even my father would have considered asking for. Not that I needed the money, but this case was murky, and if I was going to get my hands dirty, I was going to make a dent in this rich asshole's pocket while doing it.

I wasn't above playing the game and was a pro at finding the loopholes in our Swiss cheese like justice system, but there were boundaries. I refused to be like my father, who never had time for things like standards or integrity, in or out of the court-room. The day our board of directors voted to give me majority control and added another Charles to the firm's name was the happiest of my life. Mainly because I suspected it was Langston's worst. I didn't care what he portrayed to the public.

But my father was the furthest from my mind as I looked over the information my investigator Sloan had dug up on Naomi Vine. The sun setting through my wall to wall glass windows always added an orange glow to my expansive office in the evening, but the hue was doing nothing to shine a light on the woman I couldn't get out of my mind.

I flipped through the measly pages and narrowed my eyes. The woman was boring.

She graduated from Whitmore for both undergrad and law school, and then accepted the job at the district attorney's office four years ago, despite offers from prestigious, higher-paying law firms. She owned a one-bedroom home in Mid-City, with her dog Mac as her only companion.

No husband, no kids, no boyfriend. From what Sloan could gather, her last relationship had ended two years ago with some chef, and she didn't have a social life. I scanned the infor-mation on her ex and came to the same conclusion I had the other four times I had read his bio. Theodore Williams seemed vanilla on paper, and he quickly moved on from Naomi because he had a one-year-old child with another woman. *Why did they break up?* I chucked the useless thought with a scowl and kept reading.

The most exciting thing about Naomi was her family. Her mother, Frances, was a fantastic prosecutor in her day, now a small claims judge. Her father, Augustine, owned Vine, one of the best restaurants in Crestwood, and her brother, Dante, was an entertainment lawyer for some of the biggest names in sports.

I took another look at the picture included in the file of her brother. He was engaged to Annalise Taylor, a well-known model and influencer, but that's not how I recognized him. We had crossed paths during my last year in undergrad when he had been a freshman, finding ourselves at a lot of the same parties and events for future Black lawyers. I ran into him more recently at our shared gym a few times, but we never talked past shallow greetings. Maybe it was time I changed that.

My assistant Camden walked into my office unannounced, rattling off information as he always did with his eyes locked on an iPad. "Before you leave, I'm reminding you that you have a Zoom with O'shea Hamilton and his team tomorrow morning at eight and then a lunch with May Johnson at La Boheme, so try not to make it a late night." Camden had been with me since my first day at the firm and kept track of my entire life. He was also an impeccable dresser, so I let him organize my suits for numerous galas, court appearances, and other camera-guaranteed events. Today he wore a perfectly fitted cream colored Zegna suit that I probably wouldn't see again this year.

I wasn't under the illusion that I was easy to work for. I kept long hours, and Camden had to manage my substantial business and social calendars, while also handling the women who were bold enough to track him down when they couldn't reach me anymore. He earned his bonus every year. "Cancel the lunch with May and push O'shea to noon. Also, get me Kris Sloan now." Camden eyed me curiously but headed back out of my office. "Done and done. Mr. Sloan will be on line two in three minutes."

I looked back down at Naomi's file for the fifth time, hoping it would somehow answer the weird feeling I had. The woman I met in Judge Lee's office wasn't boring. She was fiery, self-assured, and definitely had a stick up her ass, but not boring. There was something else about Naomi that these pages weren't telling me, and Sloan was going to find it.

Chapter 3

NAOMI

"I have a large Americano with an extra shot and a splash of milk for Naomi!"

I thanked the barista and cradled the only thing keeping my eyes open for nearly eighteen hours. Since the disastrous meeting with the judge yesterday afternoon, I had been doing prep interviews with our first two witnesses, while also staying in contact with our detectives all day as they confirmed Drayman's new alibi.

They hadn't talked to everyone yet, but at least three people were confident that they had seen him at Marlow's, and that was enough to cause doubt in our case. I tried hard not to curse out loud as I walked the short distance back to the office.

The obvious fabrication of the alibi was frustrating, but the truly irritating thing that had long sighs spilling from my lips every few minutes was the audacity of Malcolm Charles! Every time I involuntarily pictured the man staring down at me, I wanted to punch something.

It wasn't like me to lose my cool, and definitely not in a professional setting, but Malcolm got under my skin in a way that made it hard to think straight.

I had tried to apologize to Coleman for my outbursts, but he didn't seem to mind. He was more concerned with how we were going to prove Drayman's guilt. Without a body, prosecuting this case was already difficult, and all our witnesses focused on Drayman's past dealings to showcase his deplorable character. We didn't have a scene of the crime or any physical evidence, so our case would be over if Langston and Malcolm convinced the jury of that alibi. Malcolm's cocky smirk crossed my mind again as I clicked the button for the elevator in the office lobby, and a few colorful words flew, getting a gasp and wide eyes from the woman I hadn't noticed beside me. I would wipe that smile off his face, even if it meant never sleeping again.

My phone buzzed, alerting me I only had twenty percent battery life left, and I rolled my eyes. I needed to get a new phone as soon as this case was over. It had started dying halfway through the day, and I rarely remembered to eat, let alone charge the thing. I made it to our floor, and my phone buzzed again.

"I get it, you're dying. Join the club!" I moaned and then stopped short when I saw Myra's smile pop up on my screen. I had barely seen my best friend since I'd taken on the Drayman case, and she pointed it out every time I had a second to talk.

Myra was on assignment in New York trying to interview the elusive Martin Kline, who had arguably the biggest case of the year looming behind Drayman's, but she somehow was both a badass journalist and had an active social life. I was not as good at multitasking.

I hovered over the accept button, but paused when I heard distant voices coming from down the hall. It was ten at night, and I was sure the last person had left hours ago. When I heard Coleman's chuckle, I moved toward his office, forgetting all about Myra's call.

His private space took up the whole back corner of our floor, and he had his own assistant, Kate, who I noticed wasn't at her desk when I passed.

I stopped at the door when I saw Coleman pacing and, to my surprise, Dorian standing with an open file. Although the door was open, I gently knocked to get their attention. Coleman stopped his movement, giving me a huge grin, while Dorian opted for a more subdued nod of his head. He didn't look surprised to see me, but didn't seem all that happy about it either.

"Glad you're here, Ni. I was just going to call you! Dorian found our alibi killer!" The shock of his words hit me with a mixture of disbelief and mistrust, but Coleman took my expression as a match to his excitement. "That's right! It doesn't matter how much money you have, the truth can always be found!" Coleman's booming laugh filled the room as I glanced at Dorian for an explanation, but he had gone quiet.

"Dorian found a resident in Drayman's old high-rise who heard him in the building's stairwell, arguing with someone about the murder right after it happened!" I looked at our proposed savior again and caught the clenching of his jaw as he focused on the papers in his hands.

"But our detectives interviewed all the residents, and no one saw Drayman that night," I murmured, hearing the doubt in my voice. Dorian cleared his throat. "I had some time between cases...and I wasn't trying to step on anyone's toes, Naomi. I just wanted to help." He paused, waiting for me to say something, but all I could do was nod. "Well, like I said, I had some free time, so I went through the files and found a kid. They never interviewed Jack Stone, sixteen then. His parents wouldn't allow it, but with the wait for the trial, he's nineteen now."

A kid? I tried to scan my memory of the Stone family while Dorian continued. "He was easy to miss because Jack wasn't in the original files. I figured checking everyone's background in the building couldn't hurt and got lucky." Dorian handed me the folder he was holding as he spoke. "He told me he rode in the elevator with Drayman and Candace that night.

He recalled the time because he was running late for a concert."

I vaguely recalled the Stones in our information. If true, this was exactly what could take Ronan Drayman down. We could easily verify the date because of the concert. This kid would be legal now, and he was a neighbor, so his ID would be a positive one. It was perfect. So why did it feel off?

Was it because I thought it was too good to be true, or was my reluctance coming from the uncertainty that seemed to fill the room about my standing on the case?

This was my one shot to prove I belonged at that table, and I spent countless nights combing through these files and still failed. Coleman said he was planning on calling me, but what was he going to say? I smiled as much as I could muster to hide the lump growing in my throat, wishing that the words I needed to say didn't sting so much.

"This is amazing, Dorian."

He smiled for the first time since I'd walked in, and the genuineness made me feel terrible. I wished I were happy Dorian had found the smoking gun in the case. "Thanks, Naomi. It was really your organization of all the files that made it easy to look through."

He was trying to lessen the blow, and I appreciated the effort. Ronan murdered Candace Drayman, and she deserved justice, no matter who prosecuted the case. I would take the setback with grace and cry when I got home. Like an adult. Coleman was still beaming when I turned my attention back to him to begin what was sure to be his delicate dismissal speech.

"Since Dorian has gone above and beyond, I think he would do great as the third chair. You agree, Ni?"

Third chair? Relief flooded my nervous system. "Yes!" My voice was a little high, but I didn't care. I caught sight of Dorian's own relief leaving his face as he spotted me eyeing him.

"Thanks for the catch, Dorian. Looking forward to working together." I hoped he believed my words, as I tried to believe them myself. Since I had no reason to dislike Dorian, it was time to stamp down the weird feeling I had about him. "Great. Let's get to work." Coleman was too excited for me to bring up that it was inching toward eleven at night, and when I looked over at Dorian pulling up a chair, we shared a knowing smile that told me he was thinking the same. Resigned, I pulled up my seat to Coleman's desk.

It was past midnight when I pulled into my driveway and literally ran the short distance with my heavy bag to my door to get away from the cold. To anyone outside of Crestwood, this weather would have been fine, but for someone born and bred here, anything below seventy-eight degrees was winter, and the temperature had dropped. It didn't help that I had forgotten to leave my porch light on again and that my key didn't want to go into the lock. After a few jabs, I set my bag down, turned on my phone's flashlight, and saw something silver and hard lodged in the keyhole.

What the hell is that? I squinted to get a better look, but still couldn't tell what it was. My black Labrador, Mac, howled from the backyard, and I stood upright. I'd buried the remote to my overstuffed garage in one of my kitchen cabinets, and my dog would not quiet down until he saw me, so I rushed around back before he woke the entire neighborhood.

My two-year-old fur baby immediately jumped at me when I pushed open my side wooden gate. My saint of a dog walker, Lydia had left his harness on from their walk a few hours earlier and now it hung half on Mac's body, no doubt from him tugging at the pink and gray material trying to get it off so he could properly chew it to shreds. "Hush up before these people call the cops on us!" I whisper-scolded, and Mac answered with more loud barks. I shushed him as I walked, and he hurried along beside me through my sliding back door.

My bag made a loud thud on my bedroom floor, and I moved on to the kitchen to give my wild animal a dog treat so I could distract him enough to shimmy the harness off completely.

Lydia made sure Mac had his dinner and a long walk, but he always expected a little treat no matter how late I came home. I ignored the voice in my head that told me to remove whatever the obstruction was from my door's keyhole and headed to the bathroom for a long shower while Mac tried to eat his treat and jump on me at the same time.

Chapter 4

NAOMI

Coleman wanted us to ride together on the first day to show up as a unified front. It also lessened the chances of one of us getting stuck in the courthouse's gridlock-prone parking lot and being caught alone by any wayward reporters who sniffed around looking for a scoop.

He said we could sleep in, but by six am I gave up. Mac was happy for the slow morning since we went for a nice long walk as the sun came up and he got to nibble on a piece of bacon from the actual breakfast I made for myself instead of rushing out of the house scarfing down whatever granola bar was mushed in the bottom of my bag. The early start also gave me time to consider my outfit.

I usually stuck with pants suits but couldn't help the sleek professional black dress with stockings and black pumps to match. Myra had always called me a bad bitch who took no prisoners, and whether I deserved the moniker, I wanted to embody the role today.

I put my hair up in a tight bun just before I left my house and prayed it stayed together long enough for me to get through the trial before it sprang wild again. Peering at my dark laptop screen, I noticed curls on either side of my head trying to escape. With my fingers, I leaned into the poor makeshift mirror, trying to reposition the pieces without messing up the rest of my hair. It would take fifteen minutes I didn't have in the bathroom if I had to take it completely down.

"I told you to get some Curly Girl pomade!" Regina said as she appeared at my side, making me jump. "That stuff works miracles, which is what you need for them curls you don't take care of." I could hear the reproach in her voice and ignored it. Keeping up with my wayward curls was a full-time job in itself. I'd thought about cutting it, but honestly, I didn't think my face shape suited it. That, and my mother would kill me.

"Was there something you needed, Regina?" She sniffed at my brisk tone, but handed me the small brown box in her hand. "Dorian just called in and asked you to bring extra bulbs for the court projector." A groove formed between my brows while I shifted the box around in my hand. Maybe I was still worried about my standing with Coleman, but it rubbed me the wrong way that Dorian was telling me what to do.

Regina lightly tapped my shoulder and gave me a smile. "He said he forgot to grab them this morning on his way to the courthouse." Now, I was even more confused, but I worked not to telegraph my emotions and gave Regina a nod. "Okay, thank you." Instead of leaving, she leaned in, slightly hovering over me. "You're gonna kill it in that courtroom today. I see you in that 'I mean business' outfit!"

Her words didn't help the nervous energy I was pretending didn't exist, but they brought a genuine smile to my lips. Regina squeezed my shoulder again before leaving, and as soon as she moved out of my line of sight, I saw Coleman making his way down the hallway toward me. He got to my desk just as I stood to meet him. "Morning, Naomi! I hope you got some sleep."

He handed me a hot cup of office coffee, and I took it, even though I had already had two Americanos before coming in. "Enough to be alert today! I'm all set to head to the courthouse when you are." We still had plenty of time before the trial started, but there was only so much prepping I could do.

"Great, let's head out. We can go over the opening state-ment one more time on the way. Dorian reminded me that the projector always gives us trouble, so he's already at the court-house, making sure it works by the time we get there." I nodded absently, stuffing the small box of bulbs into my already stuffed bag. I had spent weeks putting together a PowerPoint to accom-pany Coleman's opening statement.

Why hadn't *I* thought of testing it out in the courtroom? Dorian had just got back on the case, but he was already three steps ahead of me. "He's been there since seven. I'm pretty sure the man doesn't need sleep!" Coleman mused. I ignored the pit in my stomach and hooked my bag on my shoulder as we both started toward the elevators.

"You know, he once stayed up for nearly forty-eight hours to hunt down a lead our detectives couldn't find. He's a machine when he wants to be." Coleman clicked the button as he spoke, and his voice took on an odd tone at the end, but his face gave nothing away. We rode the elevator in silence, and it wasn't until we were stepping out onto the parking lot that he seemed to remember I was there.

"This is perfect timing. Judge Lee tends to arrive early," he murmured as if he were saying anything to fill the quiet, but I got the sense we were both still thinking about Dorian.

I had gotten maybe four hours of sleep last night, so I knew Dorian must have been operating on near zero. I needed to accept that he was on the case now. If we had time, I would buy him a cup of coffee as a silent truce. He would probably need the jolt, and I needed to move on.

On the ride over, Coleman recited his opening while I followed along with the printed copy and navigated us to the courthouse. Coleman preferred to look at the jury while he spoke, so he tried to memorize his statement as much as possible.

By the time we were walking down the hall to the court-room, my boss had it down. He looked confident and poised as we finally took our seats, and I only hoped I looked half as good.

I glanced over at the defense table while trying to wrangle my nerves and watched the woman who sat alone in the third seat of four.

She had pulled her black hair back into a perfect bun at her nape and wore a fitted yellow skirt suit with black trim that stopped about an inch above her knee, showing long bare legs dipped into four-inch black heels. Small black-rimmed glasses sat against her smooth, golden skin.

She must have felt me gawking because she turned in my direction, meeting my stare with her hazel eyes and a curt smile that made me turn away and pretend to look through some papers. Dorian popped up from behind the large projector in the corner, giving me a reason to look elsewhere.

Despite his creased tan suit and puffy eyes, Dorian seemed in good spirits. He took his seat, and I pushed the coffee I'd gotten from the cart in the lobby toward him.

"Thank you. I feel like I've been up for a week."

Coleman leaned over me slightly to grab Dorian's attention. "Is it working?"

Dorian only nodded, taking a big sip.

Even with the slight traffic we couldn't avoid, we had shown up a good forty-five minutes earlier than we needed to, but just as Coleman had predicted, Judge Lee entered the court-room, and the bailiff quickly announced him. Everyone rose, then sat down, waiting for the judge. He took one look at the defendant's table, and the woman stood.

"Your Honor, my team and our client are on their way. Traffic delayed them." She sat without looking our way at all.

Judge Lee grunted and glanced at his watch. As he was

about to speak, the doors to the courtroom pushed open and the missing defense team appeared. Langston was first down the short walkway, dressed impeccably in an all black suit, followed by Drayman, who wore white. I tried not to grimace as I imagined the conversation his counsel had with him about how his first appearance outfit should convey his innocence. Following a little behind his client, Malcolm wore a forest green suit that looked like it came straight from a runway.

He knocked open the small swinging doors that separated the trial from the gallery and winked at me before turning to his table. I cut my eyes to my hands and took a breath not to scoff out loud.

The spicy dark aroma of smoked jasmine lingered in the air from their arrival, and while I couldn't say who it belonged to, I had a feeling the culprit was a too tall asshole who took nothing seriously.

"I'm sorry, Your Honor—" Judge Lee waved his hand to hush Langston Charles.

"Ms. Scott already explained. Let's start, shall we?"

Coleman gave my shoulder a soft squeeze as he stood, and I gave him a confident nod. I watched on as he took his place at the ready podium in front of the jury and turned on the Power-Point with a small clicker. The wedding photo of Ronan and Candace Drayman popped up on the large screen. "Ladies and gentlemen of the jury, we are here to—"

I tried hard to follow Coleman even though I knew every word he was going to say, anything to stop me from thinking about Malcolm's cologne assaulting my nose. I glanced at Dorian, who was dutifully concentrating on the jury, and decided to snap out of it and do the same.

Coleman had gotten to the part about Candace's many charitable organizations, and all twelve of them watched him as he spoke, some shifting in their seats and getting comfortable with what would be a long trial. I was watching number five scrunch his nose at something my boss said when I felt someone staring at me. Though I refused to look over, from the corner of my eye, I saw Langston looking at our table.

Unless I turned, I couldn't be sure, but it felt like he was looking directly at me. I squared my shoulders, readying my best Fuck Off face, but as soon as I moved, my eyes locked with another Charles.

Malcolm's eyes narrowed, and when they ticked down to my mouth, I felt my lips trapped between my teeth and released them at the same time I gripped a file I was pretending to need and forced my eyes down.

Like waking from a fever dream, Coleman's voice and my surroundings came floating back, and I realized he was finishing up, telling the jury how we would prove Drayman had murdered his wife and then sailed around the world without a care.

Coleman took his seat, and I was grateful for the barrier as Langston stood. I didn't know what it was about Malcolm, but he had already taken up way too much of my headspace, and I would not let him have anymore. I focused all of my attention on Langston as he leisurely made his way to the podium. Instead of using the pillar to speak, he moved it to the side, stood right in front of the jury, and smiled.

Coleman grumbled something under his breath, and I braced myself for whatever slime was about to come out of the defense attorney's mouth.

"Good afternoon, ladies and gentlemen. I apologize for keeping you waiting and won't take too much more of your time." Langston turned away from the jury to give Coleman that same cocky smirk Malcolm possessed. "My client, Ronan Drayman, is a dedicated philanthropist, and he co-founded many of the charities the prosecution mentioned with Candace.

He is also a loving husband of twenty years, who hired his own private investigator when the police decided they didn't want to do their due diligence, and instead went with the usual 'the husband did it.'"

"He owns prominent nightclubs all around the world and has had his fair share of bad press, but that doesn't make him a killer. My client hasn't been able to grieve the last three years because he's been under constant harassment for a crime the prosecution knows he could not have committed. Just because Ronan Drayman is a successful man does not mean we should make him pay for something he did not do."

I watched the jurors as Langston said the last of his statement, my nerves mounting as they hung on his every word. He finished with a simple nod to the jury before turning to direct his annoying smirk at me this time. I heard a chair move on the defending side, and Langston's smirk dropped as he turned the small corner to sit. Against my better judgment, I snuck another quick glance at Malcolm and saw him leaning over, listening to something Ms. Scott was saying too close to his ear. I looked away and shifted in my seat as Coleman slipped me a piece of paper.

We have to look into this private investigator nonsense.

I passed the note to Dorian, and he wrote something down for himself. The jury then filed out on instruction from the judge as we patiently waited for our own dismissal. "See everyone at nine am, Monday. On time. Court Adjourned." Judge Lee stood, disappearing back into his chambers. Dorian and Coleman stood immediately, but I tried to stay in my seat as long as possible to avoid speaking with Malcolm and his team. It was clear they liked to mess with me, and I didn't want to give either of them the satisfaction.

I shuffled papers and then slowly scooped them up, tapping them on the desk more than necessary to make them uniform. "Thanks again for the coffee. I'll buy you one on the way out." I looked up to find Dorian hovering over me. "No need. You had to wrestle with that ancient projector. You deserved it." He laughed in agreement.

"Avoiding me, Ms. Vine?" I didn't have to look away from Dorian to see who was rude enough to interrupt our conversation, but I did anyway and found Malcolm and Ms. Scott standing directly in front of our table.

I stood, abandoning my stalling tactics, since they clearly hadn't worked. "You would have to cross my mind for me to think to avoid you, Malcolm." I grabbed my neatly stacked papers along with my bag and turned to catch up with Coleman, but saw that he was sequestered at the court doors by Langston. It looked like the older Mr. Charles was talking while Coleman was tolerating him. Drayman was nowhere to be seen.

"Despite facing each other in several cases, I don't believe we've formally met. I'm Dorian Keates." Dorian shot out his hand for Malcolm to take, but the smug defense attorney never took his eyes off me while Ms. Scott looked at Dorian's hand like the entire conversation was beneath her.

"By design." Malcolm spoke nonchalantly in Dorian's direction, and my brows went up.

I fought to ignore the heat prickling my skin at their blatant disrespect. Langston was also likely trying to provoke Coleman, so rather than confronting Malcolm, I turned my attention back to Dorian, pointedly ignoring both him and Ms. Scott.

"If you're still offering, I'll take that coffee." Dorian had dropped his hand, but I could tell Malcolm's disregard had bothered him because it took him a moment to look at me.

"Absolutely. I can take your bag." I allowed him to take it so we could get out of the courtroom as fast as possible.

Dorian went out ahead of me to hold open the gallery exit, but I felt Malcolm's eyes until the large courtroom doors closed.

CHAPTER 5

NAOMI

It was a quiet ride back to the office. Coleman was in his own head, and I wasn't in much of a mood to talk while I tried and failed to remove Malcolm from my thoughts. The point was to get under my skin, and it was annoying how well it was working. By the time we returned to the office, I had again resolved to banish Malcolm Charles from my mind and concentrate on the case.

Coleman tasked me and Dorian with figuring out who this private investigator was and what he might have dug up before disappearing into his office.

I looked up to see Dorian walk in with two canned coffees to add to the many we had accumulated. He had bought me a proper cup as promised, but that was hours ago. Now, we were sitting in the conference room, rehashing what little details we had come up with.

I graciously took the can as he took his seat close by. "So, Joe Castro is a fifty-year-old private eye who works mostly out of New York." I sipped my drink as Dorian continued our recap, hoping to jiggle something loose. "We haven't been able to find when Drayman hired Mr. Castro, which could put his employment into question—"

"Except for the plane ticket to Crestwood under the private eyes' name, dated the day after the murder," I interrupted with a sigh.

Dorian exhaled. "Yeah, except for that."

I typed Castro's name into our database for the tenth time, looking for anything out of the ordinary, and still found nothing.

Dorian took a big swallow of his coffee and glanced at his phone. "It's nearly nine on a Friday night, and I'm surrounded by papers and empty cans. Not quite how I pictured my law career." I laughed, not wanting to admit that this was pretty much how I pictured mine. Hunkering down past regular business hours, looking for the perfect angle or clue to bring justice to the victim.

"This case though..." Dorian stared down into his can before continuing. "Okay, I'm going to say something really petty, but I don't want you to get the wrong idea. I want justice in this case first and foremost." I arched a brow, and he smiled. "Like I said in the courtroom, I worked a few cases against Malcolm and his father with Coleman, and Langston is a piece of work, but Malcolm Charles has always been the biggest pain in my ass." He looked relieved to get the words out. "It doesn't help that the jerk seems to be everywhere! Last year, Coleman bought me a plate at one of those fancy galas that he's always invited to and it was my first one, so I wore an old tux I had buried in my closet."

Dorian sat his coffee on the table between us and leaned in as he spoke like we were co-conspirators, and I followed. "And somehow we had ended up in the same circle. A bunch of us complaining about the usual stuff Crestwood lawyers talk about. The busted air conditioning in courtroom four, Judge Carter sustaining every objection no matter what the circumstances, that weird courtroom reporter Daniel, who stares directly at the defense table the whole trial while typing."

Dorian was staring at me, but his gaze seemed distant, like he was right back at the gala. "Malcolm chimed in and said that 'at least Daniel doesn't try to be something he's not in a knock-off department store suit, trying to fit in where it's painfully obvious he doesn't belong'." Dorian huffed a barely heard laugh, and my eyes widened.

"You know, he didn't look at me then either." I touched my hand to my mouth and sat back in my chair.

I knew the kind of gala Dorian was talking about. After my parents' respective careers took off, they received plenty of invitations. The upper echelons of society loved to throw money at causes while closing ranks on anyone who they thought didn't fit in, but to call someone out like that at a public event for no reason was plain cruel.

Dorian smiled as if the story didn't still bother him. "So, it would be nice to beat him at least once, just to wipe that stupid smirk off his face." I saw my frustration with Malcolm reflected in Dorian's thin frown before he downed the last of his drink. "The man is obsessed with himself. If he didn't have all that money, he'd be nothing. Don't let him get to you."

He nodded at my words, but I could tell Dorian thought about that moment a lot. I looked around at our empty cans and all the paper scattered between our laptops. Malcolm was probably off fucking some model while we were here agonizing over work and letting him live rent free in our heads.

"There's not much else we can pull up on the private eye tonight, and I already called the detectives to do some digging of their own. Wanna call it?"

Dorian closed his laptop, and I followed. We quickly shuffled papers into their appropriate filing cabinets and turned off the light in the conference room. We were the last ones on our floor, with Coleman tapping out around six for his son's recital. He looked to be in better spirits when he left, and I wondered again what Coleman had said to put him in such a mood. He had invited Dorian and me to his house for dinner tomorrow, which meant we would probably work at some point, so I felt better about calling it a night.

Even with a few lights still on, the office was pretty dim, and while I was used to navigating the building by myself this late, I was grateful to have Dorian there. He wasn't as bad as I had imagined, and I guess stressing out together trying to find something on the private detective had let my guard down a little.

"Do you want me to grab your bag?" Dorian asked while I prepared to lift it onto my shoulder. I really needed to go through and clean out any unnecessary stuff because it was becoming unbearable. "No, you already carried it through the courthouse. I think you've done enough heavy lifting." Dorian skewed his mouth sideways into a smirk. "I wasn't going to say it, but that thing nearly broke my shoulder when I picked it up earlier. You're stronger than you look." We both laughed as we made our way to the elevator.

Without the building's usual bustle, it moved quickly, and since Dorian and I parked on the same floor, we walked between the cars together.

"I'm going to reach out to a few private detectives tomorrow and see if they can find something on Castro."

It was a great idea, and for the first time, I didn't feel threatened by Dorian. We were partners. "That's great. I'll see if our detectives have any contacts we can use, too." Dorian smiled as he slid his hands into his slacks. "I'm glad you're on this case, Naomi." We approached my car and Dorian slowed to a stop. I was curious how he knew which car was mine, but the question came and went as he stepped closer to me.

"Uh, I wanted to—" He cut himself off with a laugh that I didn't match. I was ready for bed, and the last thing I wanted to do was have a late-night conversation in a parking garage.

"I just want to clear the air officially," he pushed out, and my brows bunched together. "Maybe I'm wrong, but I got the vibe that you might have felt weird around me since I got back on the case...and possibly before, too." I took a moment to consider my response.

"I'll admit, I wasn't sure how our dynamic would work." His laughter at my honesty eased the tension in the air. "I really didn't want to step on your toes. Sorry again for springing up in your case. Me and Coleman parted ways for various reasons and...well, I'm just happy to be given another shot at helping people in a big way." Dorian rubbed the back of his neck. "Anyway, thanks for not hating me, at least not out loud, without giving me a shot." He laughed again.

I gave him a small smile. "I'm glad you're on the case, too." It felt nice to mean it this time.

He stared at me for a few seconds more, and the weight of my bag almost had me telling him to spit it out already. "Uh, also, I was hoping to grab your number?" I couldn't help frowning before he added, "I just realized I have no way of contacting you if my private investigators have any leads. Regina likely doesn't want me to contact her this weekend to reach you." My cheeks burned for thinking Dorian was trying something, but if he noticed, he had the decency not to say anything. "Sorry, of course!" I rambled off my number as I stepped past him to get to my door.

"Alright, get home safe, and I'll see you tomorrow," he said, walking backward. "Yeah, see you." I waved with an awkward laugh. He turned and continued back in the direction we came, disappearing behind a large SUV's bumper. I sighed with relief as I opened my door. The day had been long, but it was the first time in the last couple that I felt like myself. The most exhausted version, but it still felt good. I slid into my car, ready for my bed and a weekend without fear of bumping into annoying defense attorneys.

CHAPTER 6

MALCOLM

Her scent hit me before I opened my eyes. It was honey and citrus and instantly made my dick hard. I reached out and pulled her in to feel what a great morning I had planned when the scent changed. Still sweet; but not nearly as appealing. I opened my eyes to find my arms wrapped around Gabby, my nose in her hair.

"Good morning to you too." Gabby pushed her naked body into my erection, and I nearly fell out of bed trying to get some distance.

What the fuck?

After work, I took Gabby out to dinner, and she came back to my place. It wasn't out of the ordinary for us to hook up. She was gorgeous and outstanding in bed, but I thought I had just smelled someone else. A smart mouthed beauty that made me want to see what else that mouth could do. I groaned as Gabby pushed up against me again. It was a disappointed groan, but she didn't know the difference.

I placed my hands on her hips gently to move her away, and she turned to face me, her dark hair still perfect even after sleeping. It made me think of Naomi's untamed curls that didn't seem to stay contained for more than an hour. Stray tight ringlets had popped out of her precarious bun by the time the opening statements were done. Gabby tilted her head, no doubt waiting for an explanation, and I came up empty as I looked at her body, trying to understand whatever insanity I was currently going through.

"Are you sure?" She reached out her hand and slowly slid it down my still slightly hard dick.

Gabby was a defense attorney, and more importantly, she understood what we were, which meant I didn't have to worry about her being clingy or spreading our business through the office. She was perfect, and still my dick barely stirred as she stroked me, and I closed my eyes, trying to be in the moment. I had sex with her last night; I could have sex with her again. I would fuck the entire female population if that's what it took to get Naomi off my dick's mind.

But as Gabby pressed me into the bed and mounted me, Naomi's doe-like brown eyes crept in and I was back in court. As soon as our eyes locked, her glare went from murderous to something that made me forget where we were. Women had looked at me that way before. Like I was the last bottle of water in the world and they desperately needed a drink, but from Naomi, it felt like nothing else in the world mattered beyond me giving her every drop.

My dick was definitely at attention now, but it wasn't for the woman in my bed. I tapped her thigh softly, and Gabby slid off me, wrapping herself in the comforter as I pulled myself up and sat with my back to her.

Yesterday after I returned from court, I told Camden to cancel all my weekend plans. My assistant had stared at me as if I had three heads, but held his tongue. I had always filled my life with parties, women, and work. I thought I preferred it that way right up until the second I laid eyes on Naomi Vine. Now, it felt like everything not in her presence was a nuisance. Which made no sense. I thought of the way she tried to ignore me in court yesterday and that annoying worm she calls a colleague.

Dorian Keates was a subpar attorney, and now he had somehow slinked his way onto Naomi's case.

I didn't know what Coleman was doing over there at the DA's office, but he needed to retire if he thought Dorian could help them beyond tinkering with an out-of-date projector. "If you want to grab brunch, my morning is free." I turned to see Gabby studying her phone. She looked the picture of nonchalance, but I had dealt with enough women to know the invitation was anything but.

My phone rang, saving me from whatever lie was on the tip of my tongue to get Gabby to leave. She was a great woman, but so were my past ten other hookups. They were never the problem.

"Hello?" Gabby moved to the other side of my king-sized bed as I answered the phone. "Mr. Charles? I have an Avery Cartwright here at the North Crestwood Police Station." I pulled the phone from my face to look down at the number before getting back on the line. "What's happened to Avery?" I demanded as I stood. "Well, he was suspected of shoplifting but refused to speak to anyone, so they brought him down to the station, and he just keeps waving your card around." I already had pants on by the time the officer stopped talking. "Suspected shoplifting?" My voice was calm, but my blood was boiling. "And why am I speaking to you and not to him?" The officer sighed, and I hoped he understood the trouble that was about to rain down on him. "Well, the thing is...we know your firm, and we didn't think that he really... well—" I cut him off, having heard enough. "You didn't think a boy like him could afford my services, correct? You're right, officer, you didn't think. But don't worry, I'm happy to provide a proper lesson once I arrive."

I hung up, pressed another button, and put the phone back to my ear. "Yes, I need a car at my house. Passenger is Gabriella

Scott." Once I got the confirmation that it would arrive in five minutes, I tossed my phone on the bed so I could button up the shirt I had put on. "Everything alright?" Gabby was up too, having read the situation, and was slipping into the silky red dress she had worn at dinner. "I have to go."

Gabby didn't push me for an explanation and slid on her tall black heels. "Thanks for last night, and I guess rain check for this morning?" Even with the stilettos, she was a few inches shorter than I was and looked up at me with those expectant hazel eyes. "Your car will be here soon," was all I could say. Still, she smiled and caressed my chest as she walked past me, and I followed her out. Watching her hips sway, I wondered again what the hell was wrong with me.

"Wearing a sweater in eighty-degree weather. Why not just turn yourself in?" I was trying to contain my anger while Avery mumbled to himself as he hopped into my Mercedes.

During my final year of law school, I helped my professor represent Avery's dad in a pro-bono case and got along with the smart-mouthed ten-year-old kid. The court acquitted his dad, but he returned to jail for another petty theft a couple of years later. Now, at fifteen, Avery and I kept a loose relationship, mostly filled with me getting my ass whooped on a basketball court once a month.

"You said if I were ever in trouble to use your card, so I did. Drop it." The anger was building. "Drop it? I just spent three hours at a police station convincing them to *drop* charges of you shoplifting some earbuds. Fucking earbuds, Avery." I slammed the door as I got in with no intention of starting the car until I got an explanation. "I didn't have them when they searched me, did I?" He looked at me like I was the dumb one, and I had to take a breath to stop from exploding. "They had video of you distracting the clerk to snatch them out of the protective case and bypassing checkout with them on! How did you even get the security tag off them?" The kid looked proud of himself before he caught my eye and then let out an aggravated sigh. "Look, things like earbuds may not be that big of a deal to you, billionaire, but my mom has a new boyfriend, and the apartment gets... loud. I need to focus on homework, and my other ones broke last week."

We both fell silent as we scowled at each other. I didn't have a ready response, which was rare for me. I didn't ask him why he couldn't study at a coffee shop because I knew getting home before dark in his neighborhood was beneficial, and I didn't ask why he didn't call me because I knew I was the asshole who barely picked up.

They had nothing on Avery that they could make stick without him talking, but I knew that wouldn't have mattered. As much as I gave every officer that touched Avery shit and planned to give them more, their assumption that he wasn't the type to be protected from the legal system was usually true, and that pissed me off. My father had always been ambitious to a fault, choosing success over everything, and while he turned into someone that I never wanted to be, he had started from the bottom. A Black kid with no parents and no options in the eyes of the public until he made his own. How he did it, however, was the reason we would never see eye to eye.

Avery was an intelligent kid. He had already moved up a grade and could easily move up another, but I suspected he held off because he didn't want to leave his mother any sooner than he had to. He was also a genius on the basketball court, and schools were already eyeing him for academic and sports scholarships. I had offered to send him to the same boarding school I'd attended in London, but he declined. After he realized I wouldn't take no for an answer, we compromised on a private school in the city, and I footed the bill.

Otherwise, he never accepted money from me. I still gave his mom some cash here and there, but if he was stealing headphones, who knows what the fuck Reba was doing with it. "You have less than two more years of high school, and then you're out of here." I tossed him an AirPods box, and he looked prepared to protest, but I cut him off.

"Consider it part of the school curriculum. And if you have anything else that you need—" I made sure he was looking in my eyes, "school or otherwise, call me." His chin dipped toward his throat, and then he turned toward the window, letting me know that was the only response I was going to get.

CHAPTER 7

NAOMI

"Thanks, Lloyd, let me know if you find anything." I hung up the phone and rubbed Mac's soft head resting on my thigh. His eyes perked up, but he stayed where he was, content with me trailing my finger up and down his nose while we sat on my long couch. It was by far the biggest piece of furniture I had, but I loved the idea of Mac and I being able to both spread out on either side. As I looked down at my clingy dog, I realized I could have gotten a smaller one.

The last thing I wanted to do was disturb Mac's rare moment of tranquility, but I had three minutes left before my phone would start blaring, alerting me I had to get ready for Coleman's dinner. After failing to sleep in this morning, I took Mac to the dog park for a good run and then focused on work. Between calling the few detectives I trusted to find a connection to Joe Castro, eating takeout, and drinking too much coffee, the Saturday had passed in a blur.

As expected, my phone screeched, and Mac groaned as I scooted his body completely onto the couch as I stood. "Yeah, me too, buddy." As I picked out a simple long-sleeved gold knit dress that went to my ankles, I hoped Dorian had a better day tracking something down. He hadn't reached out, but maybe he would have some good news after the dinner.

I parked my car on Coleman's street and speed walked to his door, happy I was wearing flats. It was ten minutes till, so I wasn't exactly late, but Coleman had invited me for seven, and I knew how promptly his wife Charlotte liked to eat. I rang the doorbell and tried to get my heavy breathing under control, silently promising myself I would get back to the gym in the distant future when I had free time. The door swung open as I made my mental pact, and I came face to face with Dorian.

"Naomi, there you are! Mrs. Coleman was getting worried."

I gave him a small smile, wondering why he would be answering their door. Dorian stepped to the side so I could enter past him, and since I knew my way around, I continued toward the living room while he shut it.

"Naomi, welcome! We were just setting the table." Coleman gave me a slight nod and then led the way into the dining room, where his wife was setting a gorgeous china plate down between silver utensils.

"Oh Ni, it feels like forever since I last saw you. You look lovely as ever!"

Coleman was a strict man who wasn't one for affection toward his employees, but his Southern wife was the complete opposite and gathered me into a full embrace. I returned her hug and hoped she didn't notice the fast beating of my heart.

"Sorry, I'm a little late. Do you need help with anything?" She clicked her tongue before heading back toward the kitchen.

"Nonsense, you're right on time. Take your seat and relax. We'll be eating in just a minute." Coleman took his place at the head of the table while Dorian sat across from me.

"Sierra and Thomas won't be joining us. Teenagers." Coleman said the last part with a shrug that made me laugh as I thought about the adult dinners I had to attend at my parents' home when I was their age. I completely understood.

Charlotte entered again with a dish of several Cornish hens, their amazing smell filling the room as she set them on the table. I had the urge to stand up and help, but Coleman beat me to it. "Open the wine, you two. We'll have the rest of the food out in a second."

The bottle was closer to Dorian, who reached for it and easily unscrewed the cork. "Have you been to many of these?" He whispered as he poured me a healthy glass.

"A couple, you?"

"Yea, Charlotte's cooking is too good to turn down an invite. I used to come over once a month before ...well, before."

Dorian chuckled as he poured his own glass and sat back down in his seat, and Coleman and his wife returned with their hands full with trays of mashed potatoes and asparagus to complete the meal. "Enjoy!" Charlotte's accent sang as they took their seats at opposite ends of the table, and we all reached to get what we wanted.

"Dorian, how's the car restoration going?"

I looked up as he scooped some mashed potatoes onto his plate before answering Coleman's question.

"As well as expected. I got the engine a couple of weeks back, so I'm working on getting it installed."

My eyes must have asked what I was thinking because Dorian quickly followed up with, "I've been rebuilding a 1964 Chevy Impala for the past few years."

I didn't know much about cars, but I knew older model muscle ones were expensive to maintain, let alone build.

"Wow, are you close to being finished?"

Dorian shrugged. "Not really, but I don't mind. I'm a patient guy."

"Certainly more patient than my husband. If that car weren't up and running in a week, he would give it away." We all laughed, and I thought back to the story Dorian had told me the night before. Malcolm tossed insults in every direction without bothering to get to know a person. Dorian spent his money on his passions, and I warmed to him even more. "Naomi, John and I went to your father's restaurant a couple of weeks ago, and it was heavenly! I could easily gain five pounds eating there and still be happy!" I grinned at Charlotte. "Try growing up with him! Every day I complained about the fried catfish or fluffy cornbread, but I could never resist."

She nodded knowingly, but Dorian spoke before she had a chance. "Well, you still turned out looking perfect, so I guess food cooked with love can't be all that bad."

Everyone laughed at his comment, but the way Dorian looked at me afterward made me quickly break eye contact.

Maybe he was just being friendly. Dorian wasn't a bad-looking guy, but I was nowhere close to being available and was definitely not into the idea of a messy office romance. "How was Thomas's violin recital?" I changed the subject to banish my thoughts, and soon Coleman and his wife were telling Dorian and me about the crazy prices of colleges and their kids' plans.

After we finished and said goodnight to Charlotte, Dorian and I followed Coleman to his study to discuss the case. Dorian had no better luck than I had, but Coleman reached out to some of his contacts and found that Drayman's alleged private investigator, Joe Castro, was an ex-cop fired for some shady dealings. The files were sealed, but this was good information, and I felt better about our cross-examination chances when the time came. Tomorrow, we had our first two witnesses, and I had coached both to be ready for anything the prosecution might throw at them during the trial.

"What about Jack? We should get him in soon to go over exactly what his testimony will be." Dorian was leafing through papers deep in thought but looked up at the quiet surrounding my question.

"Yeah, of course. He's a little skittish, but I'll get him in sometime next week."

I wanted to reach out to Jack myself, but it was Dorian's lead, so I let it go. When it finally happened, I was eager to hear the story from the kid's mouth.

After deciding that we should all meet at the courthouse on Monday since it was an early start, Coleman told us to head home and enjoy the rest of our weekend.

A slight breeze blew past as Dorian and I stepped outside, and I cursed under my breath. "Would you like my coat?" Dorian was already taking his peacoat off before I could get the words out.

"Oh no, it's fine. My car's right up here."

I wasn't sure if I was reading his signals right or not, but I didn't want to send any of my own. He stopped with his jacket in his hands, ready to cover me, and gave a tight smile before putting it back on himself.

I laughed to fill the quiet and racked my brain for a topic while we walked along the quiet street at the glacial pace Dorian had set. "What made you want to rebuild an old car?" Dorian's smile turned genuine, and I relaxed. "My dad is a mechanic and had this rich customer who used to buy these half-finished classic cars at auctions and then come to him to get them running. When I was about fifteen and had nothing better to do than hang around his shop, this guy had a 1964 Chevy towed in. The entire front was missing, but I fell in love anyway. Wanted one ever since." We stopped at my car, but he still lingered.

"That's a great story of determination."

I clicked the lock and reached for my handle, but Dorian beat me to it, opening the door wide for me to get in.

"I'm nothing if not determined." He teased, and I huffed a laugh. Either he was unaware of how he sounded, or Dorian was definitely shooting his shot. It could respect the attempt, but it was wasted on me. "Dorian, I've enjoyed working with you so far and hope we can continue to work together in the future...as great colleagues."

He scratched his eyebrow as he laughed and looked away down the long, lit street while his other hand stayed firmly on my open door. "Yes, great colleagues. Now, have a good night, Ms. Vine." When Dorian turned back to me, his smile was still intact, and I hoped we were on the same page as I slid into my car.

"Goodnight," I returned, but it still took him a second to close my door. Once he did, I pushed the start button, igniting my needed heater, and watched as he walked back onto the sidewalk. I waved as I pulled off, but when I turned the corner at the end of the street, Dorian was still in the same spot, watching me go.

CHAPTER 8

NAOMI

Sunday afternoon traffic to the other side of town was light, but Vine was packed as usual, with almost all the tables taken and even more guests waiting at the entrance while delicious smells and laughter filled the space.

After being a no-show last week, I had promised my dad that I'd come by to taste the new menu and there was no way I could miss it again without my mother showing up at my doorstep. Getting out of Sunday dinner with the family this evening, however, might be in the cards since I wanted to get some rest and be at the courthouse early for the over punctual Judge Lee.

Jeffrey, my dad's host for the better part of fifteen years, waved me up when I walked in and surrounded me in one of his signature bear hugs before I could say hello.

Standing at six-foot-two with a massive frame, Jeffrey's hugs always took my breath away.

"My love! I haven't seen you in a dog's age!" He released me only at arm's length. "Where have you been?"

I was still breathless, but I couldn't help but smile at his warm welcome. "Working."

He gave me a chastising look, then briefly searched his seating map when a couple walked past to the exit. "You're too young to be working all the time, sweetness. Live a little!" I bit my lip and pushed down the sting of not having come sooner. I knew I worked a lot, but my job meant something to victims who deserved justice. They deserved my full attention.

"Sit at your regular table, and I'll let your dad know you're here."

I scooted past all the waiting guests, ignoring the whispers and eye daggers being thrown at me for bypassing the line. Jeffrey's loud throat-clearing quieted the discourse, making me laugh as I moved through the busy restaurant to our family's designated table. No matter how booked up Vine was, our table was always free.

I slid into a seat and observed the busy hum of the restaurant. Families had animated conversations while eating my dad's signature chicken wings, couples eyed each other lovingly while sipping wine, and groups of friends at the bar debated over the muted game on the overhead television. A glass of red wine brought my focus back to my table, and I glanced up to see my father. His smiling face stirred nerves I didn't know were so close to the surface, and I couldn't help but squeeze him tighter when he opened himself up for a hug. "Whoa, everything alright, kiddo?"

I smiled sheepishly as we both sat down. "I'm okay." He looked unconvinced, but didn't push.

"I'm glad you came! The menu goes live next week, but I couldn't let it happen without my baby girl tasting first."

As if on cue, a waiter appeared with a tray of three small plates. My dad smiled at my gasp when I saw each delicious dish.

"These are the new entrees. We have a Cajun seasoned pulled beef with penne pasta and a white wine sauce, my new spicier red beans and rice with braised pork belly, and an oven-roasted blackened chicken."

My mouth watered just looking at the food, and I started in

on the red beans and rice before he had finished the descriptions. "Oh. My. Lord."

My dad chuckled as I devoured the pasta in a matter of minutes. "Have you been feeding yourself?"

I paused as I tasted the blackened chicken, savoring the smoky flavor. "Nothing like your cooking."

My father told me about the upcoming renovations he had planned for Vine and how he could finally buy the property next door to expand while I switched to lemonade, because I still had to drive, and devoured the additional dishes I asked for. Because of research, of course.

I loved listening to my dad talk about the restaurant. His eyes lit up almost as bright as when he talked about my mom. I imagined that this excitement was the same reason he always had at least one stain on his chef coat when I visited.

After a few more plates and laughs, time had flown by and Vine was only getting busier with the dinner rush starting. My dad had retreated to the kitchen, checking on me periodically, but now I sat alone, savoring a rare calm even while a small part of me still thought about work. "How was everything, love?" Jeffrey's voice drew my attention.

"Delicious, as always," I grinned as he slid into the seat opposite me.

"Must have been because you look much better now than when you got here."

Unsure of how to respond, I took another sip of my sweet drink. "How's Fred?" I pushed out.

"Oh, you know my Fred, a worker bee like you! He just became head concierge at the Cambridge Hotel Downtown!"

I was relieved Fred was doing well. A couple of years ago, he had been diagnosed with liver cancer, and the whole restaurant staff rallied behind Jeffrey. My dad had even catered a charity benefit in their honor to help with medical bills. Fortunately, Fred had recently received a clean bill of health.

"That's great to hear! Has he gotten his boat yet?"

Jeffrey rolled his eyes playfully. "Not yet, but I'll be happy when he does. I'm so tired of hearing all the little facts about boats without being on one!"

We both laughed as my father approached. "Hey, baby girl, what time will you be at the house tonight? Your mom is already there if you want to head over now."

I stiffened and then tried to relax to play it off. "I'm not sure...I still have a lot of work to do and—" My father's rare stern expression made me swallow the rest of my excuse. "I have to stop back home, but I'll be there by eight."

My father and Jeffrey exchanged a look before Jeffrey stood up. "Well, I better get back to it. Lovely seeing you, Ni."

My dad replaced Jeffrey in the seat in front of me, and I couldn't meet his eyes. When it was clear he was waiting for me, I looked up and saw the face. The Tell Me What's Wrong face that I could never deny. I swallowed and briefly thought about how much to reveal.

"This case is really important to me."

My dad rubbed his chin, thinking.

"You know, your mother was like this too in the early days. She had calmed down a little after she had you, but she went to work a month after having Dante." The admission shocked me. My mom had always been so present during my childhood and was such a badass in the courtroom, I didn't even question how she could do both. My parents were pretty well off now, but growing up we were middle class at best, with my dad trying to get Vine off the ground and my mom working for the district attorney's office.

I couldn't imagine trying to do my job and raise a family. I could barely remember to shower. "She worked so hard because she cared about her job, but she also understood that she needed to care for herself too." My dad pulled one of my wayward curls, and it bounced when he let it go.

"Listen, baby girl, I don't know much about this case, but I do know that you've waited a long time for it, so I would never tell you to not make it a priority, but make sure it's not getting in the way of you living your life. More than just surviving."

My father's eyes were reassuring. "But I know my daughter is smart, so I'm not worried." Tears pricked at the corners of my lashes, and all I could do was nod.

"Alright, let me get back in this kitchen. I'll see you tonight."

We both stood, and my dad gave me a hug and a kiss on the cheek before disappearing through the crowd.

Dad was right. I needed to build some kind of life outside of work. History had taught me that romance was off the table, but it couldn't hurt to hang out with Myra more and enjoy my beautiful city. I started for the exit, reminding myself that I still needed to catch up with my best friend, when a voice called out my name and my mind went blank.

His usual all-white kitchen uniform was on, but his buttons were undone, revealing a black V-neck undershirt and curly chest hair. He had what looked like two-day scruff on his jaw that had found its way up into his loose, curly brown hair, a single curl resting on his forehead. Teddy paused for a second when his gray eyes met mine, but then continued the short distance toward me, his pink lips arching into a smile.

"It's good to see you, Ni. You look amazing." His voice wrapped me up like a warm blanket, and it took me a second to make my voice work.

"Hey," was all I could manage. He seemed like he expected a hug, but I stayed glued to my spot. I wasn't sure I was even blinking. Teddy's smile widened, and he took his full bottom lip between his teeth. The motion made me focus on them, and my stomach did a somersault. "What are you doing here?" I blurted, my tone between a whisper and a shrill shriek. He took my question in stride, eyeing me up and down slowly before answering.

"Your dad asked me back to help with the expansion. I thought he would have told you." Heat scorched my cheeks at his appraisal, but I raised my chin to focus. "Good for you. I was just leaving." Teddy's smile fell as I stepped around him. "Okay, well, maybe we can catch up sometime soon. Properly."

I waved my hand as I continued walking, my heart rate deescalating as I made it further away from my ex. I was grateful Jeffrey wasn't at his post, making for an easy exit, and I took a deep gulp of air as soon as I was outside.

My mother could have it all, but Teddy was proof that a love like my parents' wasn't in the cards for me. I tried to ignore the lump in my throat at the reminder.

CHAPTER 9

NAOMI

"So she does live?!" I rolled my eyes at Myra's fake shocked face on FaceTime. "I know, I know. How's New York?" I asked, and she side-eyed me. "I'll let the subject change slide because I gotta tell you about the terrible men in this city! Not one good one, Ni!" I propped my phone on my bathroom counter so I could get my hair semi together for family dinner.

Instead of working, I came home and took a nap, and it was already six thirty.

"That's what you said about Crestwood."

"But at least in Crestwood, vapid fine men roam the land to be ogled at. Everyone covers themselves up in New York. It's real winter out here!" I laughed as I slicked my hair up to the top of my head, where I let the curls poof out in any direction that wanted. "How about the man you're actually supposed to be looking for? Have you met Martin Kline yet?" Myra huffed. "Can't find him either!" She grumbled. "My contacts are saying he might not be in the city, but I think he is. I have a feeling he's not a runner."

Kline had been in the news almost as much as Drayman, with an upcoming trial of his own. He was a Wall Street mogul accused of so many white-collar counts, they would need to spend the whole first day in court listing them out. Myra had begged her bosses for the okay to go to New York and get an exclusive before the case started, but she had had little luck so far.

I carried our conversation back into my room to grab my cardigan and take one last look in the mirror. To appease my mother, I had dressed in a long sapphire-colored skirt and a flowing white silk blouse. It was as casual as I was allowed. She was very adamant that the next time I showed up in sweats, she would burn them.

"Ohhh, we going on a date??" Myra's excitement got her another eye roll. "It's Sunday, Myra. If I'm not working or hanging out with you, there's one other place I'm going, and you know that." Myra laughed and picked up her phone so that I could see more of her hotel room.

"Tell Poppa and Momma Vine I said hello and that I've been dreaming of your dad's catfish. When you pick me up from the airport, I hope you know that's our next stop." She wasn't coming back for another week, but she knew how hard it was to make plans with me, so was putting me on notice.

"Anyway, I just thought since you've been in the same courtroom with that fine ass Malcolm Charles that you might have thought about knocking off those cobwebs." I almost tripped over Myra's audacity walking into my living room. "Please be serious," I muttered, and Myra brought the phone closer to her face.

"Serious as hell, Ni. That man is 90s leading man fine and you can't tell me you don't think so." I ignored her while I put on my flats. "Exactly. Now that we've stopped pretending, let's strategize how to get Malcolm on top of you."

"Myra!" I shrieked, and my cheeks burned for no reason. "No, girl, we're trying to get you to scream his name, not mine," she giggled, and I sighed. "He defends rich murderers for money, My. Even if there were a chance that I could get past that, which there isn't, he's also a rich, arrogant asshole himself." Myra clicked her tongue.

"Okay, his firm *has* worked for some shady people."

"Mmhm!"

"And *allegedly* his father has done some shady things to keep those people out of prison."

"Mmmhmm!"

"Actually, I heard rumors of his grandfather being shady as hell back in his day too..."

"Mmm—wait, his grandfather?!"

Myra waved my perplexed expression away. "But it's just his job, Ni, and you can't blame Malcolm for being born into a rich family."

"And the arrogant asshole part?" Myra smiled with a twinkle in her eye that told me she wasn't on my side at all. "I mean, if he looks that good, and the rumors are true about him between the sheets...he's allowed."

I thought about hanging up as I grabbed my purse and keys from the table by my front door. I still hadn't found time to fix whatever was in my keyhole, so I was going to have to go around back. "Disagree. Anyway, I'm off men, you know that." As expected, Mac acted like he hadn't seen me most of the day, and I had to shoo him away all the way to the gate. "It's been two years, Ni. Forget Teddy's bum ass." His name conjured him up from earlier, and I looked away from the camera, but my face must have given me away.

"What happened?" I secured my back gate and took my time getting into my car to avoid Myra's question. "Helloooo?" Finally, I looked at her. "I saw Teddy at Vine today. He's working with my dad again." While Myra looked genuinely shocked this time, I propped her on my phone holder and started my car. I knew what she was thinking and hoped she would let it go this one time, but knew my friend too well to expect that.

"Your dad would have never let him come back if you had told your family the truth about the breakup." I pulled onto the street without glancing at Myra. There was no point in airing our dirty laundry to everyone. I just wanted to move on. "It's fine, My. I barely go to Vine, and my father trusts him." Myra sighed big and dramatic. "Your face at the mention of his name makes it not fine, but okay. Just promise me you won't let him weasel his way back into your life." I stopped at a red light and looked over at my friend.

"Absolutely not. I promise." Myra smiled at my response.

"Now back to Malcolm. Does he smell as good as he looks? I bet that man's aroma alone could soak panties." I failed to hold in a laugh as I drove onto the freeway and let Myra continue to talk bullshit all the way to my parents' house.

As promised, I pulled up to my parents' home right as the clock struck seven fifty-five. We always ate late since my dad only left Vine to start dinner after the Sunday evening rush. He talked about me being glued to my job, but Augustine Vine didn't trust many to handle his kitchen without him. In the twenty years the restaurant has been in business, only Teddy came to mind.

I took off my seatbelt and leaned my head back against the headrest. Myra had nothing to worry about on the Teddy front. Even though I had been the bigger person in our situation and decided not to tell my family about his indiscretions, there was no way I could take him back. There was a part of me that would never heal from the way he ended things, but I wasn't the same person anymore. She was also crazy to think anything would happen between Malcolm and me. He was the antithesis of everything I believed in, and nothing would change my mind. I didn't care how fine he was.

My phone buzzed, and instead of moving my head, I

brought the phone up to my eye line and then blinked rapidly when I saw a text from a number not in my contacts.

Long day, Goody?

I looked around. The street was quiet, and there weren't many cars on either side of the tree-lined sidewalk, but it still felt like someone was watching me. I stared back at the message. The area code was Crestwood, and I had never gotten a message from them before. It was probably a spam caller. I tapped the message to delete it, but it disappeared, and my father's picture filled my phone screen. Coltrane's soft notes played as his personal ringtone, which reminded me what I was really supposed to be doing. I answered as I opened my door and stepped out into the brisk night.

"Hi Dad, I'm right outside. Coming in now." I smoothed out my skirt, dropped my phone into my small purse, and headed for the door. The lightweight cardigan was not helping me the few feet, and I knew I needed to order a real coat or be perpetually cold. A bush rustled somewhere behind me, and I turned as a car passed, going way too fast in a residential area.

The red lights disappeared around a corner. Nothing stirred, but I walked faster to the door anyway, pushing it open without hesitation. No matter how many times I argued with my parents about keeping it locked, they always left the door open for their children on Sundays. It was ridiculous, but I was glad of their stubbornness as I easily clicked the door back in place and turned the lock.

Music and mouthwatering smells hit me instantaneously. Jazz was playing softly in the living room, and what smelled like the best gumbo in the world was cooking in the kitchen. I heard voices coming from the dining room and smiled, wondering why I didn't want to come. My family was exactly what I needed.

I rounded the walkway to find five people sitting at the dining table. My brother, Dante, and his fiancée sat together, listening intently as my mother and father told the story of how they met in college to Malcolm Charles.

CHAPTER 10

NAOMI

Everyone glanced up and smiled, all somehow blind to the blatant anomaly that was Malcolm sitting at my parents' dinner table. My eyes remained locked on him as I walked toward my mom, and he had the nerve not only to hold my gaze but curve those lips of his into that stupid smirk. I felt my mother's arms around me and gingerly squeezed her back, working hard to fathom what I had just walked into.

My father kissed my forehead and headed toward the kitchen, saying something about the main course, and Annalise was laughing, but for the life of me, I couldn't focus on anyone else.

Malcolm was pushed out from the table, as if he had just taken his seat, with one leg crossed over the other and a hand resting on his ankle. He looked very comfortable being in enemy territory.

"Naomi, we've only had salad. We waited for you for the gumbo." With a struggle, I pulled my eyes off Malcolm as my mother gestured to the table where everyone's half-eaten plates sat in front of them. There was a large glass bowl of leafy greens and vegetables in the middle, with a smaller bowl of vinaigrette on the side.

"Ni, this is Malcolm. We went to Whitmore together." Now that I'd looked away, it was impossible to look back at him. My body was on fire, and I knew I would begin to visibly smoke if I met his eyes again.

I considered leaving, but it annoyed me that he knew I would be surprised. He was enjoying himself, and I'd be damned if I brought him any kind of amusement. With my lips pursed in a thin line, I kept my eyes firmly on my brother.

"We've met." Without further explanation, I made my way across the table to the empty place setting next to Annalise. There were two people between us, but Malcolm's direct gaze made him feel closer. I disregarded his stare and began making myself a salad, willing my hands to stop shaking.

"I actually ran into your brother at the gym today. Rumor has it Vine is the best soul food restaurant in the city, but I've never had the pleasure of eating there, so I couldn't pass on the invite." Malcolm spoke cordially, as if we had been friends for years. I let out a small noise of acknowledgment, but never looked up from my now full salad plate.

"I love your skirt, Ni. That would have been the perfect color for the bridesmaid dresses!" I internally thanked Annalise for being wedding crazy. Their wedding was only a few months away, so she talked about little else.

"Thanks, I got it from a small boutique shop on Melbourne. But, you know the royal blue color you chose is beautiful." My father returned from the kitchen with a deep metal pot in his hands, setting it down at the edge of the table. The gumbo smoldered, and its amazing smell filled the room as my mother stood.

"I'm going to grab some extra silverware. Naomi, come and help me." I caught her gaze and saw that it wasn't a request I could deny, so I quietly followed her out of the room.

As soon as we had crossed the hall into the kitchen, out of earshot of anyone at the table, she turned and faced me, just as I suspected she would. "What's wrong?"

I could never keep much from my mother. She could sense the rain before God knew, a fact that helped her be a fantastic attorney and now judge, but was annoying as hell for a kid. It wasn't helping now, either. "I just didn't know we had company."

She looked skeptical, but turned her back to me and pulled out a drawer by the stove, grabbing a handful of spoons and forks. "Malcolm is an attractive young man." She didn't look up, but her smile told me she knew I would agree. I tried to keep my expression impassive, but my cheeks were heating against my will.

I quickly made a noncommittal sound and walked past to get out of her eyesight, grabbing some extra paper towels from the counter. She closed the drawer and turned to me with the silverware in hand.

"He seems nice, and he's a lawyer, so you should have a lot in common." It was clear she had morphed into Matchmaker Mom, and I turned to her to stamp down whatever plan she was hatching.

"He's the opposing counsel for the case I'm working on." I tried to keep my face neutral while she processed what I said.

"Trials don't last forever."

Her smirk was infectious, and I couldn't help my own, but I added an eye roll before walking back toward the dining room. No one was on my side!

My smile quickly dissipated when I met eyes with Malcolm again. It was as if they sought him out without my permission. I looked away and took my seat. "And we're debuting a new menu soon. Ni finally came by today and tried some after ghosting me." I huffed out a laugh. Who was teaching him new words?! "Sorry, work is intense right now. The defense is doing everything in its power to avoid the inevitable." Malcolm muffled what sounded like a cough with a napkin, and I shot him a quick smile.

"Careful. It's spicy."

My mother cleared her throat, but I avoided what were sure to be her disapproving eyes and took a spoonful of my own gumbo. "It's alright baby, I know your hard work will pay off. My daughter is a winner!" I glanced at Malcolm with a smirk, but said nothing, for my mother's sake. "Malcolm, if you're free, you should come by as well. The more guinea pigs, the better." My father said.

Malcolm chuckled politely. "I would love to. I'll see what's on my plate, Ni's—"

"Naomi." It was bad enough he was in my family home, I'd be damned if he thought he could use my nickname too.

"Sorry. Naomi is not the only one who has a case to win."

I looked up from my food to that half-smirk, and I wanted to leap across the table and smack it off his face. "Darling, this food is delicious. You've outdone yourself." My mother said hurriedly.

She kissed my father on the cheek, and I nodded in agreement as I stuck a spoonful in my mouth to keep my hand busy.

"I have to agree, sir. This might be the best gumbo I've ever had. Just don't tell my mom I said that." Everyone else found him amusing.

"How is your mom? She had a heart problem, right?" I glanced at Malcolm and saw him stiffen at my brother's questions. "Actually, Malcolm and I would never have met in college if he hadn't taken that time off to go home. He missed an entire year to take care of her." The air shifted, and Malcolm wore a different expression from the forever calm and cocky he usually exuded.

"Is something wrong with Jacklyn?" My mom gasped, concern lacing her question.

"You know his mom?" I asked, but Malcolm cleared his throat, and everyone turned in his direction.

"She's great," he announced through a tight smile. His tone

was curt, and it was clear he didn't like this subject. My curiosity piqued, but he was already out of his chair. "Speaking of which, I promised I would stop by for a visit in the morning before work, so I'd better call it a night. My apology face isn't nearly as forgivable as Naomi's."

It seemed he was avoiding *my* eye contact this time.

"Well, if the gumbo was really that good, what kind of hosts would we be if we didn't send you off with some? Ni, take Malcolm into the kitchen and get him sorted." Annalise stifled a laugh at what I can only assume was the expression of horror on my face at my mother's request.

"I'm sure Dante could help him." My brother stood to put me out of my misery, but my mother put her hand up.

"I'm sure he could, but I didn't ask Dante." I looked from my mother to my father, who didn't seem at all interested in getting in the middle.

As a last-ditch effort, I looked to Malcolm for a way out. Instead, he extended his hand. "After you."

Ass. Hole. Shoving my chair back, I started walking toward the kitchen, thinking long and hard about what age I actually was. I never looked back to see if he had followed, not that I needed to, because I could feel his alarming closeness with each step. The walk only took a second, but it felt like an eternity, and I spent the time desperately wishing I had skipped tonight and ruined Malcolm's little plan or had at least taken a sip of water because I realized my throat had become painfully dry.

"What are you doing here?" I hissed as I crossed the kitchen to get to the cabinet with the plastic containers. When he didn't respond, I had no choice but to look at him. He had kept his distance, settling his shoulder against a close wall.

"I saw your brother at our gym, and he invited me to dinner." *Bullshit.* I turned to the cabinet, avoiding his gaze. "Dorian and you seem close. Is that your type? Lanky?" I jerked my body back around and glared at him. His calmness was back intact, just as mine was unraveling. "It's none of your business what my type is." I said through gritted teeth.

Malcolm moved slowly. Righting himself from the wall, he took the few necessary steps for him to tower over me. I held my ground, but I wasn't sure if it was because I refused to move or that the counter was already pushing against my back. "That's too bad. I would like it to be my business."

His voice was low, gravely, and I had to tilt my head back to look at him. All the anger he pulled out of me morphed, and I gripped the counter. Malcolm leaned down so that we were almost eye to eye, and a voice somewhere far away in my brain was telling me to move, slap him, *something*, but all I could do was stare back into those dark brown eyes. My whole body was alert to his attention; it felt like he was probing for something with his gaze, and I had the urge to give him whatever it was.

"Why do you hate me so much?" Malcolm asked, his bunched brow making him look genuinely curious. Mustering all the strength I had to get my libido in check, I turned around in the small space he had given me to move. "Oh, I don't know. Could it be because I don't enjoy being around privileged dicks who make it their job to defend murderers?" As soon as the words left my mouth, I regretted them, but I ignored the urge to take them back. Instead, I took out a container and walked over to the remaining pot of gumbo simmering on the stove with the large metal spoon still sticking out of the top.

"Aren't we a little presumptuous, Goody? Innocent until proven guilty." *Goody?* Guilt from my comment faded as Malcolm's odd nickname sunk in. He was the unknown number. Instead of getting mad like he wanted me to, I pushed the gumbo filled container closed a little too hard and turned around with a smile. "My name is Naomi, Ms. Vine to you. Lose the nickname and lose my number."

Without waiting for a response, I shoved the Tupperware into Malcolm's chest. I expected to see his smirk when I glanced up at him, but his mouth formed a straight line instead. It threw my anger off a little, but I didn't hesitate as I turned and walked out of the kitchen.

I was usually a calm person, but somehow he got under my skin, and I couldn't think straight.

I made it back to my seat as Malcolm appeared at the edge of the table, all smiles again, like nothing had happened. "Thank you for your generous hospitality." Everyone gave their goodbyes, and Dante stood to walk Malcolm out. I should've been heading out as well, but there was no way I was walking out at the same time as him. Waiting ten minutes was the safer option.

"I look forward to seeing you tomorrow, Ms. Vine." Inappropriate heat spread between my thighs at Malcolm's tone. It was even more seductive than it had been in the kitchen, if that was even possible. "Oh," Annalise gasped, and I looked over to see her covering her mouth with a hand, her eyes wide. My hands balled into fists to keep me from turning to Malcolm, even though his voice called to me like a siren song. My brother was laughing hysterically, and I couldn't risk a glance at my parents. "Damn, Malcolm, I think you broke my sister!" Dante thought he was funny.

"I'm going to the bathroom." Murmuring to no one in particular, I made a beeline for the room that was in the opposite direction from Malcolm. I heard some brief murmurs of more goodbyes and my brother's damn laugh. but I remained right where I was, staring at myself in the mirror, trying to gain some sort of composure. My brain had short-circuited just from Malcolm's voice.

"Ni, the man is gone!" Dante shouted from the dining room, and I was delighted to hear my mother scold him to quiet down. My eyes looked as wild as I felt, but I took another breath and smoothed down my blouse until I was steady enough to face my family again.

Everyone had finished their food and was chatting when I took my seat, which was perfect since I wasn't hungry anymore, but desperately needed water. I took a few large gulps from my glass, feigning interest in the conversation.

"Thirsty, huh?" Dante chirped, and my mom gave him a glare as she continued telling her story of meeting Morgan Freeman.

Dante shut up, but the smile never left his face.

We had all heard my mom's story at least a dozen times, but it was a comfort one she pulled out whenever she wanted to reset the mood, and I was grateful. As she was detailing how she told Mr. Freeman that she was a happily married woman, I reached for my phone to check the time and found another text from Malcolm.

I love a good chase, Goody.

I tossed my phone back in my bag and ignored the lingering tingle of his words.

CHAPTER 11

NAOMI

I was on autopilot the entire way home, trying my best not to think about Malcolm and failing miserably. *He loved a good chase.* I scoffed in my empty car. It was good that my phone died before I left my parents' home because, despite all my resolve, I wanted to text him back. He was infuriating, but he also fanned a flame that I thought had gone out long ago.

I had no shame in admitting to myself that he was easy on the eyes, had a way with words, and could soak my panties without a single touch. As long as I didn't say it out loud, I was fine. Malcolm was off limits, and there wasn't anything his fine ass could do that would make me go against my morals. He would chase forever.

High beams pierced my rearview mirror, pulling me out of what must have been a twenty-minute daydream as I came to the last traffic light before my house. We were the only ones on the road, but they were practically on my bumper, with their lights illuminating the inside of my car intensely. I put my hand up to block the glare in the mirror and flashed my lights as a notice to turn theirs down. They revved their engine in response.

I was in no mood for a street racer, and as soon as the light switched green, I sped up to get out of the way. Instead of going around, the impatient car matched my speed and continued following too closely. I ignored my quickening pulse as I clicked on my blinker to make the left onto my street. As if on command, the dark car followed suit, staying nearly on top of me with its glaring lights. All I wanted to do was snuggle my pillow and my dog, but I couldn't shake the ominous feeling that something was wrong. Was it a prank? My neighborhood wasn't dangerous, but it was an occupational hazard to jump to grim conclusions.

I started turning to the left and made an abrupt swing of the wheel to continue straight, and was relieved to see the mystery car continued its turn.

My pounding heart made me roll my eyes. My lack of sleep was getting to me. I looked around for a good street to turn down for my impromptu detour when I heard tires screeching. Glancing in the rearview mirror, I saw the sedan barreling back around the corner, coming dangerously close to my bumper. My breath came out in short, fast bursts as I accepted I was being followed.

I couldn't see who was driving the car, and they had rushed too close too fast for me to get a good look at their license plate. The driver kept a weird pace of slow and fast that let up on my bumper only long enough for them to speed up extremely close again without ever actually hitting me. I reached into my center compartment but couldn't feel the cord that was normally there. My entire body was rigid as I pictured my designated car and work phone charger on my office desk. Why hadn't I put it in my bag like I always did? I cursed into the darkness, but stopped when the car suddenly slowed, giving me a suspicious amount of space.

I kept a steady speed, careful not to go too fast and encourage whoever was in the sedan to follow suit. Keeping an eye on the rearview mirror, I hoped this was some sick joke that the driver would get bored with and drive off. Instead, the car swerved hard to my right and edged up the side of me, almost bringing us side by side. I looked over, but all I saw was darkness. The windows were so black, I couldn't even make out a shape. "I've called the cops!" I shouted, unsure if they could even hear my lie through both of our windows. Just as quick as they were beside me, they were behind me again, so close that I braced and accelerated for a bumper hit that didn't come. Tears formed at the corners of my eyes, but I shook my head. "Cry later, Naomi." It was a whisper out loud, but I continued screaming the words in my mind as I wiped away stray tears and focused.

My phone was dead, but I knew there was a police station ten minutes away. I was terrible with directions, but I had been to the station a few times for work and was almost sure it was a couple of streets over. The roads were empty, and any confidence of other cars appearing dwindled by the minute. My decision made; I approached the next intersection and needed to make a right turn. I was on the far left and would have to swerve hard if I was going to make the maneuver.

My heart was beating too hard, and I had no idea what the driver had in mind. I couldn't be sure I wasn't driving into some kind of trap.

I looked at the street timer, counting down the walking allowance left. *Three.* I took a deep breath. *Two.* I jerked my wheel to the right and jammed my foot on the gas, skirting across the three lanes to the far-right corner of the intersection. I didn't make the turn, skidding to a stop to avoid hopping over the curb and ramming into the pole on the sidewalk. The driver screeched to a halt in the lane I had abandoned before flooring it, heading straight through the red light. I watched their red taillights as they sped into the night, turning down a distant street. My hands stayed gripped on my steering wheel, and my lungs burned with the exhale I couldn't seem to let out.

I wanted to close my eyes and attempt to calm the shaking that attacked my entire body, but even after the lights faded, I couldn't look away. I didn't see the license plate or the driver, but it was a black sedan that looked like it had seen better days. Before they sped down the street, I saw a long white scratch on the side of the car. Maybe I wasn't the first person they had done this to?

But who would want to scare me... *or worse?* I snapped back to reality. I was still staring down the quiet road. My car sat crooked between lanes, inches from the curb. I persuaded myself to glance at my car clock and saw that it was well past one in the morning. At least forty-five minutes had passed while I was frozen there. My eyes gradually slid from the clock to my hands — which were clutching the wheel for dear life — and my feet, the right one still diligently smashed into the brake.

I released the wheel, and my hands sprang to life with a stinging pain. I tightened and released them a few times until the shocks lessened enough for me to bring them gingerly to my temples. My right hand touched sticky moisture where my hairline met my forehead, and my heart kicked up again. I yanked the car into park, taking my foot off the brake, inviting another shot of pain from my stiff muscles trying to work again.

I mumbled a few colorful words as I turned off the ignition and pulled down my visor with my left hand, softly trying to move the hair out of the wound with my right to get a better look.

The two dim lights on the side of the mirror made the blood on my forehead shine a vivid red. As soon as I saw it, the throbbing increased, rhythmically thumping like the dutiful second hand of a clock. It looked as if the blood had stopped, and the amount that was present didn't go further than the crease of my eyelid, but I couldn't see the actual wound. Pushing up my curls and arching forward as far as I could while still buckled resulted in searing pain that made my eyes water. "Fuck!" I slammed closed the visor and slapped the steering wheel, my hand meeting more blood from the impact I couldn't remember.

Driving home and taking aspirin until the pain dulled enough for me to sleep seemed like the easiest solution, but what if I had internal bleeding or a concussion? It would be reckless not to file a police report, and I could get that handled at the hospital while they were examining me.

Always the planner. Malcolm's voice floated through my mind. *Goody.* So what if I liked to follow the rules?! They were there for a reason! I sighed my frustration and looked around my car.

Residual fear prickled my skin as I noticed my disheveled things strewn across the floor.

I couldn't keep sitting here. Craning my head to the backseat, I tried to find something to clean the blood, but couldn't see anything. I started to take off my seat belt to slip out of my cardigan to use, but the attempt made the throbbing increase in half seconds.

I angrily slapped the steering wheel again. "If the stop was strong enough to injure me, then it should have been strong enough for an airbag!" I shouted into the night.

"I'm suing," I whispered in a much saner tone as I hit my steering wheel once more with less conviction and started my car back up, hoping I could find an urgent care without my GPS.

CHAPTER 12

NAOMI

It was nearly four in the morning when I walked through my door. Convincing the doctor I only needed a small flesh-colored band-aid instead of the stark white gauze he was trying to put above my left eye was the only high point of my visit to the hospital. The cops offered almost no help, claiming that since my car wasn't damaged and the driver did nothing illegal, their hands were tied. They agreed to check the traffic light footage only when I mentioned working for the DA's office.

The doctor gave me a clean bill of health before sending me home with instructions to keep my wound covered. I barely had time to nap, shower, and look somewhat presentable in a basic black suit before I left again.

I pacified Mac with one of his big bone treats and scheduled Lydia for an extra-long walk as an apology for my night away.

Even with my disastrous morning, I arrived at the courthouse with enough time to get the biggest coffee they would allow at the snack stand. While waiting, I caught eyes with a few people and realized they were all glancing at my bandage. Removing it was tempting, but my forehead looked worse without it, so I pushed my hair more into my face and prayed that my curls could work a miracle.

Coffee in hand, I headed for the courtroom and saw that everyone except the judge had already taken their seats. As always, my eyes found Malcolm, but I shifted my gaze immediately, smiling at Coleman as he stood to meet me at the end of the gallery. Before my boss could open the small swinging door, another hand beat him to it.

Malcolm's smirk fell when he saw my bandage, and I passed by him to avoid whatever annoying comment he had planned. The concern was apparent on both Coleman and Dorian's faces as I sat down between them, and I decided to get ahead of the speculation. "I'm fine, just tripped over my dog," I murmured low, hoping the defense table couldn't hear me. Instinctively, my eyes flicked up to see Malcolm still standing by the door watching me.

The last thing I needed was him joking about my clumsiness. I shot a warning glare to send him away, but he didn't move. "Are you sure you're okay?" Dorian's hand touched mine on the table, but I moved from under him and grabbed some folders from my bag that I had set on the floor. "All good, truly."

When I came back up, Malcolm's hand was in front of my face with a card. "She's a prominent doctor in Beverly Hills and can work around a busy schedule. She can also make house calls."

I stared at the embossed card he held for Dr. Sherry Sleuth. A likely expensive doctor I had no desire to go see—and he presented it without a snide remark. I couldn't tell what his angle was, but I *could* sense everyone in the room staring at us, including my boss. Malcolm either didn't notice or didn't care.

When I hadn't moved to take the card, he leaned in, laying the thin paper on the table and slowly sliding it toward me. "Call her." Malcolm wasn't loud, but authoritative, like I was one of his subordinates that he was giving a warning. I narrowed my eyes, but he only arched a brow and returned to his full height, his back to me before I could even scoff at his inappropriate behavior. "That was...interesting," Dorian said, and I willed my cheeks not to betray me even as I felt them heating. Instead of glaring at Malcolm or standing up and ripping the card in front of his face like I wanted to, I tossed it in my bag to make the whole situation disappear.

"How was the rest of your weekend?" I asked Dorian, my voice a picture perfect fake calm to ensure Malcolm understood he had no effect on me. Dorian looked between me and the defense table twice, but thankfully moved on. "Good! Worked on Cassy—that's what I've named the Chevy." He smiled, and I was thankful he hadn't changed his demeanor since our talk. I liked his friendliness, I just wanted to make sure he knew that's all we would be. "What about you, boss? Did Charlotte successfully keep you away from your study?" Coleman chuckled as he flipped through the papers in front of him. "She hustled a few hours out of me. We saw some talented jazz musicians performing in Leiman Park." I smiled at his amused tone. He really loved his wife.

Feeling like the eyes of the courtroom were finally elsewhere, I glanced back to see both of our witnesses for the day sitting on our side of the gallery. Neither of them knew each other, but both had unpleasant encounters with Drayman, and without a body, our case was vastly circumstantial, so character witnesses were important. We would show what type of person Ronan Drayman was, no matter how much the defense tried to paint him as a good-natured philanthropist.

The door opened to the judge's chambers as I turned back, and Coleman shook an encouraging fist at both me and Dorian before we all stood. The judge waved us back down and immediately asked for the first witness, so Coleman remained standing.

"We call Deanne Rudolf to the stand, Your Honor." Deanne stood, visibly nervous in her slightly wrinkled and too big purple dress, but made the short walk to the witness stand in black flats.

Our eyes met after she had taken her oath, and I tried to send some encouragement her way with a small smile that she weakly returned. Coleman walked up to the stand, but didn't start until she consented.

"Ms. Rudolf, can you please tell us how you came to know the defendant?" Deanne took a deep breath. "I used to work for Mr. Drayman at the Cathouse downtown as a waitress." Her voice was steady, and I unclenched my fists under the table.

She calmly recounted her experience filing a sexual harassment report against Draymen and how she was at first urged against saying anything and then promptly fired the day after doing so. "And what happened when you told the defendant that you would take him to court?" Deanne looked down briefly but met Coleman's eyes again. "He stepped really close to me, blocking the exit, and said that 'poor sluts like you should be grateful when a man hits on them'."

I looked over at the jury, and some were glancing at Drayman with disdain. "Then the calls started."

Deanne spoke about the many nights of intimidating phone calls and the knocks on her door at three in the morning. "When did these things stop?" Coleman asked, looking at the jury. "The day I dropped the case against Mr. Drayman." The room was so quiet everyone could hear Deanne's anxious shuffling in her seat. "No further questions, Your Honor."

Coleman came to sit next to me, and I slid him my scribbled observation that the jury seemed swayed by the testimony. He nodded and then focused on Langston Charles as he stood with a closed file in his hand, making his way to Deanne. The defense's silence during her testimony surprised me, but as Langston slowly smiled toward the jury, I suspected he had something up his sleeve.

"Ms. Rudolf, you said that you were fired from the Cathouse for filing a sexual harassment complaint, correct?" Deanne grimaced.

"Yes, that's what happened."

"How many years did you sell drugs, Ms. Rudolf?" Coleman was up before Deanna even gasped. "Objection, Your Honor! Relevance?" Judge Lee looked to Langston.

"The prosecution had a chance to establish character, Your Honor. I am simply doing the same." Coleman tried to speak again, but the judge put up his hand. "Overruled."

Coleman sat silently, but the frustration radiated off him.

"Do you need me to repeat the question, Ms. Rudolf?" Langston tapped the file, and Deanne seemed glued to it. We had discussed the possibility that they would bring up her past drug conviction—years before she took the job at Cathouse—and she knew what to say.

"On and off for a couple of years."

Since standing, Langston had primarily focused on the jury, but now he turned his full attention to Deanne. "And would you say you were 'on' while working at the Cathouse?" Deanne closed her eyes, and I wanted to object, but there was no sound reason to do so. I was pretty sure Langston was using the file as a scare tactic, but the fact that Deanne could get scared told me what was coming. She had lied to us.

"Yes, but only—"

"—Didn't they fire you for selling drugs at the Cathouse, and not because of sexual harassment, as you claimed?" Deanne was looking anywhere but our table, and my hands were in fists again as Langston closed the file with a smirk. "No! That man is a pig! He harassed me for months!"

"Ms. Rudolf, isn't it true that you demanded one million dollars from my client, or you would tell his wife about an affair that never happened?" Someone gasped, and I realized it was one of the jurors. "It wasn't like that!" Langston turned from Deanne, discarding her excuse. Coleman stood again. "Objection, Your Honor, this line of questioning—"

"Sit down, John," Judge Lee said, his attention still on the witness. "Please tell us what it was like and be aware that we have a witness to the conversation. A Ms. Everton." Deanne's face paled at the name.

"After I filed the claim and they fired me, I didn't know what to do. It's hard to get a job with a conviction on your record!"

Langston still had his back turned to Deanne, watching the jury and patiently waiting for her to continue. "I went to the club and spoke to Drayman." She paused again, and Langston lost his patience. "And you told him to give you a million dollars, correct?" Her response was so low that the judge had to tell her to speak up.

"Yes."

"And if he didn't give in, you would tell his wife that you were having an affair?" Deanne met my eyes.

"My lawyer said that all the harassment I had endured wasn't concrete enough." Tears started streaming down her face, but she kept her eyes locked on mine.

"All he does is use people." Langston was already walking back to his seat. "It seems like you were the one trying to use someone, Ms. Rudolf. No further questions." Deanne stood, barely waiting to be dismissed, and raced out of the courtroom.

"A brief recess, Your Honor?" Coleman asked, sounding defeated. "Ten minutes." Judge Lee struck his gavel and then disappeared to his chambers.

Coleman stood immediately, heading for the exit with Dorian and me trying to keep up. I couldn't even stomach a glance toward the defense table as we passed in a rush.

~

The day fared no better after Deanne's escape. Coleman couldn't understand why Deanne omitted such important information. Dorian searched for her to check that she was okay, understanding that even though she hadn't told us the whole truth, being up there seemed to have dredged up terrible memories. Unfortunately, he couldn't find her.

Once we were back, our second witness Tom Buchanan gave his testimony, and while Langston wasn't able to downright discredit him, he twisted some of Buchanan's words, making it sound like the business deal that had gone wrong between him and Drayman was a difference of opinion rather than an all-out strategy on Drayman's part to keep most of the profits.

By the time Buchanan had left the witness stand, exhaustion was pulling at my eyelids while frustration was the only thing keeping me upright as I packed up.

While we had more witnesses who could speak to Drayman's indecent behavior both in and out of the workplace, Dorian's miracle witness was becoming more pivotal by the second. We had to get his formal statement. I turned to him to ask if we could get Jack in this evening, but Dorian looked just as defeated as I felt, and I figured it could wait until we got back to the office.

My phone buzzed in my bag, and I retrieved it as I lifted the case onto my shoulder.

Call the doctor.

I looked up to see that Malcolm was no longer in the courtroom, with only Gabby left behind, packing up at their table. I had expected him to pester me about the abysmal day our side had.

"You good, Ni?" Dorian was so close to my side, his voice startled me. I hurried forward, embarrassed that I had expected anything from Malcolm Charles. "Fine, sorry. See you at the office!" I pushed the doors too hard as I rushed out of the court-room, making them clang hard against the hallway walls.

CHAPTER 13

MALCOLM

"Ms. Monroe left you another message. She asked if your phone number had changed because there couldn't be any other reason you weren't returning her calls." Camden rolled his eyes just enough to show his disdain for Jada Monroe without being unprofessional before moving on.

If I had been paying attention, I would have found it amusing. As it stood, I was more wrapped up in the same question I'd had since Naomi walked into the courtroom. Why the fuck did she have a bandage on her forehead?

"Also, your father has put your name on the list for the Sheffield's gala next month. $10,000 a plate, and you're expected to give a speech representing the firm in his stead." I could tell Camden braced for my father-induced temper to flare, but even Langston Charles and his time-sucking antics couldn't deviate my thoughts. "What about the other thing?" Camden looked up from his iPad and eyed me curiously. "The other thing?" I raised a brow to stress that I would not spell it out, no matter how much it entertained my assistant.

"Oh, the Dr. Sleuth thing?" He drawled with mock remembrance. "I called, and after some *cajoling*, the receptionist said that Ms. Vine hadn't made an appointment, but she would let me know if she did." I didn't bother asking what he'd done to get the receptionist to talk. Getting information was one of the reasons Camden was my assistant, but the news wasn't what I wanted to hear.

Naomi had been fine the night before. I had stared at every inch of her, so whatever happened had been after I left her parents' house. I thought about calling her brother, but stopped myself.

Last night was supposed to be innocent fun. Naomi riled me up, and I wanted to do the same, but something about her genuinely not liking me doesn't sit right. Yes, she's an uppity know it all, whose ethics belonged somewhere in another century, but her thoughts on my character bothered me, and I wanted to prove how wrong she was instead of just dismissing them as I should have.

"Avery also called. Something about a basketball related 'ass whoopin' you have coming. That child is a menace." Camden was huffing out a breath, but I saw the humor in his eyes. I needed to call the kid back. We hadn't spoken since the police station, and I knew talking shit was his way of reaching out. "I'll call him back." I murmured. Camden pursed his lips, but said nothing, as he nodded and left my office.

I stared at my computer, but the words weren't registering. It had been nearly five hours since I'd seen that woman in court, and it still took an extreme exercise of willpower not to track Naomi down and demand she tell me the truth about her injury. Her colleagues might've fallen for her ridiculous dog story, but Naomi was a terrible liar and if I hadn't forced myself to leave the courtroom at the sound of the gavel, I knew I would've pushed her into some dark corner of the courthouse and *incentivize* her to tell me what happened. The fact that I was ninety percent sure she would have slapped the shit out of me instead of giving an explanation be damned.

But it didn't stop the question from nagging at me. A family quarrel? I tossed the thought. Although Dante's chirps were definitely getting to her last night, Naomi didn't seem the scrappy type. At least not physically. Verbally, the woman could kill you faster than a bullet. No, something she didn't want to talk about gave her whatever was hiding under that bandage. A fleeting image of Naomi entangled in the sheets made me swallow. My dick was hard, but it was unmatched by a wrath I couldn't explain. There was no way. Naomi was as vanilla as they came. There was no chance in hell she got hurt fucking some guy. I took a deep breath and tried to think rationally.

There was no mention of a current man in Naomi's life from Sloan's background check. As if to torture me, another image surfaced, and the faceless man slowly came into focus as Dorian's bitch ass. I gripped the bridge of my nose to shake the ridiculous thought, but it had tentacles that wouldn't let go. A secret relationship? Naomi was a straight arrow. Sex with a coworker would be taboo for her.

Taboo enough to lie?

I racked my mind to remember their interactions earlier in the morning, but the man was like human static and I couldn't recall what he said to Naomi, other than it had probably been an excuse to get her eyes on him.

Either speculation or Naomi was going to kill me, and I'd take my chances with Goody. My cell phone rang, and the tightness in my shoulders eased as my brain cleared from my momentary insanity.

"Sloan, what do you know?" I appreciated he didn't need any preamble and got straight to the point. "She went to a hospital near her home around two a.m. because of a car accident. She had a small laceration along her hairline on the left side." Something feral rumbled in my chest, but I clenched my jaw to remain silent. The injury was even worse than I'd thought, and Naomi worked just a few hours later? I knew she was obsessed with her job, but did she not care about herself at all?

"She also filed a police report." My legs bolted me upright of their own accord. "Why?" I roared.

Camden had closed my door behind him, but I was sure half the floor still heard me. "She said someone was following her on the road, and she had the accident trying to escape them." I tightened and loosened my fists, trying to get hold of myself. "There's been little movement from the police so far. The cops who caught the case seem to think it was a one-off. Some kids playing a prank."

A prank? The theory didn't sit well with me. "Do you want me to track down the driver?" Sloan's tone made it clear he already knew the answer, and the 'yes' was on the tip of my tongue, but I refrained. I knew cops were idiots, but there was also no logical reason for me to have Sloan track down whoever did this.

What if he found them? What would I do next for a woman I had known for less than a week? The rage tingling just under my skin made my answer easy. "No. Let the police deal with it." Sloan gave no indication of surprise. "Understood, boss. She's currently leaving work. Would you like me to tail her?" The thought was tempting. The woman made it obvious she didn't care what happened to her.

But Sloan asking this question told me I needed to take a step back and get to what was important. "No. Any progress on Fuller?" This time he did pause before speaking. "Another dead end, but my team is working another angle. I'll keep you updated." Frustration soured my mood further. "Please do," I said, and hung up, annoyed for the wrong reason.

My focus should have been on removing the stain that was my father from my law firm, and it was. I ran my tongue along my teeth and blew out a breath to expel the sudden unease I felt in my chest. Naomi was an adult and could take care of herself.

I was moving toward my door. Sloan following her was a

bad idea, but checking on Naomi myself might be the only way to quell this distraction.

I walked out of my office, thinking through different rationales of showing up at her home, none of them good, when I slowed my pace as I saw my father coming toward me. Camden stood, but I motioned for him to sit back down. This would be quick.

"Son, where are you off to in such a rush?" My office was private, but we were out in the open with associates not too far away roaming the halls, so I swallowed my irritation and slid my hands into my pockets. "Dinner plans with a potential client." Done with the conversation, I took a step forward, but Langston moved to stop me. "Oh, potential client? Perhaps the head of the firm should come along to seal the deal? We could talk about what a great day we had in court." I restrained a sigh. My father's courthouse step sermon made sure that everyone in the nation knew how well we had done in court. He was trying to get under my skin as always, but today was not the day.

"I'm sure you have other pressing matters. Isn't Rosalind in town?" The tick of my father's jaw brought a delight that almost made me want to keep talking to him. I rarely brought up his long-time mistress, and never in mixed company, but I was busy and he was getting too comfortable. Langston took a step toward me, an irritating smile developing on his face.

"You're right, I am busy. But make sure our potential client knows that we only handle high-profile cases. The ones that get handled by the best prosecutors Crestwood has to offer."

He tilted his head to the side, and his smile got broader. Before I had realized that my father wasn't worthy of adoration, I had been obsessed with studying his cases so I could be just like him. In doing so, I could pinpoint exactly when he was going for the jugular. "You know, it's a wonder the crime rate hasn't gone up with the hope of a Naomi Vine cross-examination. There must be more than a few men who would kill simply to breathe the same air as her." The glint in his eye told me I had given him what he wanted with my nostril flare and bunched fists in my pockets.

"Uh, Mr. Charles, You're going to be late for your dinner." Neither I nor my father looked Camden's way, but his reminder was enough, and I schooled my features.

"I'll inform them, though I suspect anyone unfortunate enough to face Ms. Vine will regret it." I turned from my father to the ready Camden. "I'll be gone for the rest of the evening. Go home." I walked past the miraculously silent Langston, but saw the fire dancing in his eyes. He was having fun.

I made my way to the bank of elevators and slammed the button a little too hard. I didn't want another word to come out of his mouth about Naomi, and it bothered me that my father thought he could make me angry just by mentioning her. Realizing he had been correct was something I was going to have to think more about later.

CHAPTER 14

NAOMI

I drove down my quiet street and slid into my driveway, stopping at the closed garage I had yet to clean out. It was just another thing on a list that never got any shorter. I turned my car off and sat, working up the mental fortitude to carry my bag until I couldn't take Mac's howling anymore.

With a tired sigh, I stepped out of the warmth of my car into the chilled night, bringing a sharp tingle up my spine. The road was lined with streetlights, but the night swallowed anything lacking an orange hue. Hauling my bag onto my shoulder, I hustled to my front door, remembering too late that I still had something stuck in the keyhole.

What should have been a tired groan leaving my lips, was a confused gasp at the white printer-sized paper that could've been a weird ad, except the capitalized bold lettering included my name.

I spun around and saw a dark figure just at the edge of my driveway, out of range of the street light illumination and I slinked back into my door, knocking my back hard into the brass knob while my bag scraped down my shoulder before landing hard on the ground. The shock of pain kick-started my legs, and I leaped toward my car.

"Stay back!" I screamed. "Naomi, wait!" The low, familiar voice had a startled tremor to it, and I paused with my hand clutching my car door handle.

"Malcolm?" I sputtered, still in disbelief until he came fully into the light by the trunk of my car.

"What the hell are you doing out here?" I rasped, my heart beating so hard I wondered how I could even talk without it wobbling my words. As if he hadn't heard me, Malcolm continued walking, closing the distance between us and wrapping me in his arms. The warm closeness of him called to my frayed nerves, and I leaned in for only a second before I realized this situation was inappropriate and didn't make sense.

I pushed off of him abruptly and took a couple of steps back for good measure. "You're shivering. We should go inside." Calm as ever, Malcolm's tone was even. "I asked you a question." I said, trying to ignore the way he was looking at me like I could break from a strong gust of wind.

"What scared you?" His question brought the reminder of the note on my door, and I turned my head towards it before thinking better. Malcolm had caught the motion because, of course he had, and narrowed his eyes. I rolled mine and folded my arms across my chest. "You did. Leave."

I turned from him with the slim hope that he would actually listen to me, but I felt Malcolm at my back as I made my way to my front door to grab my bag.

"What part of leave did you—" I started, but he was already bypassing me, snatching the ominous note off the olive green wood before I could get to it. He clutched the paper so tight that when I grabbed it from him, a piece of it stayed lodged between his thumb and forefinger. The menacing words were still legible, however.

DANGEROUS THINGS COME OUT AT NIGHT, MS. VINE.

Though the panic that had seized me lingered, my anger and embarrassment significantly lessened it. Why was Malcolm here? Wasn't it bad enough he invaded every other thought I had? I looked up from the note to see his stern glint. "Who wrote that?" He breathed. His voice was only an octave above a whisper, but the clinch of his jaw and the way the torn corner of the paper crinkled in his tightly wound fist made me take a step back and my throat seemed to contract and relax rapidly, forming no words.

His brown eyes shone like obsidian even under my porch light, and for the first time, the only emotion I felt toward Malcolm Charles was fear.

"I don't know." I shrieked, taking another step back toward my car, with him tracking my every movement. Malcolm blinked once, slow and deliberate, and then his mask slid back into place. "Are you okay?" He asked as he hid his hands in his pockets. He kept the distance between us and gave me that annoying smirk. Against my will, I could feel the steady loosening of my muscles at the sight. "Why are you here?" I asked exasperated, trying to keep my guard up. Malcolm looked from my bandage to my eyes.

"You were in a car accident." I fixed my mouth to deny it, but Malcolm held up a steady hand. "You're a terrible liar, Goody."

I pinched my lips between my teeth. I wanted to ask how he knew about the accident, but the man evaded questions like the defense attorney he was, and he was rich anyway. He could probably find out who my elementary school crush was if he wanted to. I was more concerned about something else.

"Malcolm, why do you care?" He was a flirt. I got that. I had gotten under his skin by not begging to sleep with him, so maybe that explained needing to rile me up from time to time. But coming here tonight didn't track. From the rare, genuine expression on his face, I could tell his presence confused him as well.

Mac let out a long howl in the silence, making me puff out a breath I could see in the dark. My neighbors probably hated me. "We should go inside." Malcolm said again and had already turned back to the door, lifting my bag before I could protest. "*I* should go inside." I said, even as anxiety swirled through my chest. The house I loved suddenly felt foreign and dangerous.

Was whoever left that note inside? I clenched my chilly hands at the thought. We were close enough now that I had to look up to meet Malcolm's calm gaze. "Let me look around and then I'll go." His tone was so smooth he could have been talking about dinner plans instead of asking to search my house for a psychopath.

"I'll be fine," I mustered. He leaned down even further, so that we were almost at the same height, my bag looking like a small knapsack on his side instead of the behemoth it was.

"Here are the facts. Someone caused your accident last night and put that—" Malcolm looked up briefly at my forehead, and the quick change in his features was inhuman. But just as quickly, he was looking back at me. All cold fury vanished as if it had been a trick of the light. "—you were injured. Now, you have an intimidating note on your door, a loud dog who's stuck outside and, if I had to guess, no alarm." Malcolm raised an eyebrow to dare me to object. I opened my mouth to do just that, but he spoke again.

"Please."

Malcolm looked down at my lips as he spoke the word, and I wasn't sure how much access he was asking for. I nodded anyway, but didn't move from my spot, looking up at those no longer fearsome eyes. The brown almost sparkled now.

I heard him swallow hard, and my pulse drummed against my throat. This was some kind of trauma response, I was sure, but my brain was hazy about why I should feel anything other than the need that was warming my core.

"You'll have to open the door first, Naomi." His words made me frown. I looked down at my ill-equipped thin jacket, and I knew I was going to give in. I was freezing and scared.

"The front door isn't working right now. We'll have to go through the back." I didn't answer the question in his eyes and instead turned on my heel and walked to the side gate. Mac was on the other side, ready to attack with love, but his bark became more pronounced when he saw Malcolm behind me. "It's okay, Mac. He's not staying long." I heard Malcolm chuckle as I kept moving while Mac circled us both, alternating between trying to jump on me and barking furiously at Malcolm.

We rounded the corner, and I left Mac behind my mini gate before my bedroom sliding door, much to his chagrin. Before I opened it, I swiveled to find Malcolm very close, looking at my ass. He didn't seem apologetic when he met my eyes with that smirk of his.

"In and out, Mr. Charles." He smiled, the full-blown power of it drawing my eyes to his mouth, and he used the moment to walk past me, opening the sliding glass door with ease. He put up a hand for me not to follow him, and while every contrary bone in my body wanted to swat it away, what he'd said had been true. Someone did cause my accident, and that note was real. I stepped in to close the door behind me and lock out the cold and Mac's yapping, but hung back watching as Malcolm slowly moved about my personal space in the dark.

The man was fine without trying. Even crouching down to check under my bed with his flexed muscles thinly veiled under a too expensive suit. He disappeared into the living room, and I stepped in further to get away from the still very vocal Mac.

It should have bothered me more that Malcolm was roaming around my home, but as I watched him open cabinets and check crevices, I felt an ease I hadn't since the accident. It was ridiculous, since I had feared him moments ago, and I sighed at my useless emotions as I walked to meet Malcolm at my front door.

He had opened it and was trying to turn the bottom knob. "I told you it doesn't work." He didn't look up, but closed the door and crouched down to peer inside. "There's something stuck inside." I folded my arms across my chest. "Yes, I know." He was using his phone's flashlight to see what it was, and for some reason, it was making me uncomfortable.

"Give me a knife."

"Mal—"

"A knife, Goody. Something small." His attention never wavered from the doorknob.

An ache knotted in my chest. It felt spiky, and my eyes burned as I watched him examining the keyhole. I turned from him in a rush to the kitchen, shaking my head as I went to get a hold of myself. He was looking at a doorknob. This wasn't a big deal. The knot in my chest only tightened.

I found a knife and had to stop my hand from tossing it at him, instead getting close enough that he grabbed the backend from me with a smile. "Hold this light here." He pulled me down to him in a swift motion and placed his phone in my hand, directing it to the side of the door frame.

I wanted to speak, to protest, but something about the interaction sealed my lips shut. His warm hand lingered on my skin, and I glanced at him to find his jaw ticking again. From this proximity, I could confirm the spicy smell in the courtroom originated from Malcolm, and I squeezed my thighs together, waiting for him to turn to me.

We were so close that if he chose to, he could wrap his arm around my waist and close the distance between us with little effort.

Did I want him to? Since neither of us had turned on the lights, we were shaded in darkness, and I could almost pretend that this moment existed outside of my real life. Something fantastical and immaterial. Free of consequences.

Malcolm looked at me then, as if he had heard my thoughts crystal clear. But rather than drop his lips down to mine, he dropped my hand and went back to his task. "Hold the light still." His voice was rough, and I noticed my hand was shaking. I took a breath and scooted a little farther away while keeping the light trained on his hands as he tried to work the knife into the keyhole. How many times would I have to shake off my feelings for him? It was getting exhausting. Maybe what I needed was an outlet. Teddy floated to mind, and I frowned. A *different* outlet.

Malcolm jiggled the knife in the hole a few times, but whatever was stuck in there wasn't budging. "How did this happen?" He asked, and I shrugged, jostling the light slightly. "No idea. I came home one night, and it was jammed." Malcolm's hands paused for a second, but then he was back at it, doing more scratching than anything. "It's late, and this isn't working. I'll call someone to come out and fix it." Malcolm kept working. "No, you won't. You'll just keep using your unlocked sliding door late at night." He murmured, his attention mostly on pushing the knife through. Agitation nipped at the churning in my chest.

"Could there be a world where you don't despise me so much?" His question caught me off guard. Malcolm's voice was just as calm as always while he tinkered with the knob, but I got the feeling he wasn't looking at me on purpose. I shifted my body to sit on my hip, suddenly feeling uncomfortable on my knees.

"I don't despise you." I pushed out. That garnered a look from him that made me grab my top lip between my teeth to stop from smiling. Malcolm clocked the action and gave me a smile of his own before going back to twisting around the knife. It didn't look like he was making any progress. "We're on opposing sides. We don't need to be friendly." I said curtly. Malcolm nodded as if it was a boring answer, and I rolled my eyes.

He worked in silence for a moment, and we both stared at the knob he was just tapping at this point. "What if I wanted to be friendly?" He asked, his voice pitched low. A breath hung in my chest. This was dangerous territory.

I don't know what I had been thinking letting Malcolm Charles into my home, into my head, but I needed him out of both. His being here, *attempting* to fix my things, made me feel something I hadn't felt in so long; it startled me.

A security that I shouldn't be feeling with the defense attorney in the biggest case of my life. "Are you almost done?" I squeaked. Actually squeaked. My cheeks burned as I sat his phone on the floor beside him and stood, happy to have some distance. With half the visibility he had before, Malcolm's laugh was easy as he held the knife steady against the keyhole with one hand and then slammed his other palm into the base.

A small metallic sound clanked on the other side of the door before he stood as well. He gave me ample space, and I flicked on the foyer light because it wasn't enough. "All I'm saying is, who says we have to hate each other?" *My sanity*. If I stripped away all the righteous anger and indignation, all I had left was temptation. A powerful force that had almost won more times than I wanted to admit. And this was my career. My life's work.

"Malcolm, I can't do this." I whispered. The smile playing on his lips disappeared, and his entire demeanor changed, from amused to stoic in a breath, and even though I meant what I said, it didn't feel good. "I think you should go."

Malcolm nodded once, scooped up his phone and the knife, handing the slightly battered kitchen tool back to me. He opened the door and walked over the threshold but turned back. "As non-friends, could I convince you to talk to a man I know? He could take your statement and find who did this." For the first time, Malcolm sounded worried. Or at least I thought he did. I looked up at him, surprised by his earnest expression. "No, I know a detective I trust. He'll take care of it." When Malcolm lingered with an unconvinced scowl, I sighed. "I'll go first thing in the morning. I know this is serious." Even saying it out loud made me feel vulnerable. I hated it.

Malcolm nodded again, accepting my words. He leaned over briefly and picked up the thing I had forgotten had fallen out of my door. It was a slender piece of silver with a tiny slope that made its end a point. I didn't recognize it, but the piece was in Malcolm's pocket before I could inspect it more. I narrowed my eyes at him, but his mask was back in place, so I was sure I wouldn't get it back.

"I'll see you in court tomorrow, Ms. Vine." His smooth voice held a hard edge, yet his face betrayed nothing. "Goodbye, Mr. Charles."

I shut the door and leaned against it. All the exhaustion that had melted away at Malcolm's presence charged back with a vengeance, mixed now with a little trepidation. This *was* serious. As I scrubbed a hand down my face, I knew I was talking about two different situations at the same time.

CHAPTER 15

MALCOLM

I had worked my whole life to contain my anger and not become like the men in my family. I thought I had been successful, but the moment I read that note and saw the fear in Naomi's eyes, I was ready to go down the darkest depths to ensure whoever had written those words could never write again.

I squeezed the steering wheel at the memory of how I had also scared her. Made her move back at just the look on my face. If only she knew my thoughts.

Naomi was becoming a liability, but I didn't know how to stop it from happening. Every second I wasn't with her, I was thinking about her, and every second in her presence made me want more. It was a problem. However, I was a problem solver. First, I needed to handle the issues I could fix right now.

I had suspicions after I heard about the car accident, but now I knew. I made a hard right turn and heard a car honking in the background as I sped onto the freeway. My speedometer crept past eighty as I tried to regulate my growing rage. Naomi was smart to deny the pull between us. Outside of the obvious conflict of interest, she didn't know me. And she damn sure didn't know my family.

She might've thought she did with the constant media coverage and my father's shameless showboating, but if she knew a shred of my actual family history, she would go the opposite direction whenever she caught sight of me. Hell, if she ever really got to know who I was, she would have every right to be afraid.

I eased on the gas to make the exit for my parents' home. Despite his antics, my father never stayed out late during a case. One of the few professional things left about him. I pulled into the circular driveway, and Samuel, the head of my family's staff at the mansion, met me at the door. He had been around since I was ten, and my mother finally understood our past stewardess had gone above and beyond her duties concerning my father.

Samuel was a svelte, light brown-skinned man now in his sixties, his white hair trimmed close to his head. He was more of a father to me than mine had ever been and had taught me how to tamp down a lot of my anger when I was a child. Right now, even he couldn't cool the fire I'm sure was clear on my face.

"Good evening, Malcolm." He looked down at his watch and cocked his head to the side, but didn't mention the late hour. He extended his hand, and I shook it, but was already looking down the hall to where I knew Langston would be. "Sorry for the late and unexpected arrival." The security at the gate of my parents' estate would have called Samuel to let him know I was approaching, and I imagined the call had woken him up. "No apology needed. This is your home." I wanted to laugh at how absurd that was, but was in no mood.

Samuel closed the door behind us and merely motioned down the hall. "Your mother is sleeping," he murmured, a quiet sternness etched on his features. I nodded my acknowledgement and turned to walk toward Langston's study. Light spilled into the hallway from the cracked door, and I paused before pushing it open.

Confronting my father right now wasn't a good plan, but the image of Naomi's frightened face had my hand on the door.

Langston looked up from a file and stared at me over the top of his reading glasses, his confusion apparent.

"Mal—"

"Who do you have following the prosecution?" His mouth clamped shut, and he dropped the file before taking off his glasses to twirl them in his hand.

"I don't—" I walked right up to his mahogany desk before he could finish his lie. "You may need bullshit scare tactics to win cases, but I don't. Call it off." The twirling stopped, my father's fingertips now tightly gripping the thin temple. I slid my hands into my pockets to appear calm as I hovered over him. I also tried to release the clench of my jaw but failed.

He stood, never taking his eyes off me as that smile I hated spread across his face. "Malcolm, I'm not sure what's got you so worked up, but I can assure you I don't have anyone following the prosecution. Despite what you might think of my ability to practice law, I was winning bigger cases than this before you were old enough to read." I wanted to reach across the desk and knock the smile off his face.

I took the small metal tip of a locksmith pick that had fallen from Naomi's door from my pocket and dropped it on top of his papers. Langston looked at the piece leisurely, holding his glasses close to his face so he could pretend to analyze it. "And what's this? Your evidence?" Animosity was building to a pitch that I wasn't sure I could control much longer. "You're having the prosecution followed and harassed. Put an end to it. Immediately. Or need I remind you what happened in the Fuller case?" The slip of the name finally caused the smile to drop from my father's proud face.

I knew I had shown my hand too soon, and Langston assessed me with an edge that proved me right. "And how did you come by this evidence?" I had hit a nerve, and he was hitting one right back. I retreated a step, and my father smiled.

If he had someone following Naomi, Langston could know I'd been there tonight. Or maybe he'd known even before that. My mind went back to my uncharacteristic interest in Naomi in the courtroom and how my father had talked about her.

With his assessment done, Langston's mouth turned downward as if he had eaten something bad. "In any case, I'm not having anyone followed, and my advice to you would be to focus your energy on our side of the case. I couldn't think of a reason I would need to monitor the prosecution. Do you?" Like most of my father's questions outside of a courtroom, he wasn't looking for an answer. Only an emotion.

I seethed inside but remained impassive. He pointed his glasses at me—a gesture that wouldn't seem threatening unless you knew Langston Charles. "As for the Fuller case..."

That smile was gradually coming back. "That was before your time, so I haven't the foggiest idea what you could be referring to. Whoever has been bending your ear is lying to you." The gleam in his eye told me he intended to find out who.

I put on a smile of my own and pushed past the hatred as I clenched my fists in my pockets. "People tell me all kinds of things." I regained the ground I had lost. "But don't worry, Dad, I always do my due diligence. Call them off." With his smile still intact, my dad let out a small chuckle before sitting back down in his chair.

"Whatever you say, son." I turned and walked out of the study before crossing the line I had worked so hard to maintain.

I walked past Samuel with a curt nod before making it to my car, slamming the door shut and jamming the ignition button. Telling my father I knew about what had gone on during the Fuller case would only bring his guard up and make it that much harder to execute my plan of ousting him from the firm.

It was an irrational move. I'd done it anyway, all because of *her*.

Every ounce of control I'd built over the years was slipping. I gripped the steering wheel as I hit the gas. Sloan's contact rang as I sped down the road.

"Boss?"

"Change of plans."

CHAPTER 16

NAOMI

I pulled into a spot at the already busy police station. Grabbing the unsettling note, now protected in a plastic bag from my passenger seat, I wondered for the hundredth time if I was making the right decision.

High clouds muted the early morning sun, and the air was still chilly. I'd worn my slate gray trench coat, but as I walked across the lot to the entrance, I prayed the building's heater was active. The last time I visited this station for a case, the air conditioning had been down in the middle of summer. Upon entering, I was disappointed to find it only a couple of degrees warmer than outside.

When it was my turn at the counter, I asked for Detective Cruz and then sat in one of the few seats available to wait for him to come down. I had court in a couple of hours, so if he wasn't available, I would have to come back, but I wanted to get it over with before I lost my nerve. Filing a report was the right thing to do, but the longer I thought about the incidents, the more exposed I felt. To distract myself, I looked down at the navy pantsuit and lavender blouse I had picked out for court. I hoped the outfit gave the air of confidence I didn't feel. We needed a win today.

I caught sight of Cruz making his way down the corridor and stood to meet him halfway. "Hey, Naomi, I didn't know we had something today. Come on up." I smiled but didn't correct him, delaying the lecture I was bound to get. Cruz had been a detective for fifteen years and had three daughters he worried about constantly. I knew when I gave him all the details, he would think I had been reckless not coming to him sooner.

We rode the elevator up in silence; the nerves rolling off me. Cruz glanced my way, eyeing the note I hid behind my back, but made no attempt to start a conversation. He wore brown slacks and a white dress shirt, standard detective attire, and a bushy beard perpetually dusted with crumbs.

We had cobbled together a loose friendship over the last few years; him being lead on a couple of my cases and me reaching out to him for advice on others. He talked about his family often, and while he was definitely a no-nonsense cop, he was fair, and I knew I could trust him with whatever this turned out to be.

We walked right past his desk, but I kept quiet as he led me into a conference room and closed the door behind us. "What's up?" I handed him the ziplock and sat in one of the available chairs while he read it.

He sat too, measuring me with that classic detective stare. "Where did you find this?" I pinched my lips together and then pushed it out, knowing I couldn't back out anymore. "On my front door last night." He gave me an admonishing face only a father could give and then looked at the note again. My injury had lost much of the swelling, and I'd used a smaller bandage, but I still pushed more curls into my face in case Cruz caught sight of it.

"Is this the only thing you've received?" I thought about brushing over the other incident, but figured I might as well say it all since I was already here. "A few days ago, a driver tailgated me pretty aggressively in the middle of the night on an empty road." Cruz's face hardened. "I reported that!" I rushed. His expression eased up only a tick.

"Were you able to see the driver?" I shook my head no,

but the image of the car surfaced in my mind. "I know it was a black sedan. Older, I think." Cruz waited for a second to see if I remembered anything else and then sat the note down on the conference table. He mentioned nothing about the torn edge. "It's not much to go on, but we can test the paper for prints and see if anything pops up." I cut my eyes, and Cruz grunted.

"What is it?" I smiled to assure him it wasn't a big deal. "Just that my prints will be on the paper for sure...and possibly another attorney's." Cruz waited for me to continue, and my fake smile got brighter.

"Malcolm Charles. I don't know if you know him, but he happened to be there when I found the note. He was just passing by." Cruz tilted his head and sized me up like he could tell I would rather have my teeth pulled with a rusty wrench than delve further into this conversation.

"Good to know." The detective gave me a reluctant smile, and I felt a weight lift. "I'll call you if we get something. Until then, don't go anywhere alone." I nodded as I stood. "And stay at a friend's or your parents' house if you can." I was less quick to agree to that but nodded anyway when Cruz pursed his lips. "Thank you for this. With the Drayman trial, I don't want to cause a scene if it turns out to be nothing." His face went back stony as he shook his head.

"It's always the smart ones who make the dumbest decisions. If anything else happens," he lowered his eyes for emphasis. "Anything, call me immediately." I had a strange urge to hug Cruz, but resisted and smiled instead.

After I promised, I gave him a wave goodbye and headed for the elevator, suddenly happy I wasn't handling this alone anymore. Malcolm's worried face, as if summoned, crossed my mind. Well, I was finally getting the help I was willing to accept, anyway.

~

The courthouse garage was always busy. This morning, the line stretched nearly two streetlights, so I scoured the narrow roads looking for parking, grumbling to myself with every block I had to pass.

Finally finding a spot three blocks away, I rummaged through my bag for my wallet, knowing that the meter would cost almost the same amount as the much closer garage. I dreaded carrying my bag all the way to the courthouse, but whatever I left behind would somehow be the thing I needed the most.

My phone dinged in my bag just as I was getting out of the car, but I ignored it as I headed to the machine. I inserted my card and tried to figure out what the tiny sun warped screen was telling me as a large black Suburban crept down the street, taking my attention. It came to a slow stop two cars before mine, its engine still on.

I focused back on the meter, finishing my transaction, but couldn't help glancing back at the car that stayed idle in the middle of the lane. The street was one-way, and they were bound to have cars piling up behind them if they didn't move, but they seemed in no rush.

Their stillness put me on edge, and I began walking, stealing glances behind me every few seconds to check that they weren't following me, but they hadn't moved. I wanted to believe I was being ridiculous, but too much had happened in the past few days that made me clutch my bag tighter while I walked as fast as I could. We were in a densely populated residential area with homes built almost on top of each other, but the street was quiet, and I wondered if I ran to a house, would anyone answer.

I glanced back in time to see the driver's side door pop open and my heart hopscotched a couple of extra beats. I picked up my pace, keeping my eyes glued on the towering figure that exited the car. The man might have been the largest person I had ever seen in my life. He wore all black, his muscles protruding out of his short-sleeve shirt, and was a head clear of the already tall Suburban he had gotten out of.

"Ms. Vine, Mr. Charles has asked me to drop you off at the courthouse." Alarm turned to confusion. None of those words were computing in my brain. "I think he called you." My gaze dropped to my bag before returning to the man. I wasn't sure if this was some kind of trick.

I glanced around, again contemplating whether I could make it to a house when he held up his own phone.

"Naomi, get in the car." Malcolm's smooth voice projected through the man's speaker, and I rolled my eyes, but the panic drained from my body. Was this the man he was talking about last night? "I believe I said I didn't need your help, Mr. Charles." I shouted. I felt absurd being so far away, but the man didn't move closer. "And I believe you're a twenty-minute walk from the courthouse, and Judge Lee will arrive in the next ten." I huffed and turned from the man, but riffled through my bag until I found my phone. Malcolm had texted me, not called, with a simple

Get in the car.

I sent the middle-finger emoji. I had forty-five minutes before the start of the trial, but could I risk Judge Lee showing up earlier? Malcolm knew I couldn't. I turned without another word, almost stomping my way back to the man's Suburban. He was saying something I couldn't hear into his phone, which was to his ear now, then he hung up and had the door opened by the time I made it to him. Pausing, I looked up at the giant.

"I don't care what he told you; this is a one time thing." I seethed. He only nodded and then looked above my head, waiting patiently for me to get in.

I practically threw my bag into the elevated vehicle and then stepped up myself. He closed the door with a soft click and then promptly slid into the driver's side, getting us on our way in a matter of seconds. The anger dissipated fast since its catalyst wasn't around, but I would give Malcolm a piece of my mind when I saw him. For now, I would concentrate on the behemoth I was riding with. The man's profile was just as staggering. His head almost touched the top of the car roof, and his dark skin blended perfectly into his black fade.

"Sorry, I was rude." I conceded. This man didn't deserve my ire. He caught my eye in the rearview mirror and nodded before staring back at the road. I guess he was a man of few words. Giving up, I looked out the window as the courthouse came into view.

As we pulled up, I could see a dozen reporters all gathered in a somewhat neat clump on the steps, with Langston a few above them. I stifled a groan as we stopped. Today was a big deal because we had Candace Drayman's sister, Marie, testifying for the prosecution. There was no love lost between Marie and Ronan Drayman. She had been the first person to come to us and offer her testimony, and we hoped she would burst any ideas that Drayman had ever been good to Candace. It was also the first time I would question a witness in the courtroom for this trial. I rubbed my clammy hands together at the thought. The driver motioned to exit the car, pulling me from my introspection, but I put up a hand. "Um..." He paused and met my eye again. "Sloan," he prompted. "Thank you, Sloan, but I can hop out on my own." He sat back in his seat as a response, and I let go of my breath.

The last thing I needed was for Langston to see me being

chauffeured to the courthouse. Who knows how he would spin it in the media? 'Lowly public servant uses tax dollars' or some such nonsense. I weaved my way through the open pockets on the steps and passed as Langston was just finishing up. "We expect a great day in court, as we are one day closer to my client's proven innocence." I kept my head down not to attract his attention, but I knew I had failed when he was behind me in the security line. "Ah, Ms. Vine. How lovely to see you this morning." I kept walking, eyeing the doors to the courtroom and my exit from this conversation. "Mr. Charles." He chuckled beside me. "It is a shame that we met under these circumstances. I have a feeling we could be great friends." I thought of Malcolm's talk of friendship and how I didn't feel as noxious at the sentiment as I did now.

"However, the circumstances can not be changed." My tone was flat, all business. I pulled the court door open, but he held it as I entered. "Yes, a pity. But if you decide to give a Charles a try, I would recommend the seasoned version. Malcolm might be fun to take to a dinner party, but I suspect you want more than just a pretty face."

CHAPTER 17

NAOMI

I stopped moving, and Langston almost hit me in the back, but swiftly avoided my frozen body. "Are you alright, Ms. Vine?" He exclaimed, checking me over with mock concern that made bile travel up my throat. He continued to his table where everyone sat, including Malcolm, who was staring at me with that blank, calm face. I swallowed down the lump in my throat and forced my limbs to make the distance to our area and sat down hard, my chair arms bumping the table.

Coleman and Dorian were greeting me, and I nodded in acknowledgment, but their words were hushed as Langston's voice was loud in my head. Warring thoughts between what he meant by what he said and me knowing damn well what he meant made my temples throb. I coughed to dislodge his words. *Focus on the case,* I whispered to myself. I would spiral later.

I felt Malcolm's eyes on me, but kept mine forward. Had he told his father he'd come to my parents' house? To *my* house? A swift kick of nausea puffed out my cheeks, and I sucked in a breath to hide it. Judge Lee entered, and my limbs moved of their own accord, lifting me upward. "Mr. Coleman, your next witness, please." The judge spoke as if this were any other day. Like it wasn't obvious my anxiety was trying to suffocate me.

I cleared my throat to make sure it would cooperate. "The prosecution calls Marie Chapman," I croaked and spun to see Marie making her way down the aisle to the witness stand, her black knee-high dress wrinkled but neat and her long blonde hair pulled back into a tight, low ponytail. I ignored everyone as I followed her to the witness stand and focused on what was important—Marie's testimony.

She looked like her sister, except weathered, like she had been through a lot more than her tired blue eyes cared to mention. She sat and stared directly at Drayman with a glare that showed she wasn't afraid of him, even while she was being sworn in by the bailiff. I used her determination to ground me. We were here to get justice for her family.

I stood in front of Marie, breaking her connection with Drayman, but she gave me a smile to let me know I could start. "Marie, what was your relationship to the victim, Candace Drayman?" She leaned into the slender mic attached to her seat. "Candace *Chapman* was my younger sister," she said, her voice even and confident. I gave a fleeting look at the jury, and they were all fixated on Marie.

"Can you tell me about the day your sister got married?"

"Objection, Your Honor. Relevance?" Malcolm's voice shouldn't have caught me off guard, but I jumped at his interruption. Langston had frayed my nerves to the point of distraction, which I knew was his intention. Looking up at the judge, I clasped my shaky hands behind my back.

"If the defense would give me beyond a single question, they will know the relevance, Your Honor." I said cooly, even as the questions of what Langston thought he knew still ricocheted in my head. "It's been two questions. Would the defense be able to get to a point in three?" Adrenaline and irritation hit my system in a wave that was doing a great job of hushing the turmoil. Malcolm Charles had to be the most infuriating person on this planet.

I smiled at judge Lee hoping it didn't come across too menacing, "I'm happy the defense is good at counting, perhaps they would also be good at sitting down and allowing a grieving sister to speak about the victim we are all here to seek justice for?" The lack of retort had me glance at the defense table to see Malcolm taking his seat with a smirk. "Perhaps. Withdrawn." He murmured, his eyes alight. I worked to contain my unwanted smile and turned back to the judge.

"Please continue, Ms. Chapman." I came back to Marie with a clearer mind. "We were really close, so I was Candace's maid of honor. She was young when she got married, twenty-two, and our parents had already passed, so it was just me and her until she met Ronan." Marie spat his name out like it was sour on her tongue. "And was she happy on her wedding day?" I prompted. "She was so excited," she breathed. "She didn't have many people to invite, so it was mostly Ronan's *associates*, as he called them. And it was perfect until a woman barged into the bridal suite a few minutes before the ceremony." This time it was Langston who stood.

"Your Honor, we've given leeway, but Ms. Chapman has no point in sight." His tone was flippant, and from the corner of my eye, I saw some of the jury nod in agreement. I turned to the judge, but Marie filled the silence before I could. "My point is, Ronan is a rapist, and my sister unfortunately ignored it." Whispers filled both the jury box and the few people allowed in the gallery. Langston, Coleman and I all said, "Your Honor," in unison, but Judge Lee was already hitting his gavel. "Langston and Naomi, approach the bench." I didn't want to be anywhere near Langston, but squared my shoulders and met him at the judge's seat.

Judge Lee looked at us with mild annoyance and moved his mic out of the way so no one else could hear our conversation. "Ms. Vine, get a hold of your witness. No more outbursts." I nodded my acquiescence and did my best to ignore Langston, who I was sure had a smile on his face. The judge eyed him next. "Mr. Charles, it's clear your team enjoys speaking. The witness was clearly getting there, albeit leisurely." Judge Lee's short, stern glance my way sent the message. "And she will have her rightful say. I will hear your voice again only if necessary. Is that clear?" I couldn't help but turn to see how Langston handled the judge's scrutiny. It shouldn't have surprised me that he looked like he was having a conversation with an old friend. "Of course, Judge Lee. Best behavior," he trilled. The judge leaned back, used to Langston's antics, and hit his gavel again to dismiss us.

When I turned, I caught eyes with Coleman, who motioned for me to come to our table. My first major case with him and I was blowing it. The moisture in my mouth dissipated, and I swallowed hard as I approached him. He leaned in close so that our conversation stayed at our table. "You're handling yourself well. That firm is a bunch of assholes. Don't let them get to you," he whispered, and I couldn't help the shock of a smile. I had never heard Coleman speak a bad word about anyone, let alone with such disdain clear on his face. Dorian contributed with a thumbs-up, and the nerves that were building ebbed.

I returned Dorian's gesture and then turned back to the judge as he was addressing the booth. "The jury will disregard Ms. Chapman's outburst." Marie pursed her lips as the judge looked down at her next. "And Ms. Chapman, you will only answer the questions being asked. Do you understand?" She scowled but agreed with a nod. I allowed the courtroom to settle for a moment before continuing. "Ms. Chapman, you said a woman showed up at the wedding who was unknown to you or your sister, correct?" It took her a second, but she leaned in. "Correct." I turned to the jury. "And what did this woman want?" I watched their faces as she spoke. "She wanted to tell my sister that she had met Ronan two weeks prior in a hotel lobby.

They had drinks, agreed on a price for sex, and he took her to his room."

I waited for someone at the opposite table to speak up, but they remained quiet. We had to submit our evidence to them, so they already knew what was coming, but I wanted the jury to hear the accusation and lack of defense. I walked to our table and, on the way, looked over at Malcolm. His face was impassive, but I felt the electric spark that seemed to jolt me whenever our eyes met.

"Your Honor, I would like to submit the following voice recording into evidence. Marie, what does this audio say?" Marie was ready to answer almost before I had finished the question. "As soon as she said Ronan paid her for sex, I started recording on my phone. I didn't know what was happening, but I'd had a bad feeling about Ronan and—", Malcolm was up before I could stop Marie.

"Your Honor, Ms. Chapman is illustrating an entertaining *story*, but if we could do without her so-called feelings on the matter, this day might eventually end." Judge Lee's stare was rigid toward Malcolm, but he soon looked at me. "Ms. Vine, he has a point." I nodded, but went right back to the jury to not lose momentum. "This woman claimed to have had sex with Mr. Drayman two weeks before his wedding, but adultery is not a crime. It's certainly frowned upon and no doubt less than an ideal thing for a woman to hear about on what is supposed to be the happiest day of her life, but not a crime."

Juror number four, an older Black woman, shook her head. "What else did the woman say?" I asked Marie. "She said that after their first night together, he asked her to come back the next night outside of her escort service. That he would pay her triple, and she accepted."

I glanced at Marie, who was gripping the front of the

witness stand so hard, all the blood had rushed out of her finger-tips. I knew this was difficult for her, no matter the bravado she was trying to show. We had the audio, but the jury needed to hear her testimony the same way I had heard it in the office for the first time. "What happened the next night?" I prompted. "She said he invited her into his hotel room and everything was normal until he pushed her up against a wall hard and...and." I moved from the jury to stand in front of Marie, whose eyes were filling with tears as she looked at Drayman. I made her focus on me. "And what?" She took a small breath.

"She said he raped her and then left her in the room." I touched Marie's hand and hoped she could feel my gratitude. "Ronan rushed in then with security and ushered her out, claiming she was lying." The courtroom was quiet, with only a shuffle of papers on the defense side that I didn't turn to acknowledge. "She was being pushed out screaming, and he thought we couldn't hear him," Marie looked Drayman in the eye as she spoke the last words. "He called her by her first name, Jessica, and told her she was embarrassing herself."

When the jurors stopped scribbling in their notepads, I turned to the judge. "Your Honor, we would like to play the audio in question." This time, it was Ms. Scott who stood. "Your Honor, we request the audio be played in your chambers first to confirm its validity." I turned, but she was looking past me as if I didn't exist. "We have just heard testimony about what is on the said audio. Surely playing it will confirm what the witness said," I retorted. Ms. Scott paid me no mind and instead directed her statement to Judge Lee.

"We have reason to believe this audio may not be accurate, bringing into question Ms. Chapman's testimony as well." Marie stood, and I immediately ushered her back down. She pinned me with a molten stare. "I'm not lying!" I tried to calm her, showing my agreement with a nod.

"Objection!" Coleman exclaimed, just as the judge banged his gavel. "Control your witness, Ms. Vine!" Marie was ready to stand again, but I held her shoulder gently, imploring her to stay down. "This is outrageous, Your Honor! If they have reason to question Ms. Chapman, that's what cross-examination is for!" I didn't turn from Marie, fearing she would use the opportunity to shout, but I could tell Coleman had moved to the front of our table as he ranted. The judge slammed his gavel again, clanging my nerves with it.

"Enough!" Judge Lee turned to Marie and me. "Ms. Chapman," Judge Lee said, "one more word out of turn, and I will hold you in contempt." Marie grunted but remained silent.

She'd been a saint in the witness practice sessions we had for weeks leading up to the trial, but I was kicking myself for not seeing her unbridled hatred for Drayman. From the shaking heads of the jury, it was hurting us more than helping. "Ms. Scott, your motion is denied. You'll have your chance in a moment."

Ms. Scott gracefully tipped her head and then sat, never once glancing my way. Her random assertion was irrelevant and unfounded. I'm sure she realized the judge wouldn't agree with her. It was obvious the line of inquiry was a ruse to get under Marie's skin, and it had worked just as the defense intended. When it was their turn to question her, Marie would be a ticking time bomb, more than willing to go off.

I pushed forward, having the audio played for the jury a few times so that they heard every disturbing word, including Drayman's ice cold voice and Candace's low sobs after her future husband had left the room. I thanked Marie when I was done and made my way back to my seat, passing Ms. Scott on the way. Again, she ignored me, and I sat down with a grunt. While Coleman was already focused on her approach to Marie, Dorian handed me a small piece of paper.

In his small handwriting, he'd written, **That was brutal**, to which I added an exclamation mark before handing it back. I didn't want to think about what had already happened. I could sulk and ruminate when the day was over. Right now, I needed to look for any angle I could use to bolster our case and weaken the defense. "Ms. Chapman, you mentioned 'the woman said' when referring to a woman you assert is on that tape." Marie huffed at Gabriella's statement. "I'm not *asserting* anything. It's what happened."

Ms. Scott stood tall, her tight bun brushing the collar of her white silk blouse without releasing a single hair. "I haven't asked a question yet, Ms. Chapman." Marie glared but quieted. "Have you seen this woman since that day?"

"No."

"Had you seen this mysterious woman before that day?"

"No," Marie muttered. Ms. Scott switched her attention to the jury. "Do you even know her last name?" Marie rolled her shoulders, visibly irritated. "She never gave her name. It was Drayman who said it. You heard her on the tape. She was hysterical." Ms. Scott tapped the jury booth lightly. Every single one of the male jurors and even a few female ones followed her in the movement.

"Yes, so you would consider her 'hysterical', as you put it? Out of sorts, a little crazy even?"

"No, that's not what—"

"But you trusted a random woman's word on the most important day of your sister's life with no evidence?"

Marie sputtered. "She was telling the truth; I could tell!" Ms. Scott didn't seem to even be paying attention to Marie anymore, focused solely on the jurors. "Right. Of course, because you're such a good judge of character." I stood to object, but Ms. Scott held up a hand without looking my way. "Withdrawn."

I sat back down and tried to hide my scorn. "Ms. Chapman, what you're telling the court is that a woman you had never seen before or since came to your sister's wedding and *asserted* that she had some kind of illicit interaction with Mr. Drayman. And that your sister still married him. Because, contrary to what you implied at the start of your testimony, your sister is Mrs. Candace Drayman, correct?" Marie narrowed her eyes. "She married him. Against my pleas."

Ms. Scott turned from the jury and walked the short distance to her table. She leaned over it with an elegant dip of her back and whispered something into Malcolm's ear before lifting again to get his response. His lips were a straight hard line, but he nodded to her, and Gabby smiled and turned, giving her full attention to Marie for the first time since she started.

"So, if the woman who we could assume knew him best— she was marrying him after all—trusted her future husband, why didn't you?" Marie's hands were back to gripping the witness stand. "Because he was a liar. You heard him on the tape! He knew her!" Marie's vitriol did not faze Ms. Scott. "Do you know what I heard, Ms. Chapman? That your sister was cutting you off." I was up faster than Coleman. "Objection, heresy!" Ms. Scott finally graced me with her attention.

"No more heresy than an unknown woman and a convenient audio." I smiled with no humor intended.

"An audio that has the defendant's voice clear as day, confirming the day of events and that the woman existed. Don't recall Candace saying anything about her sister, do you?" Ms. Scott cut her eyes to turn back to Marie.

"Sustained. Stay with the facts you can prove, Ms. Scott."

She nodded without looking at the judge, but Gabriella's entire demeanor changed. She stepped closer to Marie. "Your sister was giving you an allowance of four thousand dollars a month leading up to the wedding, yes or no?" Marie faltered.

"I was helping her get her life—"

"Yes or no?"

"Yes," Marie grated.

"That money stopped after her wedding day, yes or no?"

"Yes."

"In fact, before her death, you and your sister hadn't spoken in any significant way after that day, yes or no?"

Marie paused, her arms slack and hidden at her side in the box. "Ms. Chapman?" Ms. Scott prodded.

"No." Satisfied, Ms. Scott moved to the jury. "Which means you really couldn't speak to their relationship. In reality, you didn't really know your sister at all." Without another glance at Marie, Ms. Scott returned to her seat, and I stood.

"Permission to redirect, Your Honor?" He nodded, and I took a breath. "Marie, why didn't you and your sister speak after her wedding?" Everyone could hear the sniffles Marie was trying to contain, but after a moment, she looked up at me.

"I told her she couldn't marry him. That he was a terrible person and would bring her down with him." She rubbed away a tear. "A week later, I got a call from a woman claiming to be Candace's new assistant. She said my services were no longer needed and that I shouldn't talk to my sister again. I couldn't reach her after that."

CHAPTER 18

NAOMI

I fled the courtroom the moment the gavel was struck. I needed to get outside and away from everyone. The trial had been chaos, and it was my fault. Two business associates, far calmer witnesses, spoke about Drayman's cutthroat business tactics, but Coleman handled both testimonies while I worked not to sigh every five seconds when I thought about my failure.

Marie was my witness. I thought I had coached her to withstand anything the defense could throw at her. I didn't see the pain that was apparent on her face the moment she sat down in the witness seat.

Vendettas never came across well in trial, and Marie sounded like she had a grudge against Ronan, so the defense worked it to their advantage. I also hadn't forgotten Langston's comment, which was only intensifying a headache that was making it hard to see straight.

Malcolm's driver, or whatever he was, Sloan, sat outside idling at the curb of the courthouse, and I remembered then that I wanted to take the back way through the parking garage to escape the reporters who were waiting on the steps.

They were ready for Langston, but when they caught sight of me, they swarmed. "Naomi Vine, what evidence do you have that implicates Ronan Drayman in the murder of his wife?" Another almost toppled over that question with, "Without a body, isn't it only a matter of time before there is a mistrial?" I internally screamed. This was the last thing I needed. I tried to push past the horde, but the circle tightened, and it felt like they were trying to snap pictures of my soul with how close their cameras were.

Light flashed again and again in my weary eyes, and I almost stumbled forward, missing a step I couldn't see. Mounting pressure weighed on my chest, and I felt like I might faint or explode. An arm reached out through the crowd and encased me in a tight embrace that freed a strangled cry from my throat. I looked up to see Sloan, his fierce frame towering over me and looking out past the crowd.

"Naomi! Naomi!" They all hollered my name and kept clicking, even while Sloan knocked some of them so hard they almost lost their footing. He maneuvered me in front of him and kept the reporters at his broad back, becoming an effective wall until we got to his Suburban.

I slid into the back as soon as the door was open and slammed the door with such force the car rocked gently. I couldn't see the cameras anymore around Sloan, who was up against the tinted window, but I could still hear the shouting of my name and their asinine questions. My hands trembled as I moved my bag from my shoulder to the other side of the car, and I held them to my chest and concentrated on breathing. "Did I miss the show?" Malcolm's tone was sharp, and I heard the sway of yells from my name to his.

Sloan moved from the door, and I saw Malcolm standing on the highest step of the courthouse, commanding the crowd of vultures clamoring for his blood now. The lights all flashed and questions flew, but he looked poised and unfazed as he stared straight at me. There was no way he could see through the darkened window, but he stared at me like he could, and I stared back until Sloan drove us away.

~

By the time I got back to the office, it was nearly seven in the evening. Sloan had dropped me off at my car and then I just sat there for I didn't know how long, trying to get my heart rate back down. Each acute memory fought for supremacy in my mind until I finally shut them all out.

I walked onto the deserted office floor from the elevator and sat my bag at my desk. Unsure of how long Dorian and Coleman had already been working, I headed for my boss's office, where they were probably going over our options for tomorrow. Coleman was dismissing Kate when I entered, and I tipped my head to her as we passed each other. Dorian was sitting in the same chair he had been in when he joined the case less than a week before, and I couldn't believe how many things had happened in such a short period. Coleman closed the door and then rounded his desk to stare at both of us with a solemn tilt of his mouth. "Okay. We needed that to go better." I worked not to slink down in my seat.

"I finally convinced Jack to come in," Dorian murmured, perking me back up. "The witness? When?!" I didn't hide the eagerness in my voice. "He'll come in tomorrow evening after we're done with trial."

I wanted to see the boy now, but held back my exasperation. "That's great, but he may not be the slam dunk he once was." I stood at Coleman's deflated tone. I was careful not to let my emotions get the better of me as I spoke. "He saw Candace and Ronan on the day of her disappearance. It has to count for something." Dorian nodded in agreement, but he didn't seem convinced anymore.

"We still don't have a motive, and the witnesses tomorrow are just more disgruntled employees and business partners." I couldn't believe what Coleman was implying.

"But this is an eyewitness, sir!" Coleman rubbed at his eyes. "Naomi, we have to consider that our case isn't strong enough to win outright." I had so much to say, but the words caught in my throat. He wanted to give up? All the days and nights flashed before my eyes.

"We can use Jack as leverage to get a plea deal," Coleman murmured. I didn't want to have this conversation. Drayman deserved life in prison without parole, not a deal that could have him out in five years with good behavior.

I could tell my boss sympathized with me, but he had been doing this a long time; he could more or less predict the outcome. "Call his defense team and make the offer." Coleman said as he turned from us. I stared at his back, struggling to come up with an argument that would work. Calling Charles and Charles was the last thing I wanted to do for any reason, but of course it was me; I was second chair. I held in a sigh and sat back down, not at all ready to hear Langston's smarmy voice through the phone.

"I could do it." I realized I hadn't answered Coleman and glanced at Dorian, who nodded at me. The thought was appealing, but I dismissed his help. "I can do it. I'll call now." I didn't care how devastated I sounded as I walked out of my boss's office.

CHAPTER 19

MALCOLM

She's still at the office.

I ignored the paperwork in front of me and stared at Sloan's text, knowing Naomi would hunt me down if she knew my private detective was following her around. The thought shouldn't have excited me so much.

After the conversation with my father, it was clear I needed to adjust my strategy, and that started with making sure no one could get to Naomi. Sloan confirmed she had gone to the police station and asked around about the detective she had seen. Diego Cruz had a reputation for being a rare capable cop and had already pulled the CCTV footage from the night of her car accident. Since he was good at his job, I would let him continue tracking down leads until he had something I could use.

I read Sloan's message again and wondered if Naomi would pick up if I called. Her assault on the courthouse steps was only a blip on the news, with my statement taking up more coverage as I intended, but I still studied the footage and was trying to curb the urge to make anyone that touched her regret the day they put on a reporter badge. She had to be shaken by the incident, and I wanted to hear her voice to stop me from doing something stupid like going to her home again.

I couldn't take my eyes off my goal of taking Langston down, but there wasn't a minute that went by that Naomi didn't creep into my thoughts. She was mesmerizing when she got out of her own head and took control of the trial today. There wasn't a person in that room who wasn't hanging on every word she said. That her witnesses were flimsy and volatile only showed how good Naomi was at making a case from nothing. I leaned back in my office chair and swung around until I was looking out at the bright lights of the Crestwood traffic.

I wanted her. More and more by the second.

That didn't matter, though. I could continue letting Naomi shut me out and pretend like I didn't notice every time she lingered within arm's reach, waiting for me to close the distance. I could deny the feelings I had for her until I finished what I needed to do, but now that my father thought he saw blood in the water; it was better to keep her close.

My phone buzzed, distracting me from my lie.

Frustration laced the chill that ran through me at my grandfather's call. I punched ignore, but knew I would have to pick up the phone eventually. Eugene James didn't like to be kept waiting.

Camden's office phone rang once before he picked it up, and I turned back to the files on my desk. I should let him go home. Nothing productive was happening anyway. I couldn't hear his conversation through the closed door, but a knock came, and he peeked in. "Mr. Charles, Naomi Vine is on the line. She was looking to speak with your father, but since he's not here, the overnight operator transferred her to me. Should I reach out to his assistant?"

I sat up straighter. There was a clear smile in Camden's tone, but he didn't so much as quirk his lips. My dick pushed against my zipper, putting his snark in the periphery.

"Put her through to me."

"Yes, sir," Camden murmured, his smile blatant this time

before he disappeared behind my closed door. A late-night call for my father? Coleman must have seen the writing on the wall. The phone beeped, letting me know Naomi was on the other end. "Mr. Charles." She sounded like she could barely contain her anger, and my dick jumped. "Ms. Vine." There was a pause, and then when she came back, her tone remained laced with steel, but also something sultry.

"I was expecting your father." I leaned back in my chair, savoring her attention. "He's out of the office. What do you need?" I could practically hear the profanities floating through her mind as she tried to sound composed. "The prosecution would like to give Drayman a chance of a future outside of prison." I stifled my chuckle, but couldn't help the grin. "A chance of a future, huh? Well, I couldn't possibly hear such an intriguing offer over the phone." Naomi sighed, aggravated, and I felt like I could breathe again. "Mr. Charles—"

"Naomi, whatever offer you have, will need to be in person. I'm at the office for another couple of hours. Or maybe your house would be more suitable?"

When she didn't respond straight away, I sat up, concerned she might send that jackass Dorian instead. "I will only consider the offer if it comes from you, Goody." I thought I had lost her until she grumbled something under her breath. "Fine. I'll be at your office in thirty minutes." She hung up without another word, but it did nothing to damage my uplifted mood. I called to Camden and told him to take off and did a lap around the office floor to ensure everyone else had gone home as well. It was a risk to talk here, but it was time Naomi and I had a proper conversation.

Forty-five minutes passed before I got the call from security to let her up, and I smiled to myself as I turned on the building camera feeds from my computer to watch Naomi as she spoke to herself in the elevator. I couldn't hear what she said, but her bunched-up brow suggested colorful words were flying. I leaned in when she stilled, staring at herself in one of the mirrored elevator walls, lightly patting her hair before yanking her hand away. She was definitely cursing now.

"What's so funny?" Gabby's voice slid the smile off my face as I clicked off the cameras. *Shit.*

"What are you still doing here?" She made a habit of staying late but was on my father's floor below. She walked further into my office, and I noticed the file tucked under her arm. "Working on prep for the Neiman case. Here's the motion to suppress the photographs. I was going to leave it on Camden's desk, but I saw your light was on. She set the file down in front of me but didn't turn to leave. "Thank you. Head home." Gabby narrowed her eyes at my cool tone. The distant tapping of heels distracted us, and Gabby turned, but I was already rounding my desk and walking out of the room before she could ask about the noise.

The tapping grew distant, then stopped. Gabby held her questions, but I could hear her following me as I made my way to the lobby. "Hello?" Gabby halted at Naomi's voice, but I kept walking, meeting her by the reception desk. Our eyes met only briefly before she looked behind me, and a scowl I had never seen shifted onto her face. I thought I had seen Naomi angry before, but this was her pissed.

"Naomi, what can we do for you?" Gabby had made it to my side as she asked her question in a syrupy voice. Before Naomi could answer, I stepped forward. "Goodnight, Gabby." My tone was even, but it was hard to maintain as I watched Naomi's glare change from furious to surprised as she met my eyes. Gabby said something I wasn't paying attention to, but she still hadn't moved, so I reluctantly turned. "I can take care of this. I'll see you in the morning."

The last thing I needed was for Naomi to use Gabby as a buffer, so I walked back toward my office with her trailing closely behind before they could interact further. Gabby watched us go, her face impassive as we passed.

When we made it, I let Naomi walk on and then shut the door in case anyone else was around. She stood in the middle of the room in her fitted pantsuit, and I wanted to freeze time just to stare at her ass uninterrupted. I snapped out of it before Naomi caught on and rounded my desk to sit. She didn't take the hint and instead stood with her arms folded and gave me what I was realizing was my own personal glare. My dick tented my slacks, and I was glad to be sitting. "Let's get this over with." I hid my delight at her annoyance as best I could and folded my own arms at her callous tone. "We need to talk." Naomi rolled her eyes, not a hint of amusement to be found. "Yes, about a deal your client doesn't deserve." I frowned. I couldn't care less about Drayman.

"Ten to life." Naomi pushed out. When she continued to glare at me after her offer, I sighed and stood. She took a few steps back before I was even close to her. "Take it or leave it. I'm busy." I made it to the front of my desk and leaned against it, assessing her. Naomi tried to hide her hands within the folds of her arms, but I could see her fists clenched tight.

"Your witnesses aren't strong enough. He's going to walk." Naomi shifted her weight from one leg to the other and then advanced on me slightly.

"We can win this." I arched a brow but said nothing. I knew how hard this was for her, and for the first time, I hated being right about a case. Naomi's glare softened, and she shook her head. "Don't look at me like that." I cleared my throat to shove down the unfamiliar desires that threatened to choke me. "Like what?" Naomi was quiet, but she didn't step back.

"Are you taking the deal or not?" For the first time, she

sounded defeated, and I couldn't allow that. I reached out to her, closing our distance completely. She leaned into me, staring up with those big brown eyes.

"Not," I whispered. She was so close, I could cover her mouth with mine before her next breath.

"Fine," she breathed, putting both hands on my chest and lightly pushing off me. My mind was hazy with her scent, but I faintly registered that she was turning around to leave. "Wait!" I rushed out, bolting forward to reach her as she gripped the doorknob. "I'm not playing this game anymore, Malcolm." The resignation in her voice made me wrap my arm around her stomach to pull her back to me. "This isn't a game," I said into her hair and inhaled her scent hard, not caring if she noticed or not. She stilled beneath me, and I slowly turned her body so that I could look into her eyes and show her how much I meant what I was about to say.

"I want you." She looked away. "You'll get over it." Her voice was hollow, and even though her words were sharp, I wasn't giving up so easily.

"You don't want this?" I caressed the small of her back before pushing her into me more so she could feel how much I wanted her. "You don't want my hands on your body? Because I want to touch you." When she wouldn't look at me, I slid my hand up to her hip and squeezed, making her shiver. "You don't want my lips on your throat? Because I can't stop thinking about it." When she didn't pull away, I leaned in and kissed along her neck, stopping at the dip by her ear when she gripped my shoulders tightly. It was hard to keep from laying her on the desk, but I needed Naomi to know how serious I was.

I leaned back up and tilted her chin until we made eye contact. "You don't want me between those thick legs? Because all I want is to taste you." Naomi was so still I wasn't sure she was breathing, but her brown eyes looked up at me with so much need I had to restrain from pushing her up against the nearest wall.

I slowly turned and walked us back to the desk, picking her up for a second so that she was straddling the edge. Naomi made a noise of shock when I lifted her, but otherwise remained quiet. I leaned in, and she moved back until she was in danger of almost lying down, her shaky arms barely supporting her.

"Malcolm, this isn't a good idea." She practically moaned the words, but I paused. "It isn't a good idea to kiss you?" She nodded while staring at my lips. Her needy expression was proof Naomi was trying to deceive us both, but I stood up, moving out of her space. The cutest growl I'd ever heard came from her as she sat back up, and I couldn't help the smirk. The woman was fighting a losing battle.

"Those reporters were animals today," I murmured, attempting to get Naomi out of her own head. I couldn't have her trying to leave again. Her bewildered glance said it worked. "It was my fault. I shouldn't have gone outside like that." I swallowed to control the anger that lit at the memory of her surrounded by that crowd. "Those scavengers were out of line." I tilted her chin back to me when Naomi tried to break eye contact. "Were you hurt?" She had replaced the band-aid on her forehead with a fresh one, but I still wanted to look underneath. Naomi broke free of my light hold, but kept her eyes on me.

"I was a little out of it when Sloan dropped me off at my car. Could you thank him for me?" My chin lowered at her apparent familiarity. "Sloan works for me. Do I get a thank you?" She rolled her eyes, but I stepped closer between her thighs, and that got her full attention. I placed a hand on the button of her blue slacks and watched as Naomi's face morphed from exasperation to desire.

"Malcolm." Her voice was a near pant already. "Your father knows something is going on between us." That stilled my hand. "Did you tell him you came to my house?" My lust clouded mind cleared as I stared into her questioning eyes. As if a sign, I was being reminded of why this was a bad idea. Langston had already made a move, and I had been too distracted to notice.

I took my hand off Naomi's button and rested it on her thigh, not having the strength to stop touching her completely.

"Don't worry about my father." Naomi's irritation was clear on her face. I wanted to caress her cheek, but there was no way I was moving my hand when I was so close to where I wanted to be. I leaned in instead, my lips grazing her ear. "We have a... complicated relationship, but know that I would never tell Langston anything." My hand moved back to her button.

"He won't be a problem, Naomi. Trust me." I couldn't tell if she huffed or gasped, but she was opening her legs to me, so I didn't give a fuck. "There's still the trial. Someone could find out..." Her weak objections trailed off as I pulled her zipper down. I noted that fucking in my office was not one of them.

"This trial will end in two weeks either way, and then we're just two adults doing whatever the fuck we want." It would end sooner than that, but I couldn't afford to get Naomi worked up about the wrong things right now. A faint thought that this was only going to confuse matters more crossed my mind, but when I leaned back to see Naomi's dark green lace underwear, the air in my lungs seemed too hot and I had to focus. The wet, thin fabric was within reach, making my mouth water.

"This isn't real. We can't be real." She whispered the words to herself as I slid her pants and underwear down and then traveled back up to hold her gaze. Naomi's eyes were glossy, and her hands gripped my desk so tight I wouldn't be surprised if her nails left grooves in the wood. A deep ache in my chest almost overtook my need for her.

"This is real." Without taking my eyes off hers, I lowered myself down until my knees touched the floor of my office. "Tell me yes." Naomi closed her eyes, but I squeezed her thigh and she popped them back open. "Say it, Naomi, or you can leave right now." I held my breath as we stared at each other. I was bluffing. If she tried to get up, I wasn't above begging. After a few agonizing seconds, Naomi tilted her head in approval.

"Say it." I could tell even in her aroused state, Naomi wanted to roll her eyes at me, but she resisted.

"Yes."

Her smirk made me grip her thighs harder, bringing her closer to me. Naomi's eyes widened with the sudden jolt forward, watching as my face advanced on her pussy.

"Good girl, Goody."

A low moan swallowed whatever she was going to say next as I finally tasted her, and everything else ceased to exist. Naomi bucked from the desk, but I held her firm as I lapped up the sweetness waiting for me.

A whine escaped her as I gently sucked on her clit, and Naomi's hands came to my head, trying to keep me where I was. She didn't need to, though. I didn't want to leave this spot ever again. I felt her shake beneath my tongue and pulled back, not nearly ready to be done. That growl I was fast becoming addicted to slipped from her lips, but it turned into a shriek when I began tonguing her entrance the way I wanted to be fucking her right now. She recited my name over and over, catching herself when she got too loud, only to increase the volume each time again until I eased out of her completely.

I glanced up to see her wild hair, and my dick strained for freedom. Fuck, I wanted to be inside her, but I had already gotten too carried away. I went back to her clit like it called for me and licked slow and hard, making an incoherent noise come from Naomi.

"Say we're real." I laid my tongue flat on her core and licked again to show I meant business. "What are you doing?!" she huffed, and I licked again, loving the way she unraveled beneath me. "Give in." I saw the hesitation in her eyes, so I dipped down, taking her clit into my mouth and suckling softly until she was panting my name.

"I'm waiting." Even in her fog of desire, I could see the doubt. Before she could voice what I saw on her face, I took all her attention by focusing on what I knew couldn't lie. She shook violently before coming with a barely hushed shout, and I kept going until she was screaming. I wanted more.

I realized now that there weren't enough hours in a day for how much I wanted Naomi, but I forced myself to stand and walk away from her, grabbing a towel from my ensuite to clean her up as an excuse to keep touching her while she caught her breath.

Naomi let me wipe her clean; her silence loud in the room that only a moment ago had echoed with her moans. The swell of my dick made it plain what I preferred. As soon as I finished cleaning her up, Naomi slid off my desk and pulled her underwear and pants back on. She was avoiding eye contact, and I could feel the distance she was trying to put between us. I had to clench my fists at my sides not to take her in my arms.

It seemed the only time she listened to sense was when I was touching her, but maybe I had gone too far tonight. I needed her to see reason, but I also knew it was going to be hard for her to accept this.

"I'll see you in court tomorrow," she muttered as she tried to sidestep me, but I blocked her path. Finally, she looked up, and I saw the tears that were close to falling.

"I'm sorry, but I need to go." Looking down at the agony on

Naomi's face cracked something in me. I stepped aside, and she bolted for the closed door. I turned to watch her leave, but while I had stopped myself from chasing her, I couldn't let it end like this.

"This can be real." Naomi didn't look back, but I hadn't expected her to. The ache in my chest intensified as I watched her run out of my office and away from me.

CHAPTER 20

NAOMI

"You were on that man's desk, Ni?! I knew you had it in you!" My best friend was squealing and dancing around her hotel room with an excitement I didn't feel at all.

Instead, I felt like I might need to pull my car over to throw up the granola bar I had scarfed down for lunch. I couldn't believe I had crossed the line with Malcolm. What was worse was that, between my shame and embarrassment, when I thought about his hands gripping my thighs or his tongue in other places, I wanted more. It was ridiculous considering how hard Malcolm had made me come.

A car honked, and I looked up to realize the light was green. I pressed the gas a little too hard and sped onto the freeway. "Ooohhhh, you're thinking about it right now, huh?! I'm so jealous!" I glanced at Myra doing another dance on my dash-board through my phone.

"This isn't a good thing!" My face was so hot, I turned off the heater in my car. "This is a phenomenal thing! Malcolm is fine, you're gorgeous, and ya'll are going to make gorgeous babies!" I rolled my eyes at my friend's rapid escalation.

"The man is a playboy, and even if we were something, which we're not, this is probably a common occurrence for him." I thought about another woman on Malcolm's desk with him between her thighs and felt queasy again. "Yeah, yeah." Myra tossed my objection aside as if it weren't possible. "You'll need media training before ya'll go public, though. The frenzy today was a disaster." I sighed, recalling. Myra and my family had been texting me all day about the reporter scuffle that had made the news.

Myra had sent me a link to the footage earlier, and I still wanted to crawl into a hole. My hair was a mess, and before the behemoth Sloan blocked me from view, I looked like a lost child on the verge of tears. Not what I imagined my first foray into the public eye would entail.

"Trust me, there will be no publicity. This ends here. I can't be involved with him, My." The unusual silence from my friend made me glance at her.

"Why not?" Myra had stopped dancing and was looking directly into the camera, all humor gone.

"It's unethical for one."

"And for two?" I huffed at her sudden interrogation.

"For two, he has a weird relationship with his father." I frowned, thinking about how Malcolm deflected my questions about Langston. "What do you mean?" Shrugging, I tilted my head. "I don't know. They share the firm, but it's like they're against each other." Myra moved to her bed and propped me on something so she could lie down.

"Okay, so he has daddy issues. I thought you hated his dad, anyway?" I remembered Langston's smile after his disgusting comment and nodded my agreement. "Then why does it bother you if they hate each other?" I exited the freeway, and we sat in silence as I drove down a deserted street because I didn't have a ready answer. "Naomi, don't lose out on happiness because you're worried about getting hurt. I know you're scared, but you can't move on if you keep holding yourself back." A red light stopped me, and I didn't have a reason not to look at my friend.

I hadn't told her what Malcolm had said as I was leaving. I didn't even want to think about it, let alone believe it. Remembering the seriousness in his tone when he talked about us sent a shot of anxiety through my chest.

"Myra, I am scared. I just fraternized with the enemy. I should be on the phone with my boss, recusing myself from this case instead of rehashing the details of my mistake." Myra bit her lip and sighed.

"You're human, Ni. I love you, and I want you to be happy, whatever that looks like." The light turned green, but I didn't move. The tears that I'd successfully held in Malcolm's office threatened to fall again. "I just wish you could get out of your own way sometimes." Failing, tears fell, and I kept driving. "I love you, too," I murmured and shook myself to get ahold of my emotions. "Enough about me. You should finish getting ready for your interview with Kline." Myra yawned in answer.

"You're right. I need to be on my toes, and I want to watch more footage of him."

Martin Kline had a reputation for ripping reporters to shreds. He rarely gave interviews, but when he did, it was more like a battle than a conversation, and he often came out the victor. Myra surprised me when she said Kline had personally contacted her to do a sit down. I had only followed the case through the news, but if even a shred of what they were saying about him was true, he was dangerous.

"Goodnight, and tell my nephew Mac to stop being under your feet all the time! If you fall again, we fighting!" We laughed and hung up as I pulled into my driveway. I hoped that my poor dog could forgive me for lying on his name to everyone.

I wiped stray tears and headed for my door, happy to go through the front, and my phone rang again as I made it to the now locked sliding glass to let Mac in.

"Hi, Cruz." I gave my dog a couple of rubs before turning my full attention to the conversation. "The results are back from the lab, but unfortunately there weren't any usable prints on your note." I expected as much, but thanked him for the effort. Mac sniffed around the house idly, and I let his calmness relax me. He would know if someone was here who shouldn't be, and I didn't want to be scared in my own home.

"I pulled the camera footage from the night of your accident, though." He paused for effect, and I knew he must have heard about the hospital visit I should have told him about. Cruz grunted at my silence, but moved on.

"It's a black a late-model Honda, but the plates were stolen. The car was also fitted with a tint too dark to see inside." A shiver ran through me as I thought of that dark car being beside me. "Okay. Luckily, I haven't had any other issues." Mac was whining near my leg, so I grabbed a snack from the cabinet. My stomach grumbled, reminding me I was hungry too.

"Good. I'll see if I can get a new angle from another camera. They might've parked somewhere and gotten out of the car after they sped past you." I gave Cruz my thanks and hung up, and my stomach growled again with emphasis, demanding to be the next order of business. Opening my freezer, I saw very few options and regretted not bringing home some of my dad's gumbo.

I usually froze his food, having it ready since I seldom had time to grocery shop, but tonight I would have to settle for store-bought single-serving lasagna or a small box of mac and cheese. I considered having both when my phone buzzed in my hand.

Goodnight, Goody.

I still hated that nickname, but the butterflies in my stomach didn't care as they soared. *What if he doesn't give up?* A small voice questioned. I felt the same sensation I had when Malcolm was fixing my door, and frowned. Considering Myra's suggestion, I decided that whatever was going to happen; it didn't have to be figured out tonight. I ignored the message and switched to a food app, giving up on my poor excuse for dinner options. A late-night Italian spot caught my eye when my phone rang again, this time Coleman.

I had already sent him a text about Malcolm turning down our offer, and worried what the call could be about. Did he want me to push for another deal? I groaned.

"Naomi, sorry to call so late, but because the defense refused our plea, Judge Lee has granted us a full day's recess to regroup." I stifled a moan of relief while I took in what Coleman said. Judge Lee was fair, and even though I didn't want to admit it, if we didn't start gaining some traction, Drayman was going to get away with murder.

"Okay, great! I'll connect with Dorian about getting Jack to come to the office in the morning, and we can spend the day prepping him." My voice was too high, but I hoped Coleman took it as determination. "I've already let Dorian know about our recess, and he's working on getting Jack tomorrow. You get some rest, and I'll see you at the office in the morning."

I tried not to let the fact that Coleman had called Dorian first get to me. We were a team.

"And Naomi, with the busyness of today, I didn't get a chance to tell you, but you were great today. You handled every-thing well and stayed professional. You're an asset to the district attorney's office. To me." I should have felt pride, but anxiety harped on the word 'professional,' as I thought about being laid out on Malcolm's desk. John Coleman would be so disap-pointed if he knew what I had done. All I wanted now was a shower.

"Thank you, sir. It's an honor working with you." We said our goodbyes, and I hung up, vowing to make my life less complicated. I was an excellent attorney and a good person, and nothing had changed. Yes, I crossed a line with Malcolm, but nothing like that was going to happen again during this trial. I could think about what I wanted after it was over. What was important was that tomorrow our team would reframe our case, and I was going to live up to Coleman's words. I swiped back to the food app and browsed the options. A shower and shrimp Alfredo sounded perfect, and Mac yelped down at my feet, wagging his tail in agreement.

CHAPTER 21

MALCOLM

If my labored breathing and sweat-drenched t-shirt were any indication, I was dying. Avery tossed me the ball, but I let it fly past me while I zeroed in on the bench with my water and gym bag.

I worked out at least three times a week, yet every time we played one-on-one, it felt like I didn't know what running was. Collapsing on the bench, I free-poured water straight onto my face, grateful for any that actually made it into my mouth. Though I could faintly hear Avery laughing, my focus was entirely on not wheezing to death. "I thought we were going to ten?" I heard the ball fall effortlessly into the net, and then Avery's head hovered over me, blocking out the sun.

We were in a private park, with only a few people playing on the other courts. "You win," I pushed out as I gradually raised myself up. With the impromptu recess, I had time to pick Avery up from school. I'd spent the day in the office getting no work done because every time I looked down at my desk all I could think about was Naomi sprawled out on it.

Going to meetings with a hard-on was not how I wanted to spend my day. Avery laughed as he sat beside me, the ball flopping back and forth between his hands. "You can only take three games now, Billionaire? Sitting around all day has finally made you weak." I snatched the ball from Avery's grasp with all the energy I could gather and began dribbling where I sat. "Wisdom comes with age, child." He easily stole it back, choosing to rest the ball on the bench while he got his own water. "How's school?" Avery shrugged as he swallowed. "Good. You didn't come to my last game of the season, but I scored twenty-five points, and my coach said there's a basketball camp he could get me into for the summer." He appeared nonchalant, but Avery mentioned nothing unless it mattered. "Sorry I didn't come, but this basketball camp sounds promising." He nodded, looking away. When I called and told him I was picking him up, I figured I could use the time to work out the strange urge to see Naomi, but maybe I wasn't the only one who had a problem.

"What's your mom think about the camp?" He rolled the ball back and forth on the bench.

"I haven't told her yet. She's dealing with some things, so I don't wanna bother her."

"About that guy she's been seeing?" Avery stood and started dribbling the ball toward the basket, ignoring my question. I stood too, forgetting the burn in my thighs.

"Avery, if there's something going on, you shouldn't bottle it up." He shot, made it, and the ball rolled back toward him like a magnet. "What like you? You play shitty, but not that shitty. You obviously got a problem you're not dealing with." He shot again, and the swoosh of the net told me he made it without having to look. He was right. I didn't talk about my issues. Ever. I devised a plan and followed it until I achieved the desired outcome. I would do that with Naomi too as soon as I figured out how.

"It's a woman." Avery stumbled and missed his shot, making the confession worth it. He retrieved the ball but then studied me with a broad smile.

"And?"

"And she's the most frustrating person I have ever met in my life."

Avery shot again and made it. "I like her already." I retrieved the ball before he could scoop it from the ground and began dribbling around the court.

"Your turn." Avery scoffed, and I thought he would try to deflect when he put his hands on his hips and looked at the ground. "The guy's name is Carl, and he's an asshole, but my mom won't break up with him." I kept dribbling, but caught the tension in Avery's shoulders. "What's his last name?" He looked up as I shot and missed.

Once I got the ball, I stood in front of him. "Burris." I smirked.

While my life was becoming less predictable than I liked, this I knew I could handle. "And where does Carl Burris work?"

Avery made me drop him off a few blocks away from his house, claiming that he didn't want my "expensive ass car" in his driveway. He had been vague about the situation with his mom and Carl Burris, but it was a wasted effort because as soon as he had given me Carl's name and job, Sloan had dug up everything I needed to know.

I stopped in front of the thinly veiled chop shop Carl worked at, nestled in one of the forgotten streets of downtown. Sloan had offered to go to the shop to relay my message, but I declined. I thought that being with Naomi would finally quell the restlessness she brewed inside me, but it had only intensified. My fascination should have been alarming, but I was past questioning the emotions. They weren't going anywhere, and I would make Naomi see that too. I was already concocting a way to see her as soon as she was free.

For now, she was at work, thinking of ways to make me earn my billable hours, and I needed a distraction.

The doors to the large garage complex were both open, with two cars suspended in the air. Out front were a few broken-down vehicles, giving the illusion of a working mechanic shop, but the dust on the cars visible from the curb proved they hadn't been moved in years. Sloan said Carl Burris was a routine criminal who mostly stuck to stealing and selling cars. He had already been caught twice and served seven years before relocating to Crestwood. Police here also arrested him for drunken disorderly conduct, but they dropped those charges. I recognized the place where they arrested him as the bar where Avery's mother worked.

I stepped out of my car, and a rancid smell wafted through the air. Music was coming from somewhere behind the building, but no one was in either of the large open garages. "I'm looking for Carl Burris." I called. The music turned down, and I could hear voices before a man's rounded bald head came into view from an opening in a back corner.

From the photo Sloan sent over, it was Carl. A straggly beard that didn't connect marked his dry brown skin, and I stared back at him as he assessed me, confusion in his beady black eyes. "Carl, I don't have all day." That had him stepping out of the doorway, his round face scrunched up from the sun or my tone; I didn't care.

"I don't know you!" He shouted, his expression morphing between contempt and uncertainty as if he couldn't decide if I was a threat or not. He would know soon enough.

"I'll make this quick. You're seeing a woman, Reba Cartwright. That stops now. You're not to go to her house or her job again. Do you understand?" Carl stepped forward more, and I saw his worn, dirty blue jeans and what used to be a white t-shirt. The smirk he gave said he didn't want to take the easy route, and I was pleased I had come.

"Listen, I don't know who you are, but Reba's a big girl.

She can make her own decisions." I took my own step forward, only for Carl to slide back. My smile widened to show all my teeth. "Well, Reba is her own woman, but I am her lawyer and speaking with regard to her best interests." I moved my hands to my pockets but kept walking toward Carl, who was doing a piss-poor job of maintaining his ground. If he kept walking backward, he was going to trip over one of the many useless things scattered on the floor.

"Asshole—" Just as I thought, Carl lost his footing on a large metal beam and tilted backward. The scene slowed to a crawl as I watched his mouth fall open and his arms flail out at his sides. We had moved back so far that if he fell, Carl would hit his head on a discarded busted tire, its rusted rim jagged and torn from some long ago accident.

I could let nature take its course. He would fall from his own actions, permanently solving Avery's problem. Someone could argue assault or manslaughter through intimidation, and they wouldn't win, but it wouldn't look good for my firm.

There was also the witness; the other voice I had heard in the back. If they hadn't run when I announced myself, then they were still here. Watching and listening.

Most importantly, this wasn't who I was. I didn't play God like the other men in my family.

With a sigh, I snatched the middle of Carl's browned shirt and swung him forward. His oil-marked hands came to mine as an added attempt to hold himself up, his small eyes wide with fear.

"Carl, I suggest you listen to me." He tried to rip from my grasp once he got his bearings, but I held firm, bringing him in closer and ignoring the cheap liquor smell on his breath. I was going to have to give this entire suit away. Camden would be upset.

"Unless you would like me to alert my officer friends of

your illicit activities." I didn't have the evidence, but a man like Carl never learned his lesson, so I had no doubt he was still stealing cars. "Do we understand each other?" With his mouth a grim line, Carl nodded once, and I allowed him to wiggle from my fist.

I felt his glare on my back as I made my way back to my Mercedes. The hand that held him tingled as I drove away, and I ignored the regret that settled in my stomach for saving his life.

CHAPTER 22

NAOMI

"Is it possible to get a better idea of when he'll be available today?" I asked Dorian, doing my best to keep the irritation out of my voice. It was almost six in the evening, and Jack still hadn't arrived for prep.

We had been in a strategy meeting for most of the day with Coleman, reworking our remaining witnesses and going through any potential holes we might've missed, but the day was largely supposed to be about Jack's testimony. "I'm sorry, Ni, I wish I could drag him here, but he's finicky and I don't want to spook him."

I pulled my shoulders away from my ears and took a breath. Dorian was trying. He had been in and out of our meeting on the phone, hoping to pin down a time to bring him in. I'd overheard him even offer to pick the kid up, but I guess Jack had refused. "I promise he's coming in today, even if I have to pull him in by his legs." Dorian wanted a smile, and I gave it, not wanting him to feel worse than he already did.

"I understand, and sorry. I know I've been pushing. I just want him to be ready for Monday." Coleman had given the go-ahead for us to submit Jack's name to our witness list, so the defense knew he was coming next week. Whether they understood the potential weight of his testimony was their problem.

"For now, I have that witness—" I rummaged through the papers on the conference room table we had commandeered. "Lennard Curtis to call back." I had found his name from an old deal gone bad and reached out to him a few times months ago, but had just gotten word back that he would speak with me. "Is that guy a viable witness? I thought Coleman ruled him out since he's another disgruntled partner." Dorian murmured, flipping through his own paperwork. He was right, but I didn't want to give up until I talked to the man. It couldn't hurt.

"I'll reach out to let him know we're moving in a different direction. He's been in Switzerland these last few years but landed back in town last week. Worth a call back at least." Dorian glanced at me, tilting his head.

"You're amazing, Ni." He smiled through the words, and I tipped my lips up in surprise. "For what?" He shrugged and pulled out what he had been looking for from his stack. "You never stop. Always working an angle, digging for a clue. It's admirable." My cheeks reddened at his words, and I dropped my eyes. "Whatever happens, I want to know we did everything we could." Dorian didn't continue, so I looked back up just as he glanced away from me with a laugh.

"Um...anyway. We'll probably be here late with Jack. Whatever time we get out, do you want to grab dinner? I know a late-night spot nearby that's slightly less depressing to eat at if you have someone with you." The 'no' was on my tongue, but I hesitated. It would be late when we got out, and it'd be nice to eat food that wasn't in plastic containers for once this week. "They have French fries," he added, wiggling his eyebrows. I thought Dorian understood what kind of relationship we had, but as I looked at him waiting for my answer, he seemed to hold his breath. I didn't want him to get the wrong idea, so I shook my head.

"Not tonight, I have my dog to get home to. I'm already a terrible dog mom." Dorian's smile dropped, but he nodded. "Right."

I ignored his sudden terse tone and brightened my own.

"I'm going to head to my desk to call Mr. Curtis, but let me know when Jack reaches out to you." When he nodded again, I decided to leave him alone. I didn't want to upset him, but I wasn't going to change my mind.

I left Lennard a voicemail letting him know to call me back and then went back through the information we had on the detective Drayman claimed to have hired. We needed to start thinking about the other side of the case.

It was another hour before Dorian came to my desk with some good news and better spirits. "Jack's downstairs!"

I stood up too fast, knocking some papers onto the ground, but left them there. "Great, bring him in and I'll let Coleman know!" Dorian's excitement mirrored mine, as he nodded like a loon.

I was finally going to talk to the witness who could break our case wide open. I sent Coleman a text since he'd left to work from home a couple of hours prior.

> Great! Make sure he can handle himself in court.

His text sent a worried bolt through me, but I shook it off. Dorian and I would get Jack ready for anything.

I walked to the conference room, sorting papers into neat piles and scooting in the office chairs for no reason. Patience wasn't my strong suit, but it was past business hours, so the quiet of the office made it seem like Dorian was taking an hour to bring the kid up. I was sorting a random stack of papers again when Dorian rapped on the door.

I turned and met deep green, nervous eyes. Jack wore jeans and a white t-shirt with a basic zip-up hoodie, but his shoes were colorful and expensive looking, as well as the wide-faced Rolex on his thin arm. He stood at about Dorian's chin, and his wavy brown hair fell into his face as his gaze moved from me to scan the glass-lined room. Dorian had his hand firm on Jack's shoulder, and it didn't look tight enough to hurt, but the boy wasn't going anywhere.

Did Jack want to testify? I knew he was skittish, but nerves differed from involuntary. He met my eyes again, and I realized I hadn't spoken.

"Nice to meet you, Jack. I'm Naomi." He raised his chin and then looked at Dorian, who gently pushed the boy forward. "Take a seat, and we'll be right back." Dorian leaned his head toward the door, and I followed him out. We walked a few steps to be out of earshot, but he still whispered.

"Jack's nervous. He almost backed out in the elevator." I glanced at the kid now scrolling through his phone and felt for him. Going against a guy like Drayman was a big deal.

"Are you sure he's comfortable doing this?" Dorian smiled. "Absolutely! He's just..." Dorian glanced at the boy again, who had pulled out a chair and was tapping his foot on the carpet as he scrolled. "He's never gone against his parents before, but he wants to do what's right." I watched Jack playing on his phone and then met Dorian's eyes.

"Okay, I think you should ask the questions then. He might be more relaxed with you." I wanted to coach him, but I needed to put Jack's needs ahead of mine. Dorian pulled air in between his teeth.

"Actually, sorry, I totally forgot that Coleman asked me to track down a lead on Joe Castro." I narrowed my eyes. "What lead? We have something on him?" Dorian shrugged and gave me an apologetic smile. "Yeah, something about a previous client. I have to go all the way to Birch Hampton, which is going to be a bitch at this hour." My brain went fuzzy trying to understand what he was saying. Coleman hadn't mentioned a lead to me. Dorian placed his hand on my shoulder, bringing me back to our conversation.

"I mean, look, I just got back on Coleman's good side. I don't want to screw up. You're the witness whisperer, anyway! You got this. He'll relax once you get started." I wanted to mention that I had prepped our other witnesses, and they had blown up in our faces, but the words wouldn't come.

"Can you stay for the beginning?" I heard the trepidation in my voice, and Dorian squeezed my shoulder. "I mean I could, but who knows how long it'll take to get out there, plus speak to this person." *What person?* My mind screamed, but I gave a weak nod instead. Dorian's face lit up.

"Thanks, Ni. I'll keep in touch if I find anything!" He squeezed my shoulder once more and then was off, disappearing to the other side of the office without a second glance. I turned to look at Jack, who was already staring at me, and threw on a smile to hide my worry. Dorian hadn't even said goodbye to the kid before he dashed out of here, leaving him with a random woman he didn't know.

I hadn't pried into why Coleman had demoted Dorian; it wasn't my business, but this moment had me wondering.

I walked into the room, racking my brain for something to break the ice with once I got to him, but as soon as I crossed the threshold of the room, Jack sprang up. "If it's okay, I'd like to get this over with." In the fluorescent dim light of the conference room, the dark circles under his eyes were pronounced, and the hand not holding his phone was twitching seemingly without his knowledge.

As I sat down, I took a small breath, attempting to make my plastered smile more genuine. I was about to gamble with the case, but I wasn't going any further until I was sure he was ready to continue. I motioned for Jack to sit back down, and he did, his foot going back to the rhythmic tap. "Before we begin, I want you to be honest with me." I ignored how his tapping intensified.

"Do you want to testify? You can walk out of this room right now if you would like." Jack froze, his eyes unblinking. "Jack?" I murmured, trying to inject calm into my voice. "Well, I..." He looked down at his phone and then back up at me. "I do, but I'm nervous." He rushed out, and the anxiety that was clutching my heart released enough that I let out a soft laugh in relief.

"I can help with that," I said, and he gave me a small smile in return. Excitement replaced the nerves as I smiled back at our star witness.

CHAPTER 23

NAOMI

Once Jack relaxed, we found a rapport, and the mock questions went well. He was concise and didn't flinch when I threw him the curveballs I thought the defense would try.

His story was so great that by the end of our three-hour session, I was confident the prosecution would be hard-pressed to find a weakness they could manipulate. I had offered Jack a ride home, but he declined, opting for a ride-share service that I watched him jump into before I headed home myself.

We had scheduled one more meeting for Friday evening after court so that we could go over everything again and it was fresh in his mind for trial on Monday, and I planned to insist Dorian came to that one. He needed to be involved since he was the one who found Jack, and having another set of eyes to catch issues was always a good idea.

I was yawning by the time I drove onto my street, but for the first time in a while, I wasn't so exhausted. I was optimistic about our chances and wanted to hold on to that warmth for as long as I could. As I pulled up, I saw a large white van parked just past my driveway, with the words Quinn Alarm and Safes in thick black lettering on its two back doors. Exhaust floated out from the back, but I didn't see anyone around.

Who was getting an alarm system this late? I pulled to the front of my garage and shut off my car, taking another look at the van through my rearview mirror, but my eyes widened at another vehicle parked in front of it.

"It couldn't be," I whispered, and as if I conjured him, Malcolm appeared from the driver's side of the burgundy Mercedes, dressed head to toe in black and looking so good I momentarily forgot that this situation was bizarre. He smirked as he came into view, walking with ease up my driveway to my car.

Opening my door, he offered his hand, and I just stared at it, dumbfounded. "What is happening?" I thought aloud, but instead of answering, Malcolm took my hand from the steering wheel and led me out into the night. I went willingly, still waiting for an explanation. "You look beautiful. Wish I could've seen this outfit in court today." I looked down at my light green long-sleeved dress and back up at him.

I would never have worn something like this in court, and I had a feeling Malcolm knew that. "I'm sure you had fun being a nepo baby somewhere else." He laughed, and I noted he hadn't let go of my hand.

"What's going on, Malcolm?" He peered down at me, glancing between my lips and my eyes. "You're getting an alarm." I frowned and tried to step away from him, but he pulled me closer.

He tilted my chin until my stormy expression met his calm one. "But I didn't call for an alarm system," I said through gritted teeth. Malcolm unleashed his full smile on me, making my stomach flip against my will.

"I called one for you." He leaned down so close to my face I forgot what protest was on the tip of my tongue. "Not seeing you all day was less than ideal," he breathed. I had to break eye contact to make my brain work again.

Using my bag as an excuse for space, I dipped back into my car, grabbing everything I needed, and then glanced at Malcolm again. "I don't need an alarm."

"You do."

"And even if I did, I could call them myself."

"They're already here."

"Malcolm—"

"Let me keep you safe." My rebuttal got stuck in my throat. I raised my chin anyway. "Just so we're clear, you're not paying for this." Malcolm arched a brow, but I was already moving past him.

There was no use arguing, and I did want to feel safe in my home again, but I'd be damned if he thought I was going to be some kind of kept woman. I'm sure he had arrangements with other women, but that wasn't me. I heard a car door open behind me and turned to see Malcolm right on my heels, but around his large body was the alarm technician, grabbing something from the back of his van.

Malcolm waited patiently for me to unlock my front door, and the whole situation felt too domestic and natural for my liking. I pushed a little too hard and stumbled inside, but Malcolm said nothing as he walked in behind me, and I worked to get my shit together while turning on all the lights in the house and letting Mac in.

My favorite pup was excited to see me as usual, but turned surly when he caught sight of Malcolm in my bedroom doorway. The playboy made the entrance look tiny with his frame, but Mac didn't seem fazed by Malcolm's stature and ran right up to him, barking his head off. Curious how he would handle my ball of energy, I watched on as Malcolm leaned down without hesitation, allowing Mac to jump into his arms, sniffing and barking away.

Once the licking started, Malcolm seemed to have had enough, and stood back up, leaving Mac to alternate between jumping and yelping for more attention.

I met them both at the door and scooped Mac up as best I could. "Stay in here, fur ball. We have company." I was happy to let Mac sully Malcolm's expensive clothes, but the alarm tech didn't deserve to be licked to death. I grabbed a chew treat for Mac and then closed my bedroom door.

"Hi Ms. Vine. I'm Patrick, and I'll be installing your system tonight." I walked to the front door to greet Patrick, and Malcolm stepped to my side. "Hi, Patrick! Sorry you're here so late." Patrick gave me a grin that made a dimple appear on his blushed cheek. "Not at all. Mr. Charles said you work late hours, so I'm happy to accommodate. We have you down for a full lockdown, is that correct?" My brows pinched together, but Malcolm answered for me. "Yes, cameras and motion sensors on all sides of the house. Inside as well." I almost stuttered as I threw up a hand. "Hold on!" I screeched, startling Patrick. I gave him a quick smile before grabbing Malcolm by the arm and dragging him into my kitchen. It wasn't far from the front door, so I still whispered.

"I will not have cameras inside my home!" I seethed. Malcolm blew air through his nose as if I were the one being unreasonable. "What if someone comes in here when you're not home?" He asked calmly. He thought he was going to win this argument too, but he was mistaken. "My dog walker comes to my house every day, and I don't need to watch her. Cameras outside are fine, but that's it. I mean it, Malcolm." I folded my arms and readied for a fight, but he only smirked, leaning down and giving me a quick peck on the nose.

The move was disorienting, but he rose back up too fast for me to react. "Fine." All the fight deflated in me with the word. "Fine?" I repeated, unsure what game he was playing. "Fine." He smiled and walked back to Patrick, and I followed, not having anything else to do. "No cameras inside." Patrick nodded, giving me another grin.

Malcolm's firm hand pulled me to his side, and my stomach flipped with the movement. "You should get started. It's getting late." Malcolm's stern voice vanished the smile on the poor boy's face. The technician couldn't have been more than twenty-two, and he practically jumped into gear with a sudden, "Yes, sir!" before dropping his bag on the floor to rummage through it so he could begin. I shot a glare at Malcolm on Patrick's behalf, but he only squeezed me tighter to him, the genuine amusement on his face disarming my irritation.

I looked away, but didn't move from his grasp.

Chapter 24

NAOMI

Malcolm stayed during the installation, but spent most of the time working from his phone.

In a little over an hour, Patrick installed everything and guided me through it; however, when I inquired about pricing and payment, he nervously glanced at my preoccupied house guest before informing me it was already handled. I let it slide since he was only doing his job, but I would call the alarm company and get it sorted myself. Malcolm could throw his money around somewhere else.

"That's it, Ms. Vine! Please don't hesitate to call us with any questions." Patrick handed me his business card with a smile and then headed for my door. "Thank you again for coming so late, Patrick." I felt bad that I only had a ten-dollar bill to give him as a tip, but was lucky I had cash at all.

When I tried to hand it to him stealthily, Patrick shook his head as Malcolm appeared at my side. The man was quiet when he wanted to be. "No need, Ms. Vine! Have a good night!" Patrick turned and opened my front door himself, like he was running from me, so I didn't push the issue. I could add it to the bill when I called.

Malcolm followed Patrick to the door, and unease rose in my chest.

He should leave. It was late, and Malcolm shouldn't have been here in the first place. I could admit it felt nice having him in my home, even if it also brought an anxiety that I didn't want to inspect, but we had agreed to keep things professional until after the trial. This was far from professional, but Malcolm going toward the door had lies swirling in my mind to get him to stay a little longer. I clamped my lips together to keep the words from spilling out.

The van's engine hummed outside, and Malcolm stepped back over my threshold, closing the door behind him as if it weren't a question that he was staying. The longer we stared at each other in silence, the wetter my panties became.

"I could leave."

The statement hung between us until Malcolm closed the distance. "Or I could stay." Any reason for him to go didn't seem that important as I looked into those searching brown eyes, but I still held up a hand.

Myra was right. I needed to be honest with myself and stop running from what scared me. But I also wanted to be smart. "We need to talk," I asserted and took a couple of steps back for good measure. Malcolm only smiled. "I love to talk."

When I failed to hide the smile that spread across my face, I cleared my throat and tried again. "I'm being serious. This is unprofessional." Malcolm blinked twice at my response as if I had spoken a foreign language, but he nodded and then walked past me to sit on my couch. I followed him as he sat, his giant body making my sofa seem smaller than it was.

"Let's talk." His voice was so gravelly, I knew talk was the last thing on his mind, so I remained standing, crossing my arms in front of me. "We can't keep sneaking around like this while the trial is happening." Malcolm patted the seat next to him, but I raised my chin, and he sighed. "I disagree." I huffed out a breath. "This...thing we're doing is wrong. It's grounds for a mistrial and—" Malcolm's chuckle stopped me in the middle of a pace I hadn't realized I'd started.

I frowned down at him. "What's so funny?" He leaned

back, his left arm laid across the back of my couch as if we were having the most casual conversation in the world. "Goody, sleeping together won't cause a mistrial. That'll happen regardless of whether or not you admit what this is." Anger readied my tongue as I stepped closer, only for Malcolm to swiftly pull me into his body, swinging me around so that he hovered over me while my back pressed into the couch before I knew what was happening.

"Too easy," Malcolm murmured while he stared down at me. "Malcolm—" He leaned in further, quieting whatever I was going to say. "I missed you more than I thought possible." Looking down at my lips, Malcolm seemed to talk more to himself than to me. Slowly, he moved in further until his lips were grazing mine, and even though I didn't feel his weight, I was stuck, like the single place we were touching had paralyzed me. "How can you miss lips you haven't kissed yet?" he whispered against me, and I shuddered.

Malcolm raised up so that I could see his eyes, and all the warm brown had morphed into a black obsidian that reminded of that night at my front door. Instead of being afraid, my core flexed. "We do need to talk, but first could you listen to what I suggest?" He asked, and despite his usual impassivity, a strained vein in Malcolm's temple betrayed his restraint. I wanted to mention that I was the one who started this conversation, but only nodded. Malcolm smiled his appreciation.

"After this trial is over, I'm going to take you on a proper date, but for now, I agree we need to keep a low profile." I opened my mouth, and Malcolm lowered his, making my hands come to his chest on reflex. "Where was I?" He grazed my mouth again, and I almost gave in.

Malcolm rose up, and an involuntary groan escaped me. "Ah yes. We should keep seeing each other, albeit behind closed doors. There's no reason we couldn't keep our arrangement to ourselves." While I was getting more aroused by the second, Malcolm's idea was too ridiculous not to scoff at. "That's a bad idea! As you love to point out, I like to follow the rules." Malcolm raised a brow at him being literally on top of me as we spoke, but I ignored his implication. "I don't want to sneak around! We need to stop doing this for right now." He leaned further into me, sandwiching my hands between us. "For now?" He raised a brow, and my cheeks flamed. "Yes. For now. After the trial...we can talk." With that smirk I was starting not to hate so much etched on his lips, he nodded.

"I can agree to your terms if..." Malcolm paused, his eyes dipping to my breasts and making my heart race. "I stay the night." Malcolm was brushing against my lips again, ignoring my soured expression.

"Just once, Goody." I didn't know how he kept from fully lying on top of me, but he lowered himself enough to rub against my thin dress as he spoke, sending shivers through my body. "Say yes, and I promise not to lay another finger on you until after the judge slams the gavel down for the last time in this case." He pressed against my core, and I bit my lip not to moan. "Unless you ask nicely." Malcolm's eyes were swirls of black, begging me to give in, and I felt his hand on my thigh, opening me up more to him so he could hit the spot that was making my head hazy.

All rational thought gone, I leaned up to take Malcolm's mouth in mine, and we both moaned at the connection. My body trembled, and sparks burst between my thighs as I pulled away from the kiss to end the night before we hit a point of no return, but Malcolm moved to my neck, and I whimpered instead.

He moved up, licking behind my ear, making me gasp. "You're soaking my thousand-dollar suit, Goody. I already changed once today."

My cheeks burned, but Malcolm pushed his hard dick against my clit, rendering me speechless. "Might wear you around tomorrow." My breath came out in brief, hot spurts as he continued to grind us together, and I gripped his shoulders to move along with him, but he pressed me further into the couch and then stopped the movement altogether.

I scowled, but Malcolm only smiled, looking down at me with such awe, panic attempted to overcome the lust coursing through me. He moved wayward curls from my face and held me in place while nervous energy cranked my brain into overdrive as I thought of all the reasons I needed to get up right now.

My career, my reputation, my heart.

That last one wasn't supposed to be on the line at all. Malcolm tapped the place between my brows, and under his finger I felt how bunched it was. "Always thinking," he murmured, and I felt the trail of his fingers inching up my thigh to the thin fabric of my ruined panties. "Let's give your mind a break." Taking my mouth as he dove a finger into me, Malcolm absorbed my shocked groan with his kiss, while his thumb rubbed against my clit with such delicious force I was already close to shattering.

He added a second finger, and my body started rocking with his pace to help take me over the edge. "Open your eyes." I hadn't realized I'd closed them until my eyes shot open on command, and I locked on Malcolm's. His face was rigid with concentration, as if what he was doing to me was enough to make him also explode.

My body shook before it shattered, and the world went dim and then too bright all at once. I moaned as Malcolm kept up the pace and I realized I might come again.

I wasn't a multiple-orgasm kind of girl. One was a miracle for me. Still, the pleasure from release morphed and warmed my belly and rose to another crescendo. "You're gorgeous when you come undone," Malcolm sighed, and the bliss of another orgasm sent warm tingles through my whole body.

When I finally came down, he slowed his fingers and lifted himself off of me, flipping us with ease so that my boneless body rested on top of him. I felt Malcolm's stiff dick against my thigh and couldn't believe my core twitched to accept him. If the imprint was any indication, I wasn't sure he would fit. I felt the rumble of Malcolm's laugh and forced my head up to see the smirk on his face. "Calm down, Goody. When I said I wanted to stay the night, I didn't mean sex." I side-eyed Malcolm, and he sighed.

"This was *your* fault." He gestured to our current state. "I can't stop myself when you look at me like that." I let my head fall back on his chest and huffed out a breath. "Look at you how?" I questioned, and my body lifted and fell with Malcolm's long exhale. "Well...when you look at me at all, really." He murmured, and I laughed, the movement shifting my body and pulling a groan from my current pillow. "Let's go to bed before this night gets even longer." Malcolm's tone was nonchalant, but I saw the hard swallow he took as he gently sat us both up, with me straddling him.

Awareness and fear mixed and prickled along my skin at my wild thoughts. I rested my hands on Malcolm's warm chest, feeling the rapid beat of his heart beneath the hard muscle. "Or," I ventured, sliding my arms slowly around Malcolm's neck, want replacing hesitation as I moved. When I met Malcolm's eyes, I found that want reflected. "Or?" His question was a rough whisper that sent a throb to my core.

In answer, I leaned in, taking Malcolm's mouth in a soft kiss. He opened for me, but didn't try to take over as I explored his mouth with my tongue, leaning into him so our hearts beat against each other. Malcolm's arms wrapped around me, sliding my ass closer so there was no space between us, and my legs spread, feeling how hard he was against my clit. I let out a moan, and Malcolm growled. "Naomi, stop playing around before I flip you back onto this couch." I smiled into our kiss. "Who said I'm playing?" I moved my hips and saw stars. Malcolm grunted, his hands tightening on my ass. He pulled away from my lips, and I saw the sweat dotting his forehead.

"Do that again, and I will fuck you." Amusement sparked in his eyes, but I saw the hesitation too.

He didn't want me to regret this, and that only made me want him more. We still had a lot to figure out, but in this moment it was clear not only how much I wanted Malcolm, but how much he cared about me. I let go of all the doubts and allowed myself to enjoy being in his arms. I moved again, and with an agility that took my breath away, Malcolm swung me onto my back and pushed us further into the couch cushions, taking my mouth in a punishing kiss.

All too soon, he was up again, and as I sucked in air, he unbuttoned his black dress shirt and tossed it on the floor. "I'll try to go slow." His gaze was trailing down my body, his hands inching up my dress until it was up and over my arms. Instinct told me to pull him down to hide the soft parts of my body, but I kept my hands above my head, enamored with the way Malcolm was looking at me. His brow wrinkled when he came to my soaked panties. "I'll try," he mumbled before raising my legs in the air and sliding the wet fabric off. He sat between my stretched limbs, kissing each ankle softly, his eyes shut as if he were praying.

"Fucking stunning." He whispered, opening his eyes slowly as he licked down my leg, and I somehow felt the sensation between my thighs. "Malcolm," I urged, and he chuckled. "Take off your bra." Releasing me, he moved to his pants while I discarded the last piece of clothing I had on. I didn't know where I tossed it, too preoccupied watching the finest man I had ever seen slide out of his silk grey briefs. My eyes widened as his dick sprang forward, impatient and ready. When my eyes ticked up to Malcolm, he only grinned. "Don't run now, Goody." I realized my mouth was open, and I shut it, watching Malcolm slide a condom on before lowering himself back on top of me.

He took my mouth in an unhurried kiss, his hand moving to my nipple and squeezing almost to the point of pain. I whimpered against his lips, and he moved to my neck, switching to the other nipple. "I want to hear you," he rasped, pinching the soft nub, making me moan. "Good girl." Malcolm's tongue came between my breasts, licking me in the dip between my chest and stomach, and my back arched off the couch. I didn't know it was a spot for me, but Malcolm's relentless mouth was driving me crazy.

He held my torso with both hands, pushing me back down into the couch as he ventured lower, and I couldn't take it anymore. "Malcolm, please." I whined, not caring how I sounded, but he kept kissing down. "I want to taste you again." He murmured, never taking his eyes off my body.

"And I want you inside me. Now," I growled, and Malcolm froze, his hands digging into my stomach, still holding me in place. He rested his forehead on my pussy, taking a deep breath. "You're going to kill me," he whispered. Before I could respond, Malcolm was up again, his dick at my entrance as our eyes locked.

He moved his hands to my arms, holding them over the armrest of the couch as he sank into me, stretching me so far that my mouth dropped open at the impact. My whole body shook, my senses overwhelmed as I tried to take him in. "Breathe, baby," Malcolm coaxed, going to my ear as he filled me completely. I tried to listen, but waves of pleasure were drowning me, and all I could do was dig my nails into Malcolm's hands.

"Damn, Naomi, if your pussy keeps sucking me in like this, I won't—" Malcolm groaned low, cutting off whatever he was going to say, and then he was moving in and out at a speed that made me pant. The warmth in my stomach spread out to my fingers and toes as my release rushed close. "That's right, come for me, baby." My body listened, coming apart so hard I screamed. Malcolm kept moving, picking up his pace as his mouth crashed onto mine, still holding my hands above my head so that all I could do was take him. I tried moving my hips to meet Malcolm's thrusts, and he pushed me further into the couch to keep me still. I rolled my hips again, and Malcolm broke our kiss.

"Shit," he groaned, giving up on holding my arms and instead focusing on fucking me into oblivion.

My whimpers became shouts of Malcolm's name as we collided into each other and his forehead came to mine as he shuddered. "Ah fuck, Naomi," Malcolm shouted as I watched him come undone, and the sight forced another climax from me with a scream.

Our breaths mixed as we came back down together, and Malcolm's head fell on my chest. If he hadn't been on top of me, I was sure my body could have slid right off the couch, exhaustion lowering my eyes and pulling a yawn from my lips.

I could feel Malcolm's smile before he spoke. "*Now*, let's go to bed," he chuckled. "Good idea," I murmured, not sure I could walk. Malcolm pulled us both up with ease and sat me back on his lap.

I sighed, working up what little strength I had left to rise off of him, but he grabbed me at the waist to keep me seated on his thighs.

My eyes widened as I felt his stiff dick between my legs. I

didn't know what time it was, but it had to be late, and there was no way I could go again.

Malcolm took my chin in his fingers so that I met his serious gaze, interrupting my thoughts.

"Don't worry about my father." I pushed a wild curl out of my face and frowned at the sudden mention of Langston. "This trial will be over soon." Malcolm said as he stared at me, mapping my face with those hungry eyes, and I wondered what he saw. "And then you'll be mine." The words would have irked me if I had had the energy to do anything besides breathe. Still, my expression made him smile. "You heard me." As my mind tried to alert me to the seriousness of this conversation, necessary questions began bouncing around in my brain.

I vocalized none of them as Malcolm lifted me, like I weighed nothing, and we made our way to my bedroom, Mac's sleepy yips waiting on the other side. I let the madness in my head simmer to a quiet roar as I fell asleep in Malcolm's arms.

CHAPTER 25

MALCOLM

"Okay."

I shifted in bed, searching for the missing warm body. The cold sheets roused me from sleep. Darkness swallowed up everything in Naomi's room except the sliver of light underneath her closed doorframe. The honeyed smell of her was all around me, but Naomi wasn't there.

"Yes, I understand." I heard her whispered tone on the other side of the door and sat up, grabbing my phone from the nightstand. It was almost five a.m. Who was she talking to at this hour? I walked to her closed door, intending to find out, but stopped short when I heard her again.

"Right. He called me ten minutes ago and wants to meet now." I opened the door, and Naomi nearly jumped out of her skin. "What? Oh, no, sir, I'm fine! Um, my dog...scared me." She motioned for me to go back into her room, but I didn't budge, and even while she glared at me, her eyes couldn't keep from scanning my body. I had slept in only my briefs, and my dick loved her perusal. It took Herculean strength not to nestle between her legs once we got in bed, but I would keep my word. Her decision to give us a chance after the trial made the temptation tolerable.

Naomi turned her back to me and moved closer into a corner of her kitchen, but her place was small, and I could still hear her fine. "There shouldn't be traffic, so I can be in the office in thirty." *Work.* Of course. Tension tightened my shoulders. The woman never stopped. John Coleman never liked me, mostly because of the earned notoriety of my father, but I had at least a small bit of respect for the man.

He never folded to Langston, but he also wouldn't deny getting justice for a victim because of his ego, like some other prosecutors. But now, I wondered if Naomi's boss deserved my regard at all, calling a woman at four thirty in the morning to come to the office, especially on a case that was basically dead in the water.

Naomi hung up and spent another second with her back to me, probably hoping I would evaporate if she waited long enough. If I weren't so annoyed at the workaholic, I would have been amused. "It's a little early for business calls, isn't it?"

A sharp breath came from Naomi before she turned to face me with a frown. "You have to go," was all she responded before walking past me back into her room. I followed, unfazed by her expected curt tone. The throbbing in my chest, which felt like someone had plunged a knife there, was unrelated.

I watched as she moved around, selecting clothes from her closet and doing her best to pretend I wasn't there. "Where are you going?" I tried again, my patience hanging on by a thread. Without glancing my way, she sighed. "Malcolm, I don't have time for this. You need to leave."

Gathering her clothes as she spoke, Naomi tried to dodge me to go to the bathroom, but I stepped forward to block her path. I invited the scowl on her face since she was at least giving me eye contact. "Do you regret it?" I asked, hiding the odd swell of emotion that tightened my throat. I kept my voice level and waited for an answer she wasn't walking away from. She opened her mouth and then shut it, and I arched a brow to dare her to lie. With a huff, she tossed her clothes back on her bed.

"No, I don't regret it at all." I smiled to hide the relief. "But you promised you would leave me alone after last night." She grumbled, and I wanted to point out that it practically *still* was last night, but thought better of it. "I promised not to touch you. I didn't say anything about not worrying about you." She put her hands on her hips and stepped so close she had to look up to meet my eyes. "I'm going to work." Ignoring her exasperation, I leaned down and kissed the tip of her nose.

"Okay." Her eyes narrowed, but I didn't care that I had already broken my promise. She was lucky I didn't take her to bed and show her exactly what I was okay with. "Okay?" She repeated the word as if I were trying to trick her somehow. I smiled at her confusion. "Okay. I would have loved to wake up with you in my arms, but I can wait." Naomi turned quickly away from me, but I caught the tinge of red on her cheeks.

"Okay." Wild curls bounced around in spiraling wisps as she went back to her clothes, and I put mine on at a glacial pace to watch her move around her room. I stayed until she threatened never to see me again if I was still there when she got out of the shower.

Even though I had been awakened at an ungodly hour, once I'd gotten home I wasn't the least bit tired and started my day with a shower of my own where images of Naomi had me under the water for nearly an hour until my dick decided she was out of our system for now. It wasn't yet eight a.m. when I got the call that the prosecution wanted to submit a new witness, and Naomi's whispered conversation began to make sense.

Though my face revealed nothing as I entered Judge Lee's chambers, it was disappointing to see only Keates and Coleman there. They looked tired but motivated, and it piqued my interest as to what kind of witness they were trying to introduce. Ronan had told us everything about the case, good and bad, and we did our own investigation as well, so I wasn't too worried even if they thought they found something significant.

My father entered at the same time Judge Lee appeared, and we shared a single glance before he turned and smiled to everyone else. Judge Lee took the papers Dorian was holding and scanned them quickly.

I reached for the one he held out to me, but Dorian clung to it until we locked eyes. "So you *can* look up," he murmured, and I was glad that if I was forced to interact with him, I was at least getting paid.

"I guess little men have to take their power plays where they can get them." I took the paper from his tight grip with ease and moved to the other side of the room, not waiting for a response.

"This is another character witness?" The judge asked while I skimmed the paperwork. "Lennard Curtis went to school with the defendant and was also a brief business associate. He has a unique light to shine on the defendant's life that none of our other witnesses have touched."

My father pounced before Coleman could get another word in. "Your Honor, the prosecution has already tried and failed to paint my client's character. How many people do we have to catch in a lie for them to understand it won't work?" Coleman wasn't entertaining my father and instead looked to the judge, who was still reading. From what I could see in the file, Lennard Curtis didn't look different from the others they had called already.

Coleman tried to speak again, but Judge Lee held up a hand. "It says here that your witness recently flew in from Switzerland?" Coleman nodded. "Yes, which is why we are just now getting in contact. His testimony is vital and relevant to these proceedings."

I tried to hand my father the paperwork to show this wasn't an issue, but he stepped forward to grab the judge's attention.

"I'm sure that's what they thought of the myriad of other witnesses they've paraded in front of the court. This is a ploy to extend my client's time on trial. Please see through their flimsy attempt, Your Honor."

Judge Lee thought it over.

"You can call Lennard Curtis to the stand, but the defense will have an extension to prepare. Five hours." It was tight, but if there was a reason to be worried about Curtis, we had people on the payroll who could find it out in half that time. Still, my father edged closer to the judge's desk.

"Your Honor, this witness seems like a desperate Hail Mary from the prosecution. "Why should we sit through another testimony from an allegedly disgruntled associate if it amounts to nothing?!" My father was more stressed about this witness than I had ever seen him. He was also pushing the judge to retract a verdict, which was implausible and risky.

Judge Lee side-eyed Langston, but I stepped in. "We understand, Your Honor. If the prosecution wants to waste everyone's time, we're happy to oblige. We'll see you in court." I was relieved when the judge only stared at my father a beat longer before exiting.

Coleman looked like a kid in a candy store as he squeezed Dorian's shoulder, nodding. I turned to my father to talk about next steps, but he was already punching his finger on a contact in his phone.

"Curtis is through," were the only words I heard him hiss as he marched past me to the door.

CHAPTER 26

MALCOLM

I sat between Gabby and my father, going over our newly found information on Lennard Curtis and doing my best not to let my gaze land on Naomi, who was just on the other side.

When she walked into the courtroom, I noticed the dark green dress I saw her pick out this morning, and the color reminded me of her panties from that night in my office. I hated myself for not taking them that night. Next time. Knowing there would be a next time, eased the muscles in my jaw as I shuffled through papers on our table. Gabby leaned in so close I could smell her perfume, and it brought me back to the courtroom.

"Malcolm, do you have the notes about Curtis's business in Switzerland?" I handed her the papers she wanted and glanced past her to Ronan, who had been in a bad mood all day. Our strategy meeting ended with him and my father talking privately while I focused on our team getting all the information they could on Curtis that wasn't in the prosecution's diluted file. Langston was acting cagey; I wanted to know why. In the end, they hadn't come up with much other than Curtis's uncle being on the board of Drayman's father's company and contributing the seed money that made the Drayman company flourish in the early days. My grandfather had done the same for Langston when he married my mother and started the firm.

I understood better than most that money was the leading factor in most people's poor decisions, so this connection bothered me. When I pressed my father about what he and Ronan were hiding, he denied it.

I was appeased, knowing that he wouldn't let the case implode, and if we were here, it was something we could handle. Gabby hadn't moved away, and I looked down to see her eyeing the direction of the prosecution. I didn't turn, but could guess her interest. She hadn't asked about the night she saw Naomi at our office, but she was a smart woman. If she suspected something, the last thing she would do was bring it up to me.

Gabby didn't strike me as the vindictive type, but Naomi was worried enough as it is, and I didn't need any other obstacles. She caught my eye with a smirk before turning to answer a question Drayman was murmuring.

With her back still against me, I could feel Gabby stiffen. I glanced over to see Drayman had his hand on hers and was leaning in so close that if she hadn't pushed into me, he would have been right on top of her. I cleared my throat to get his attention, and he leaned back slightly to acknowledge me.

"Mr. Drayman, move your chair so that we can all breathe properly." Annoyance flashed in his eyes at my direct tone, but we had already had a conversation about him keeping his hands to himself, and I would never bother with fake respect for such a bottom feeder. He scowled, but sat back, getting out of Gabby's space, and she turned back to the files. She said nothing, but her shoulders dropped.

I held my tongue but counted the days until I completely controlled what cases we took on to eliminate predators like Drayman from our books. Shady characters were part of the job, and I didn't mind the money, but some people didn't deserve my firm. I felt my father's eyes but ignored him, knowing that he would have let Drayman do whatever he wanted for the paycheck and prestige.

"I'll cross-examine Curtis," I said sharply, trying to control my rising anger. "Whatever you say, son." Langston sounded cheery, but I could hear the disdain underneath, helping my mood. I smirked, giving him my full attention. "I'll never tire of hearing that." He gave me a tight smile, but Judge Lee emerged before he could rebut, and that made my mood even better.

It was time for Lennard to take the stand, and my gaze shot to Naomi as she stood. Was she handling this witness? My hopes were realized when she summoned Lennard Curtis and positioned herself before the witness stand. I was resolute in my attempt to avoid her table, but now I got to stare at her all I wanted, and it was both gratifying and difficult.

I took a breath to keep my dick in check and ignored Gabby when she glanced at me. Lennard Curtis wore a dark suit and had a receding hairline with sparse gray hairs that clung to his head like a U. He looked unassuming in glasses and had a polite smile, but I didn't trust the image he was portraying. He was a fairly successful proprietor, and his blue eyes were too sharp as they zeroed in on Drayman before centering on Naomi. I opened his file and looked over his background again while she began.

"Mr. Curtis, could you please tell the jury how you know the defendant?" I stopped mid-sentence at the sound of Naomi's confident tone and raised my head. She was between the jury and Curtis but not enough to block their view, and I couldn't take my eyes off her.

"We went to boarding school together our freshman through junior years, before he transferred." Naomi's heels clicked on the floor, and I remembered them behind my head at my desk and had to take another breath. "And what kind of kid was Ronan Drayman?" My father tapped his finger rhythmically on the desk, and I knew he wanted to object.

I understood his urge, but Judge Lee rarely upheld objections on character, making it pointless and Langston would never give the prosecution that satisfaction. "He was popular. We didn't run in the same circles, but I would see him out in town occasionally with his friends or girlfriends." Naomi stepped closer to Curtis. "You said 'girlfriends,' as in multiple. How did Ronan treat them from what you observed?" The tapping stopped, and Langston was up.

"Your Honor, I would ask Ms. Vine, what high school has to do with the here and now? None of us are getting any younger." The judge looked at Naomi, who didn't give my father a glance. "My apologies, Your Honor; I was trying to establish the connection between the defendant and the witness before we continued. If Mr. Charles could be so patient as to give me another five minutes of his time, he could continue to grow older in peace."

I watched in quiet amusement as my father tried to maintain his smile, but his grip on the desk tightened.

"Overruled. Continue, Ms. Vine." Naomi nodded and turned back to Lennard. "What did you see, Mr. Curtis?"

I stared at the witness but saw no shift in his emotion or movement in his seat. Whatever he was going to say, he didn't fear Drayman, unlike the other witnesses.

"He would take every single one to an ice cream shop at the beginning of their relationship and at the end."

"And how do you know this?" Curtis smiled at Naomi's question. "My girlfriend, now wife, used to work at that shop, so I would spend my free time there. It was one of the few places kids could go in the small town." Naomi turned slightly to the jury and then back to Curtis. "When you say he took them there to end things, do you mean he would break up with his girlfriends at the shop?" Curtis nodded and then caught himself and said yes. "How would he break up with them?" My father was tapping again.

"He had a little speech that he said so much I mesmerized it after a while. 'I need to focus on school. Maybe we could talk over summer break' like that. The only difference was the girl's name. And then the following week, he'd have a new girlfriend."

I glanced over at Drayman to see how he was taking the testimony, expecting him to be writing in his notepad as we had instructed him to do to look busy, but he seemed very interested in what Curtis was saying.

"Did this speech ever not work?" Naomi was facing the jury fully now, scanning each of their faces.

"Yes. Once. Marleen Edwards." It was so low, I wasn't sure anyone other than Gabby and me heard it, but Drayman grunted. "How did Marleen take it?" Naomi's voice was still confident, and it had a patient flow which must have been helping the jury paint the story. "She started shouting that he had told her if she slept with him they would spend the summer together and that she wasn't ready but did it for him." Naomi looked back at Curtis.

"How did Ronan take that?"

"He was calm and refused to engage. He got up and walked out. Rumors started about Marleen. That she was mentally ill and had never even dated Ronan. That she made the whole thing up." The testimony was bad character-wise, but nothing we couldn't come back from. They had already tried this tactic with the waitress, and the jury didn't seem swayed. "What ended up happening to Marleen, Mr. Curtis?" For the first time, Curtis looked uncomfortable.

"Someone found her hanged in her room a few days before summer break."

My swallow was subtle as I trained my head forward, but I wanted to ask Drayman why the fuck he hadn't said something about this. "They found a typed note saying that she couldn't handle school life and being away from her family so much, and everyone talked about it until the semester was over and we left to go home."

This wasn't great, but she didn't name Ronan in the note, and the prosecution didn't have anyone else to corroborate Curtis's story.

"Did you ever hear Drayman talking about Marleen again?" I hadn't noticed how tense my father had gotten until he shot up. "Objection! This is just another attempt to drag my client's name through the mud. There's nothing to say he even knew the girl!" This time, Naomi did look at my father.

"The witness has already stated the nature of their relationship."

"Overruled," Judge Lee said, and my father eased into his seat, barely hiding his displeasure. I looked between him and Drayman and gritted my teeth. This is what they had been keeping from me.

Curtis picked up like he was never interrupted. "I was packing and remembered that I still had stuff in my locker to take home." Curtis glanced at Drayman, but there was no apprehension in his eyes. "When I went out into the hall, I heard Ronan and some friends laughing and talking. I wasn't going their way, but I paused and got closer when I heard Marleen's name. They were sitting on the stairs that went up to the third floor, so they didn't see me behind the wall."

Naomi nodded for Curtis to continue. "Drayman said that Marleen's family was going bankrupt and that the sex wasn't even good." Curtis took a breath. "And that if she had shut up, maybe he wouldn't have choked her so hard."

I was happy the judge had refused press in the room because this would have been on every news channel within the hour.

My jaw tightened as I watched the jury take furtive glances

at Drayman. Gabby shoved a notepad onto the table in front of me, and I jerked my head down stiffly.

I didn't know about this!

I would consider whether she was telling the truth later. Right now, I had to discern how fucked up my firm's reputation was about to become. My father was up again, all smiles gone.

"This is hearsay, Your Honor! They weren't friends, by the witness's own admission." The judge deadpanned his ridiculous protest. Naomi continued when Judge Lee nodded to her.

"What else did he say?"

"No one really laughed except Ronan, and then everyone got quiet. He told them they could never back out of what happened because they had done most of the work getting her up on the ceiling fan."

Naomi paused and turned to the jury one last time. "Thank you, Mr. Curtis. Nothing further." My father stood as Naomi turned to walk back. He whispered something to her on his way to the stand, and the furious look on her face as she sat made my temper flare to dangerous levels.

I was furious that he and Drayman concealed this testimony and that Langston was leading the cross-examination despite my expressed wishes, but speaking to Naomi? It was time I made a move of my own.

Naomi tried to appear calm, but her hands were in fists on the table. Coleman leaned over and whispered something to her, and she took a breath. She looked like she wanted to cry, and I rose from my seat, but Gabby's firm grip on my wrist stopped me. Frozen midair, I looked up at the judge, who watched my movements with confusion. I had to calm down.

Sinking into my chair, I pointedly ignored Naomi to avoid killing my father in front of the entire courtroom. Instead, I focused on Langston, who was walking around in small circles, his hand on his chin, and his eyes tight. Coming to the jury, he stopped but kept the puzzled look.

"Mr. Curtis, you said you never spoke with my client in school, correct?" Curtis nodded again, forgetting, and then stated "yes" out loud. "How did you end up working together, then?" Some of the jury members tilted their heads, and while I had words for my father after this, I hoped he could dig us out of the hole he had attempted to hide.

"We didn't. Ronan called me out of the blue and said that he had a business venture for me and that we should talk." Langston smiled. "So, a real estate mogul like Ronan Drayman offers you, a person he doesn't know, a chance out of the blue like that. Wow. And why would you take him up on his offer if you thought he did something like what you claim in boarding school?" I slowly regained control of myself and concentrated on the testimony. My dad was trying to find faults, but Curtis seemed sturdy.

"I also wondered why he would call me, and then I thought maybe he knew I had been there that day. Fear for my family drove me to see what he wanted." My father rolled his eyes to the jury, so the judge couldn't see. "Right. And then you agreed to go into business with him because of this fear? Not because you stood to make millions of dollars?"

"I never agreed to work with him." Langston paused only for a second.

"You had a contract; construction was ready to start before your dealings with Mr. Drayman fell through, correct?"

"No. He brought me into his office, gave me a contract, and explained that the location was selected and ready, adding that he wanted to help an old classmate."

My dad tried to interrupt, but Curtis continued. "I told him I needed to review the site and other factors before I signed a contract, but he told me that guys like me who know how to keep a secret wouldn't have to worry about red tape."

This time, my father wouldn't let Curtis keep talking.

"Mr. Curtis, I didn't ask for your memory of the events that happened at least ten years ago. I don't expect you to recall that day well."

"But I do, because I had only ever been that vividly afraid one other time—the day by the stairs. When I told him I didn't want the site, he told me that if I wanted to continue to stay quiet for free, then fine, but make sure I did."

The pieces were coming together for me, and the more they did, the more I wanted to drag my father out of the courtroom. "If you're such a noble person, why exactly did you never bring up your accusation with the authorities?" Curtis looked down, and for a second, I thought we might have something. "It's my single biggest regret. I failed Marleen by not saying anything for all these years. That's why I'm here."

I shot a muted glare at Drayman. If he had even an inkling of what Curtis would say today and kept quiet, I was dropping him as a client. Fuck the contract.

"So, your testimony is that a person you consider dangerous enough to commit murder knew that you could identify him, but allowed you to walk away not once, but twice?" Curtis opened his mouth to speak, but my father cut him off. "Strike the question, Your Honor. Nothing further." My father walked back to his seat and stacked paper, willfully ignoring my heated stare. Naomi and I stood simultaneously and then looked at each other. She pivoted her attention to the judge, and I did the same.

"Redirect, Your Honor?" Shit. "Your Honor, I ask for a short recess to confer with my client first." I needed to see exactly what was going on before she delivered what was sure to be a death blow.

"We'll call it a day after Ms. Vine asks her question. Then you can have all the time in the world with your client." Naomi didn't look at me or move from her standing position. "Mr. Curtis, what conclusion did you come to about the defendant not harming you or your loved ones?" Lennard Curtis looked directly at Drayman as he spoke. "After I thought about it, I realized it must have been because my great-uncle is on the board of his family's company. He has a defining stake in the stock. I figured he couldn't risk that he would find out and bankrupt his business." Naomi smiled.

"Yes, from your testimony, we know how little the defendant thinks of those who are bankrupt. Thank you, Mr. Curtis."

The judge slammed his gavel and told us to convene at nine am sharp Monday morning before leaving.

"Office, now," I spat, and was up and through the doors before Judge Lee closed his. There would be no courthouse step conference today. We were all going to discuss what the fuck that was.

CHAPTER 27

NAOMI

I kept my composure after the trial, forcing a grin when Coleman told me I did a great job, but in my car alone on the way back to the office, I let myself worry about what Langston would do with the information he clearly had. His terrible whispered taunt made me want to vomit.

When Lennard Curtis called this morning, I didn't want to get my hopes up. He was old money, and we already had the shafted businessman angle, which didn't seem to make a dent. But spending the morning with Curtis as he told his story over and over to get it down for the jury, the excitement just kept building. Now, I couldn't enjoy the impact.

Malcolm told me not to worry about his father, so maybe he knew Langston was all talk. *Or maybe they planned this.* I shook myself, tossing the thought away as I walked into the elevator. I still wasn't sure that I could reconcile Malcolm's work with how I felt about him, but knew he wasn't evil.

Still, I couldn't bring myself to call him. The lump in my throat that appeared when Langston spoke to me, bobbed. I should write my resignation letter right now, but rationalized I had to finish the prep with Jack. It would be my last act on the case. The dread continued to choke me so much that I didn't notice Dorian before I heard him. "You really were amazing in court today, Ni!" he said almost to the entire office as I met him at my desk.

I ducked my head as a few people looked our way. Attention was the last thing I wanted right now. I cleared my throat and focused back on him, hoping I conveyed the calm I didn't feel. "Do you want to use the same conference room in the corner for Jack's interview tonight?" He pursed his lips. "He didn't call you?" I mirrored the confused look on Dorian's face. "Call me about what?" I asked, worry already rolling my stomach. Dorian put up his palms.

"Uh, well, he's not coming." I took in his defensive stance and could feel the eyes that were still glancing at us periodically. We were standing almost in the middle of the room, and Dorian wouldn't know an inside voice if it smacked him in the face, which I wondered if that's what he thought I was going to do since he had such wary behavior. I worked to smooth my features.

"When did he call you?"

"Around eleven. You were prepping Lennard, so I didn't mention it, but I figured he'd reached out to you too. He's busy at some family event, and since he's already testifying against his parents' wishes, he didn't want to rock the boat more."

Eleven? That was hours ago, and Dorian hadn't said a thing. I was mad, but outside of Malcolm igniting my temper, I never got angry enough to be unprofessional. Still, Dorian kept his hands up as if I were a ticking time bomb. I turned away from him, hoping to lose the interest of the few people paying attention to our conversation. "Does Mr. Coleman know?" I asked as nonchalantly as I could and took my laptop out of my bag to appear busy. There was no reason to stay in the office if Jack wasn't coming, but I didn't want to look at Dorian anymore.

"I thought you would have told him." That, he said in a hushed tone, feeling so close to me I startled and glanced back but found he was standing in the same spot. His palms had retreated, and he looked appropriately contrite, although an apology hadn't left his lips. "Anyway, Jack told me you prepped him well and that he'd be ready for Monday!" Back to announcing our conversation to the office, I decided to end our chat. I turned to Dorian with a tight smile.

"Fine, can you let Mr. Coleman know? I have a few things to finish up before I'm out of here." I was a team player, but he should have already said something. Dorian's amiable smile dropped. "Sure thing." He spoke in a low voice, and I felt an unwelcome chill. His congenial eyes turned hard for a split second, but then his smile was back, and he squeezed my arm before he was strolling down the aisle between office desks.

The encounter left me with a weird urge to back up a few steps even as the distance between us grew without me moving. I rubbed a hand down my face and sat to collect myself. He had done nothing outwardly hostile, but there was something about Dorian that didn't sit right with me. Once this trial was over, I would resume putting distance between us. *You won't be around for the end of the trial*, my mind whispered, and my stomach rolled again.

I tapped my phone to life and tried reaching out to Jack, but the call went straight to voicemail. Maybe his phone was off for the family event. I sent a text for him to call me if he was free at all this weekend so the questions would be fresh in his mind, but I had a feeling I wouldn't get a response.

My interactions with Dorian and Langston left me drained. I tapped Malcolm's contact and stared at his number, not sure if I should call.

What would he say?

Would he rush to my house? The thought of him being there when I got home eased some of my tension.

"There you are! I heard you had a good day in court." Regina appeared in front of my desk wrapped in her signature cardigan. "Did you tell Malcolm Charles I said hello?" I was blushing and rolling my eyes at the same time. If she had known the drastic shift in my emotions toward Malcolm, she would never let it go. "Why would I be talking to that man, Regina?" I blurted and tried to think of something to steer the conversation in a different direction. A question came to mind that was out of my mouth before I could stop it.

"Do you know why Dorian lost second chair?" I hadn't spoken loud, but I glanced around anyway. Everyone was either minding their own business or doing a good job of pretending.

Obviously, I trusted Coleman's judgment, but Dorian officially gave me the creeps, and I wanted to know what his deal was. I looked back at Regina, who scrunched her nose. Instead of answering, she surprised me by silently beckoning me to follow her.

We weaved through the desks until we were in the conference room where I had interviewed Jack. She closed the door, and her silence only put me more on edge. Regina was rarely quiet. When she spoke, it was a whisper, and I had to edge closer. "You know Coleman's receptionist, Kate?" I nodded. "Well, we chat a lot since we're both in the office the most, and she told me that about seven months ago, Coleman and Dorian were in the office after hours. Coleman had told Kate she could leave, but she had forgotten her keys in her desk. When she'd gotten back on the floor, she could hear them yelling from the elevator." I sucked in a breath. I had never heard Coleman speak above a civil tone, even to Langston.

"What were they saying?"

"Dorian shouted it wasn't true, and Coleman said he didn't believe him and that he was fired."

I bit the inside of my lip, confusion dimpling my forehead. "Kate said that they went back and forth like that for a minute, and she got scared that Dorian would see her when he left Coleman's office, so she ran to a conference room and waited."

Regina clammed up briefly as an associate walked by, but they lost interest in us as soon as they passed.

"When she thought they might be done, she headed for her desk, but heard Dorian crying through Coleman's door. He was begging Coleman not to fire him." My eyes widened.

Me begging Coleman not to let me go after he found out about my association with Malcolm ran like a loop in my mind. "What had he done?" My voice was weak, but Regina didn't seem to notice. "She doesn't know. She got her keys and ran out. The next morning, Dorian was at the office but wasn't working with Coleman." I retreated into my thoughts, working to sift through everything Regina had told me, but she touched my arm to bring my attention back.

"The thing is, later that day when Kate was about to leave, Dorian popped up at her desk telling her not to forget her keys."

"He'd seen her?" I asked, not sure why I was so worried for the woman, but worried all the same. Regina nodded. "Kate said he was perfectly nice when he said it, but something in his eyes made her shrink back. She said he laughed and walked off."

The same chill I had when I spoke to Dorian ran through me as I thought about his eyes. I had felt the same way. "You're working a case together, but be careful around him, okay?" I nodded because I didn't know what else to do. Dorian had done something bad enough that Coleman wanted to fire him, but he wavered, and now the man was on our case. I had no right to doubt my boss when I had possibly derailed our hard work.

Whatever Dorian had done couldn't have been as bad as my actions with Malcolm. Still, my unease remained. He had found Jack, but otherwise what had he done, really? Dipped out of meetings, claimed to be working, but had no additional information to bring to the table. I thought back to all the times we were all in the same room together and how Dorian liked to mimic whatever Coleman had just said. Like he agreed with him, but also everything was an idea that he had brought to the table.

I frowned and squared my shoulders. It wasn't my job to judge Coleman's choices, and I'm sure he had his reasons. I needed to concentrate on my own fuck up and come clean. Nausea pushed at the lump in my throat, but I restrained myself from showing any discomfort to Regina. I would tell Coleman the truth tomorrow and let the chips fall where they may.

As my life imploded a thousand times in my mind, one thing I knew for certain, no matter Coleman's decision; after this trial, I was staying far away from Dorian Keates.

CHAPTER 28

MALCOLM

"Let me get this straight." Gabby had cleared the entire floor before we went into the conference room, but I was sure the lower levels could hear the thunder in my voice.

Drayman stood well away from me, but my father remained close enough that I could strangle him at any moment. He was brave. Gabby sat in a chair close by, and even she looked worried for him. "Drayman consulted with you alone about Lennard Curtis, and then you didn't tell the team—me—because you didn't think it was relevant?" I was trying to temper myself, but the fire in my veins wouldn't calm.

"Son, I had eyes on him in Switzerland. He was busy with a project and wasn't supposed to come back, but—"

"But he did!" Gabby jumped, and I worked harder to control my tone before speaking again.

"Despite that, you said nothing." I thought back to his cross-examination and grimaced. "As I said, old man, your asinine antics may have worked in the past, but not anymore. Now we have a client who's going to prison." I flicked my eyes to Drayman and barely held my tongue. I didn't give a shit about him; our reputation was what I was worried about.

The press could soon have the Marleen story, which was bad, but only if they also got a guilty verdict.

Our firm being the face of a high-profile failure like this meant a conversation I couldn't afford to have. Drayman scowled, and I realized my expression perhaps conveyed what I hadn't said but didn't give a shit. "We're not damaged yet. I have this handled." My father knew better than to sound too nonchalant, but his carefree smirk made me step closer to him.

"He didn't damage us? Lennard Curtis' testimony implicates our client as a murderer. A person who decided who lived or died based on their family income." Drayman must have tired of being talked about because he stepped forward.

"You should have made sure he didn't get on that plane, Langston! What am I supposed to do now?!"

"Ten to life."

Drayman sputtered at my answer.

"Curtis was a misstep, but we still have a play. Calm down." I frowned at my father. "What play? The flimsy alibi we cobbled together?" I spat the words out, but he turned his back to me, ignoring my question.

"Ronan, get some rest this weekend, and we'll see you in court on Monday." Seconds passed as Drayman glared at both me and my father, but he stomped out without another word.

Still not answering, Langston took the seat across from Gabby and pulled out his phone as if the conversation was over.

"Gabby, file papers with Judge Lee to drop Drayman from our firm. I'll have a reason for him by morning." My father looked up at me, amused but wary, and Gabby glanced at both of us before touching my arm as she left.

"Son, we can't drop Drayman." I stared him down. "There is no 'we.' You broke our contract by crossing Curtis, and now I will toss Drayman out on his ass and work to correct the mess you made." His fingers began tapping on the desk, and I crossed my arms, waiting for whatever excuse he would try. Langston only sighed, and for a second, I thought he might give in, but then the tapping stopped, and he slid a folded manila envelope out of his jacket pocket.

He rose to stand in front of me, his bored mask betrayed by

the glint in his eyes. "I didn't want to use this so soon, but you gave me no choice." He waved the envelope in front of me, but I didn't move.

"You should've been more careful about the company you keep. Gabby was perfect for you, but you had to go after someone you couldn't have." At my silence, he pushed the envelope into my chest, and I gripped the yellow paper too tightly as I opened the small clasp and saw several photos stacked together.

I pulled them out, and each one made me more furious. They were all from the night Naomi found that threatening note on her door. They captured us standing too close together on her front porch; us going through her side gate and then me coming out of her home later that night.

The last one, where I stood outside her door as her brown eyes stared up at me like I was just Malcolm and not some murder defending lawyer, made the ache in my chest burn. She hadn't even wanted me there. I'd shown up at her house and in her life unannounced, and put her in my father's sights.

"Why would I care that you have photos of a late-night negotiation of a plea deal?" I asked. Langston nodded.

"Sure, you could probably spin these photos, but what about Naomi? Do you think she's the type to lie like that?" I heard his fake sigh, but couldn't take my eyes off the images.

"I don't think she's like us, son."

He was right. Naomi wouldn't lie, and if she knew about these photos, she would go to Coleman herself.

"And even if you used that silver tongue of yours to convince her that everything would be fine, wouldn't she worry about what *other* photos I might have?" The twinkle in his eye said my father thought he had me, but just as I had shown my hand when I came to his home that night, he had just shown his.

"Who's being fed lies now, old man?" Langston's assured smile faltered. "Ms. Vine won't know because there's nothing here." I dropped the photos on the glass conference table, and they spilled away from each other. "And there aren't any other photos."

That my father didn't know Sloan had been watching Naomi since that night implied I had someone else to thank for the invasion of privacy. I would find out who.

"As I was saying, this case is done. I'll reach out to the board about the fallout." I wanted to relish my father's defeat, but didn't have the time. If this case was over, then that meant there was no reason Naomi and I needed to hide, and it took away the only tactic Langston could use against her. She wouldn't be happy about the delay in Drayman's case, but I could think of a few ways to cheer her up.

I had almost forgotten that my father was still in the room until he sighed. "I spoke with Eugene." My eyes snapped to him. "He said he's been trying to reach you." His languid smile told me we were thinking the same thing. My grandfather was not someone you just chatted with. "I've been busy," I gritted out, and he huffed a laugh. "Yes, I let him know all about it."

Turning from my father, I walked to the window, staring at the buildings reflecting the sun back to me. Fear, cold and sharp, slithered through my chest. "He agrees with me about Drayman." I hadn't calculated that my father would be desperate enough to reach out to Eugene. You never had a conversation with that man without losing something. The higher the stakes, the worse the loss.

"So, this is your plan. You can't beat me yourself, so you run to him?" I muttered, barely hiding the trepidation in my tone. If Eugene already knew about Naomi, then my father was the least of my concerns.

Langston came to meet me at the window, taking his time

to look out at the same skyline. "I don't have plans, son. That's your obsession. All I do is survive." He turned to me. "And I recall you doing the same all those years ago." Langston watched me closely, soaking in the position he had put me in.

I couldn't go against Eugene. No one could. In our game of power, my grandfather had always been the defining factor. Dangerous as he was, if Eugene James was on your side, there were no more obstacles. I had made a deal with the devil ten years ago to take my father's firm from under him, and now he had done the same to keep me in line. I looked down at my father and met his amused gaze.

"What did you say to Naomi in court today?" His smirk spread into a smile, and my jaw ticked until it ached. "All I said was that she had chosen the wrong Charles." The words wrapped around me, and everything else muted.

Langston was still speaking, but all I heard was the rhythm of his voice and my own thoughts screaming at me to do something. My fist clenched so tight, I could feel the skin on my palms break with the tension. I said I could protect her from my father, but she had no idea of the other demons that lurked in my life.

I used to be able to withstand any button Langston pushed, calculate all his moves, and stop them before his plans metastasized, but my distraction allowed him to outmaneuver me. Naomi's face looped again and again in my mind, and I wanted nothing more than to feel Langston's face beneath my knuckles. To, for once in my life, succumb to the impulses these men had instilled in me.

"Glare at me all you want, son. I didn't put you in this situation," Langston huffed. Red seeped into my vision as violent urges bombarded my thoughts, and Langston made the smart choice to move away from my grasp as he continued to speak. "Drayman stays." Langston walked along the glass wall that separated the room from the office at large. He peered out through the closed blinds, appearing calm, but I noted the eye he kept on me as I imagined how easy it would be to wrap my hands around his neck and squeeze until he couldn't say anything to or about Naomi again. Until he couldn't speak at all. "Don't lose your head, Malcolm. The board has eyes and ears everywhere." The not so subtle threat did little to clear the fog in my mind.

My father had me by the balls, and he knew it. Everything I had been afraid of was happening before my eyes, and there was nothing I could do to stop it. After all the years I spent getting to this point, my grip on Langston was crumbling. And I had pulled Naomi into my chaos.

The anger seeped out of me as self-loathing took its place. Langston sensed my defeat and moved closer. "Now, let's go home and get some sleep. I have a feeling court is going to be exciting on Monday." With a fatherly nod that didn't fit him, he squeezed my shoulder.

"Goodnight, son." I reached up and grabbed his hand before he could release me and tightened my own. "You have her followed or speak to her again, I will kill you."

I leaned in, crowding Langston, and squeezed his hand until the smirk slipped off his face. "And if you ever talk about her to Eugene again, death will be a dream that you pray for every waking moment." Something close to fear shadowed my father's features, and I grinned.

I may not have been as dirty as they were, but I would make it clear that I could be just as ruthless. "Malcolm?" I looked up to see Gabby in the conference room doorway, concern etched on her face, and I released him. I didn't wait for Langston's reply and walked out of the room, already calculating how to shield Naomi from the mess I had put her in.

CHAPTER 29

NAOMI

I woke up with a dry mouth and a dull headache. I vaguely recalled a dream of me packing up my desk while several no-faced colleagues whispered around me. The only person I could make out was Dorian, and he was laughing his ass off.

I groaned and hoped it would become a fuzzy afterthought once I got some coffee. I should have spent the night drafting my resignation letter, and I had tried, but with a bottle of wine and too many tissues, I had only gotten as far as 'I'm so, so sorry' and decided it could wait until later today. My phone buzzed, and my stomach flipped.

Malcolm hadn't reached out to me at all yesterday. He swore to keep things professional, so it made sense that he was backing off, but the theory that he knew his father was aware of our situation wouldn't stop nagging me. Maybe he was keeping his distance to prove Langston wrong? My eyes rolled at my anxiety. I didn't know what he was doing, and at the moment, I didn't care. I had my own issues to deal with; like what I was going to do if Coleman fired me.

Mustering up the courage, I tapped the screen and saw that it was Myra. She sent me a meme of two cats bumping into each other again and again with mini wine glasses dancing in the background.

That will be us in a few hours!!

I had set a reminder to pick her up today, but Myra knew me, and this text was both a nudge and a promise. Mac barked from outside, signaling that I had enough time in bed, and I padded over to the door and let my noisy roommate in, then headed to the kitchen to start my coffee maker. My phone buzzed again, and I remembered I hadn't responded to Myra's text but paused when another name appeared.

> Don't do anything I wouldn't do, Goody.

I waited in vain for the three dots to appear that would elaborate on what Malcolm was telling me, and frustration burned my cheeks red when they never came.

I tapped his contact and listened to the drawn out rings until the call went to voicemail. Not once, but twice. I squeezed my phone so tight that the small buttons on the side left grooves in my skin. Was he back to playing games? I had gotten so swept up in this thing between us; I had forgotten that I was dealing with an entitled asshole who answered to no one.

Rage guided my fingers as I typed out a message, but I stopped before sending, chucking my phone on the counter with a loud clang I regretted. If he couldn't communicate properly, I wouldn't waste my time.

Gingerly, I grabbed my phone again, inspecting for damage. I grumbled at the new crack I saw on the side. I needed to replace the dying device, but didn't want it to give up on me before I had a chance.

Pushing the constant thoughts of Malcolm to the back of my mind, I typed out a quick message to Myra telling her I would be there. Even in my current state, I was excited to see my friend after so long.

My coffee machine beeped, and with Mac at my heels, I

sipped and ignored an impending headache so I could get dressed and out the door.

I had only circled the airport loop twice before I saw my beautiful friend. She was wearing a yellow ankle-length sundress and sandals I knew she had just changed into in the bathroom. Myra was a seasoned traveler and wouldn't be caught dead barefoot in the TSA line.

Her brown skin and dark box braids shone in the sunlight, and I matched the infectious smile she gave once she noticed me. "Niiiiiiii, I missed you!" She sang, collecting me into a hug, before we tossed her small carry-on into the backseat. I didn't know how she survived on these trips with such a tiny bag, but that was Myra.

She scrutinized my face as we slid into the car. "Your forehead looks better." I touched my now slight cut. It had healed enough for me to remove the bandage, though it was still noticeable if you knew it was there. I wasn't looking forward to the scar.

"Yeah, told you it was nothing! How was your interview?"

Her smile returned, and I slid into traffic. "Ni, Martin told me all about the upcoming trial in New York and his plans to open his own finance firm once everything blows over." I wrinkled my nose, but said nothing. Kline had allegedly embezzled some of his fortune from his clients, and Myra was on a first name basis with him.

I adjusted my face when she gave me her Don't Start glare. My perspective on most things was black and white, but Myra saw all kinds of colors. It wasn't worth getting into a debate, though. Not when my life was developing a few colors of its own.

Smiling, I switched topics to lighten the mood. "Your boss would be dumb not to give you that raise now!" She happily took my subject change with a laugh. "Damn right! Do you know how much money independent bloggers are making these days?" I didn't, but I imagined it was more than an investigative journalist at a dwindling newspaper. "So, how about we order lunch in at my house and watch a movie? We can stop at the store and grab champagne and orange juice!" My fingers were crossed that Myra would settle for a chill day inside. I was putting up a good front, but my nerves were shot, and I needed to lie on the couch and figure out my next steps.

"Um, no, girl! We are going to Vine! I was dreaming about your dad's cooking on the flight!" She opened her mouth and pretended to be salivating over the thought of my dad's food. I sighed. I would probably burst into tears if I saw my father right now, and then my whole family would be at his restaurant in ten minutes flat. Crestwood traffic wouldn't matter. "I'm not really in the mood to be around people, My," I tried, but she pouted. To be fair, I rarely was up for public gatherings that didn't involve my laptop or a courtroom.

"Ni, please, I need this. I had a great time in New York, but it was also—" She paused and looked out the window. Myra wasn't one to be pensive, and her stark change in mood concerned me. "Well, it was a lot. I just want to get food at a nice, familiar place with my best friend in the universe." Her seriousness gone as fast as it had come, Myra clasped her hands together under her chin and leaned on my shoulder. She changed to poking me in the side when I hadn't answered.

"We're going to crash," I moaned between shrieks.

"Then say yes already!"

"Fine!" I yelled, and she retreated to her side of the car, grinning.

She was quiet for the twenty minutes it took us to get to my dad's restaurant though, which also wasn't like her, but I chalked it up to being able to see the Crestwood skyline again.

Jeffrey was on the phone as we walked in, and his eyes nearly popped out of their sockets as he looked us both up and down. As always, guests filled the compact entrance while waiting to be seated, and every table was occupied except the one reserved for our family. "Tomorrow at seven for four, thank you, Ms. Melina. Now I have to go—two angels just walked into the restaurant!" I gave Jeffrey a small smile, hoping that my showing up last week meant I would not get smothered to death today, but Myra was busy striking a pose for our favorite host, garnering some chuckles from the surrounding people.

"Myra, get over here and give me a hug!" She obliged and held Jeffrey tightly. I followed suit, and Jeffrey still squeezed the life out of me. "My, my, my, Ms. Naomi. You becoming a regular now?" I gave him a kiss on the cheek as he playfully gasped. Another person entered, and I took the moment to walk past, heading straight for our family table. "See you later," I yelled over my shoulder as Myra and I navigated our way through the chairs and tables, passing animated conversations.

A server met us as we sat, and we immediately ordered two mimosas and two portions of my dad's tasting menu. Jeffrey might have been right about me becoming a regular once the items were officially on the menu.

Once the server left, Myra smiled in a way that told me she was about to say something I wouldn't like. "So, Malcolm." Heat flooded my cheeks as I stifled a groan. I didn't want to jinx it when she hadn't mentioned him in the car, but now I knew why. She wanted me trapped. "What about him?" I murmured, looking for our server and my much needed mimosa.

Myra only waited, her head cocked to the side with a grin that made my cheeks burn more. "He's a lawyer, and he's attractive. Nothing much else to know." She leaned in. "Other than him eating you out on his desk, you mean?" I choked on nothing, and the server returned with our drinks and rushed off, promising to bring water. "This is my dad's restaurant, Myra!" She frowned. "That's why I whispered."

I couldn't help a small smile at her ridiculous logic before I achieved a straight face again.

"I want to know what happened since! Did you tell Malcolm you'd give him a chance after the trial? I saw on the news that the case has been bumpy. Langston Charles hasn't met a camera he doesn't like." Our server set our water down, and I drank half of mine. "We had a good day yesterday, and I think we'll continue to gain momentum." *Coleman and Dorian will gain momentum*, I reminded myself. I would be on the sidelines, getting updates on the trial from the news like everyone else.

"What's wrong?" Myra cocked her head to the side, and I tried to wipe the mournful look off my face. I loved my best friend like a sister, but I couldn't tell her what a disappointment I'd become. That I ruined my career for a man. Tears burned at the rims of my eyes, and I snatched up my mimosa glass a little too fast, the liquid teetering dangerously close to spilling over the top.

"I know this food is good if my baby's here a second time in the same month!" Myra and I both stood and hugged my dad before all sitting back down together. We chatted about the new menu and the expansion, and my dad laughed as Myra devoured the food much like I did.

The restaurant hadn't cleared out at all since we'd been there, but the faces changed as we chatted for an hour.

"Poppa Vine, are you sure you trust Teddy in the kitchen this long? I mean, he's fumbled pretty badly before." Myra winked at me, and I rolled my eyes. My dad laughed so loudly that a few people looked our way.

"On that we agree, but he seems to fare better with food than with women." My cheeks hurt from the embarrassing smile I was holding back.

After my dad refused to let us pay the bill, we gave him hugs and headed for the exit. Jeffrey was busy at the podium but gave us air kisses on our way out the door, and as soon as we crossed the threshold, Myra gripped my forearm, stopping me from walking. I studied her, puzzled.

I stuck to one mimosa so I could drive us home, and I hoped she was happy to end the day now because pretending nothing was wrong was taking its toll.

"Tell me." Myra raised her eyebrows, waiting for a response I didn't want to give. I sighed and tried to keep walking, but she held firm. We were still at the entrance of Vine, and people were approaching.

Nudging her to the side of the building closer to where my car was parked, I grappled with what to tell her. "I just have a lot on my mind."

"Like what?" I hated when she turned investigative reporter on me. "My, I don't want to talk about it right now." I didn't want to talk about it ever, but soon everyone would know. She assessed me, her eyes softening the more she looked at me.

"Is it about Malcolm?" She asked, and the "yes" fell from my lips as a whisper.

"Did he hurt you?" Yes, he had, but not in the way she meant. In reality, I had hurt myself by allowing my feelings to get the better of me. "Whatever it is, you're stronger than you think you are, Naomi." A bitter laugh escaped me. I was weak. A strong person wouldn't be in this position. Myra moved to stand directly in front of me.

"There's nothing you can't do, and Malcolm Charles would be lucky to lick the bottom of your high heels." She was trying to make me laugh, but I couldn't manage the effort. "In New York, I made a decision I probably shouldn't have."

I was shaking my head, but she kept going before I could speak.

"I slept with Martin Kline." The sharp intake of cold air I took caught me by surprise, and I sputtered as my lungs felt like they were on fire.

Myra let me go when I started coughing, chuckling to herself. "Yep, that's about the reaction I thought you would have." When I could finally see straight, I stared back at my friend, questions whirling in my mind. Myra was a free spirit, but she took her work seriously. She never mixed business with pleasure, and she had interviewed movie stars who slipped their phone numbers to her and wouldn't leave her alone for weeks when she hadn't taken the bait.

"Why Martin?" was the question I settled on. She bit her lip and squinted her eyes as if she were trying to figure that out herself. "He's so—" Myra looked up at the sky like it had the answer and back at me when it didn't.

"To be honest, it's like there was this pull between us that was too exhausting to deny." I nodded. I understood that well. "Anyway, I'm saying whatever it is can't be as bad as me fucking my story and sullying my journalistic integrity, right?" I frowned. "Malcolm's dad knows about him and me, and it's only a matter of time before he brings it up and I get fired and maybe even disbarred."

Saying the words out loud dislodged the vice on my heart a little. It was my worst nightmare, but it felt good telling someone. Myra had the decency not to choke on air as I had, but her mouth was shaped in a perfect circle as my words sat between us.

"Wow," was all she could manage for a full minute before she shook herself. "Does Malcolm have a plan?" I wiped my hand over my eyes and laughed. "Malcolm's plan is to go radio silent." Myra scrunched her lips to the side of her face. "I mean, maybe you should just wait and see, Ni." I couldn't believe my ears. "Myra, two nights ago the man was telling me how he couldn't go a day without seeing me, and now I get one cryptic message and he's nowhere to be found?" I walked past Myra, heading for my car.

She couldn't be taking his side this time; she didn't even know him. "I'm not saying he's not an asshole, but maybe he's trying to keep his distance to help you." I had thought the same thing, but didn't want to hear that now.

"And what if he and his father came up with this to ruin the prosecution's case? Seduce me to gather intel or keep me focused on the wrong thing?" I was raising my voice, but I wanted my best friend to understand.

I opened my car and sat down, slamming the door back hard, making the car shake. Myra closed her door less dramatically. I wanted to start the car and take her home. I wanted this day to be over and for my reality to be a dream. But I was too mad to do anything other than stare out the window, seeing nothing.

"You don't really believe that, do you? That this was all some kind of game to Malcolm?" Myra's voice was placating, and I hated the sound. I looked at her, my eyes filling with tears.

"I really hope not, My," I whispered, and a sob pushed its way up my throat when I realized how much I needed that to be true.

CHAPTER 30

NAOMI

After crying my eyes out in front of my best friend for an embarrassing amount of time in Vine's parking lot, we called it a day, and I dropped her off at home.

Myra was quiet on the drive through the city, but as she got out of the car, she told me to give Malcolm the weekend. If I hadn't heard from him by Monday, I could do whatever I thought was best. I told myself that was the reason I let the two days come and go without emailing Coleman my registration.

Never mind that I still couldn't put my immense failure into words. As I tossed and turned all night and watched the dark sky turn bright, the whisper of doubt I had about Malcolm turned into a steady voice.

I walked through the halls of the courthouse with heavy steps. Sweat made the fabric of my silk black top cling to my chest, and my suit jacket was too hot and tight to breathe properly.

The echo of my heels thundered in my ears, and the dimly lit walls seemed to press in with each step. Every breath I took, my chest grew more constricted, and I rubbed my hand down my chest trying to help air enter and exit my lungs.

Looking down, the marble floor seemed to sway, making me lose balance, and the world tilted, the floor coming closer until something large and soft wrapped around me. My chest pinched tighter as I fought to breathe while the quiet hall turned into a dark, small corridor. I looked up to see brown, tired eyes searching my face.

"Baby, breathe," Malcolm whispered, and like my body was only waiting for the reminder, my breath came out in a jagged, long stream. I sucked in another and let it out while Malcolm clutched me to his steady chest.

We had maybe fifteen minutes before Judge Lee would arrive in the courtroom, and I needed to speak with Coleman, but I was content to stay nestled here with Malcolm forever in our secret cocoon that no one could rupture. The thought was sobering.

"Let me go," I eked out. Malcolm didn't loosen his arms. "Don't do it," he sighed. His tone was a plea that cracked the doubt I had forged all weekend. I hardened my resolve and pushed as hard as I could against him. He gave me some distance, but hadn't let go.

"Your father knows Malcolm." I wanted to see the surprise on his face. I wanted to be wrong in thinking he knew what I knew and still had not contacted me, but he was as calm as always, though I caught the tightening of his jaw. I twisted away, and he released me.

"I can handle my father. Trust me." I swallowed the scream that rumbled in my chest. "Trust you?" I hissed. "What have you done to warrant my trust? You defend murderers, you show up and boss me around, and then when I needed you most; when I felt like my dreams were ending because of what *we* did, what you told me would never happen, I should trust you?" Tears fell down my face and I let them because I couldn't keep my voice low and stop them. I stepped closer to Malcolm, and for the first time, he moved back.

"I have no trust in you," I seethed. I wanted to walk out of the dark nook and out of Malcolm's shadow for good, but my feet wouldn't move. My heart must have controlled them because with every beat it was begging Malcolm to prove me wrong.

He gained back the ground he lost and then some, backing us deeper into the dark until my back pressed against a wall. I let him cup my face, taking my mouth into a kiss that my whole body sighed into. Emotions that I wanted to believe were coming from Malcolm pushed down on me so heavy, my knees almost buckled from the pressure.

His lips separated from mine too soon, but he raised my chin to meet his eyes, and his face revealed the aching I felt in our kiss. "I would never let anything bad happen to you." Without another word, Malcolm turned from me, walking out of our hiding place as if it were the easiest thing in the world to do.

When I walked into the courtroom and sat in my usual seat, I didn't look up, but I could feel Malcolm's eyes. He sat first chair, his father taking the second.

I wondered whether that was what Malcolm meant by "handling his father," as both Dorian and Coleman nodded to me.

I tried to hide my trembling hands under the table.

Judge Lee would be here any minute, and if I was going to talk to Coleman, I needed to do it now.

I turned to my boss, but the words refused to come, and I looked away when he glanced at me, coughing into my hand and turning forward. Malcolm hadn't given me any confidence in his ability to leash Langston, and yet I still believed he could.

Turning to the gallery to distract myself from the nerves rolling in my stomach, I saw Jack sitting right behind us, and the man and woman he sat between. From the information I could dig up about Jack and his family, I recognized them as his parents, Mary and Jack Senior. Jack Jr. was more dressed up today, wearing a nicely tailored black suit, and looked slightly older with his brown hair swept neatly to the side.

Both his parents avoided my eyes, so I focused on Jack.

"You're really brave," I whispered, hoping to quiet whatever worries he might have while mine cascaded again and again against my chest. He gave me a small smile, then glanced at Dorian and I turned back around.

As my eyes flicked between Malcolm and Coleman, I realized Jack was stronger than I could ever hope to be.

"Are you okay, Naomi?" Coleman asked, and all the words I was afraid to say felt like they were floating on balloons up my throat to my tongue. I saw Malcolm stand, and I thought it was to stop me, but then everyone was standing, and I turned to see Judge Lee had walked in.

Quickly, I stood up and sat back down with everyone. "Could you handle Jack's testimony?" Coleman continued, and I blinked at him. "Dorian said you did his interview alone, and I know you sent me the questions, but I think a young witness like this would benefit from familiarity. You deserve it."

Coleman frowned, and I nodded to hide whatever expression I had given him. He leaned in to speak again, but the judge interrupted him. "Prosecution, your witness?" I stood and stared at Judge Lee while I smoothed my blouse down, letting the motion steady me.

If I was going to do this, I was going to do it right.

"We call Jack Stone to the stand."

After some hesitation, Jack made his way through the courtroom to his seat. After his oath, I walked up and rested my hand on his gripping the stand. Jack's eyes flew in every direction, but never to me.

"Jack," I whispered, but his eyes stayed in motion while his leg bounced, making a soft thudding sound with each quick descent. I moved my hand to speak with the judge and try to get a small recess, but Jack grabbed onto me tightly and released me just as fast with a nod to continue. He worked to appear calm, and I decided that if he wanted to do it, we would.

"Mr. Stone, please describe to the jury what you witnessed on the night of January 14, 2023?" I had told him if he ever felt scared to just look at me, but he stared somewhere over my shoulder.

"I was going to The Seminal's concert at the Paradigm and took the elevator down from our condo at nine-fifteen. I know because I was running late and kept checking the time. Mr. and Mrs. Drayman were in the elevator already, and I nodded to them, then stood close to the doors because they were at each corner in the back." He sounded robotic, as if he had rehearsed his testimony a thousand times, but I let him continue for fear that he might clam up if I stopped him.

"They were really dressed up, like she wore a really nice dress and he had on a tux, but Mrs. Drayman was upset about some woman, Carrie, and kept loudly whispering the name over and over and how she could never have a nice night out." I glanced at the jury and saw a few of them making notes.

"And what did Mr. Drayman say?"

"He didn't say anything. I didn't turn around, but it was like I was only in the elevator with Mrs. Drayman."

"What happened next?"

"The elevator suddenly stopped on the wrong floor, and the doors wouldn't open. It stayed like that for maybe five seconds, and then it continued down like nothing happened. Mrs. Drayman only got louder, saying that she wished the elevator had killed us. I think she might've been drunk or something."

"Objection, Your Honor," Malcolm's voice cut smoothly

through the courtroom. I didn't risk looking at him. "There is no way for Mr. Stone to discern whether Mrs. Drayman was drunk. He's not even sure." Judge Lee nodded.

"Sustained." I frowned, but morphed it into a small smile for Jack to let him know it was okay. "What made you think she was drunk?"

"Um... she slurred some of her words, and she didn't speak to me at all. She was usually pretty friendly."

Malcolm said nothing else, and I relaxed. Jack's tapping hadn't stopped, so I tried to push the testimony along so he could get out of the chair as soon as possible.

"Alright, so you got off the elevator and went your separate ways?"

"Yes."

"What happened when you came back home?" Jack looked behind me again. He must have been looking at his parents.

"I got home around midnight and took the stairs because I didn't want to get stuck in the elevator."

"I—" Jack trembled a little, and I stepped closer to the stand so all he could see was me. "You're okay, Jack. Just tell me what you saw." He stared at me, his eyes wide and unblinking. "I took the stairs and heard a voice, but it was way up at the top. It took a while to get to my floor, but by the time I did, I could hear the voice more clearly. It was Mr. Drayman's voice." I waited for Jack to continue on his own. "It was still above me, but the Draymans only lived two floors above us. My parents would drag me to their dinner parties sometimes. I couldn't see him, but he said that someone needed to 'get to his house and take care of it.'"

The judge leaned over to Jack, who was still trembling. "Mr. Stone, do you need a break?" Jack declined with a shake of his head. "I just want to get this over with." Judge Lee nodded and righted himself in his seat.

"Did he say anything else?" I wanted to hold Jack's hand, but knew I couldn't. "He didn't say Mrs. Drayman's name, but he said, 'She was getting too out of control. She forgot how to keep her mouth shut.'" I smiled at Jack, happy that he had gotten through it.

"Thank you." I walked to my seat, avoiding the defense table, but as Malcolm stood, he deliberately brushed past me, his scent centering me more than any breathing technique could do.

He continued walking as I made it to my table, and Coleman passed a note assuring me that the testimony was compelling.

I nodded, but my attention remained on Malcolm. He stood in front of the jury, his right hand in his pocket, but his left resting right in front of a female juror who looked up at him starry-eyed before he turned from them.

"Your Honor, I would request a fifteen-minute recess for Mr. Stone to have a moment before Mr. Charles continues." Judge Lee turned to ask Jack, but he was already shaking his head. "No, I'm fine." Malcolm smirked at me and then turned back around.

"Thank you, Mr. Stone. I only have a few questions, and then you can get out of that box." Jack nodded but was looking increasingly nervous by the second.

"You say you left your house at 9:15 pm, correct?"

"Yes."

Malcolm walked to his table and picked up a file, looking through it. "The show you were going to see started at ten, but they never scanned the ticket you purchased." Malcolm looked between Jack and the jury. "So, my question is, did you really go to the show?" The question was weak. We had photos Jack had taken of the band that night, and most venues didn't scan every single ticket, especially if you were late. This was a ploy to discredit our witness, and I had already prepared Jack for something like this, but he seemed paralyzed, staring at Malcolm with wide eyes as if he had caught him in a lie.

"Mr. Stone, I'm sorry, but I need an answer." Jack cleared his throat once, then twice, but never spoke. Coleman stood before I could. "Your Honor, the witness clearly needs a break—"

"I lied."

All sound in the courtroom seemed to stop at Jack's words, but Malcolm didn't wait long to pounce.

"You lied about going to the concert?"

"I lied about everything."

Now I was standing along with Coleman, although I didn't know what to say. Malcolm's head almost swiveled in my direction, but then he stopped, turning back to the jury.

"You understand that lying on the stand is a serious crime?"

"Yes."

Malcolm took another moment. Dorian was up now too, and it took a glare from the judge to get us seated, but I stayed focused on Malcolm. He looked at his table, and I followed his line of sight to see everyone sitting there calm. Gabby was writing something down, and Drayman had a hint of a smile on his face, like he was trying to contain it but having trouble.

Langston glanced at the jury before meeting his son's gaze. They shared a look, and then Malcolm turned back to Jack. Seconds ticked by before he spoke again, and when he did, anger laced his words.

"Why would you lie, Mr. Stone?" Jack looked behind me to his parents, but slowly our eyes met, and his lips moved slightly, but I couldn't make out what he was saying. Malcolm shifted in front of him, blocking our connection. "I withdraw the question, Your—." Malcolm's voice was rushed, almost frantic, but everyone still heard Jack fine.

"Ms. Vine told me to lie."

Malcolm was yelling something, but I couldn't hear it. I was glad I had sat down because it felt like the bones in my body had turned to jelly. I could faintly hear an echo of Coleman demanding a recess and the gavel being struck many times, but otherwise, everything was hushed.

Someone was squeezing my shoulder, but my eyes were too unfocused to see who it was. I closed them, and Jack appeared in the dark, still on the stand, his mouth moving on a single word, again and again. My brain tried to make out what he had whispered until his voice flowed with the word like magic. "Sorry."

CHAPTER 31

NAOMI

I still couldn't form words; but the world around me had stopped spinning since Jack had announced I had told him to lie on the stand. Chaos had ensued moments after Jack's confession, and the judge had excused the jury and ushered Jack and his parents into his chambers.

I didn't know how long we had been waiting, but the time brought back some of my ability to function.

Dorian and Coleman remained on each side of me in the courtroom, having at first tried to comfort me with promises of finding the truth and their belief in my innocence. But when I could only nod, they quieted down and waited for Judge Lee to come back.

The defense team had disappeared for the recess, and even through the haze of my disbelief of everything that had happened, the need to speak to Malcolm was overwhelming. Why had he tried to stop Jack from speaking? Did he know what he was going to say?

I was an idiot. At every point, my instinct had been to stay away from him, and yet Malcolm still slithered his way into my heart. A heart that was so cracked, I could feel the fracture with each beat.

"I didn't do this." My tongue was heavy, but I got the words out, and Coleman put his hand on mine. His warmth made me realize I was freezing.

He squeezed once and then let go. "Of course, I know that,

Naomi," he said, sliding a steaming coffee cup I hadn't noticed in front of me even closer. I took the cup and felt like every part of me was coming back online as the hot liquid warmed me from the inside.

"I'm so sorry, Naomi. Jack's story was concrete, and he was nervous, but never did he say he wasn't telling the truth." I glanced at Dorian and saw that his head was in his hands. When I didn't respond, he stopped hiding, and our eyes met. "When Judge Lee comes out, I'll make sure he knows I found Jack. I don't even know why he would say your name and not mine if he was going to blurt a lie like that out!"

I breathed deep, but it was still rusty and uneven in my lungs. "You found him, but I coached him. Alone. There's no one to corroborate that I didn't coax him." Dorian's face fell, but Coleman was standing. "We'll fix this, Naomi. The boy was nervous! Everyone saw it. I'm sure he's telling Lee that he misspoke right now."

I didn't have the energy to look up at him to show I appreciated the conviction in his voice, but my head shot to the court doors as they creaked open.

Malcolm walked down the aisle, looking calm and immaculate, his stride assured. He glided past our table without a glance at any of us, and I moved my hands to my lap because they were shaking. Dorian took off his coat and wrapped it around me, but I couldn't feel the weight. How had everything gotten so out of hand? I heard Malcolm flip open a file he must have had with him because there was nothing on the defense table before he had come in and, as if on cue, Judge Lee walked in and took his seat. He said nothing at first and only stared harshly in my direction, and I had an urge to rise. "Mr. Coleman, your witness wouldn't elaborate about his confession that Ms. Vine coerced him to lie on the stand today."

Coleman stood to speak, but Judge Lee put up a hand.

"However, I take these accusations seriously. Jack and his parents will come back tomorrow morning for the boy to give a formal statement about the matter, but what is your stance at this time?"

"Your Honor, we vehemently deny this accusation! Ms. Vine is an exemplary attorney and would never stoop to this degrading level." Judge Lee turned his attention to me, so I stood, praying that my legs would hold. Thankfully, they were sturdier than they had been earlier.

"Ms. Vine. Jack would not repeat what he said on the stand, but surely you understand the issue this presents both for the case and yourself." I pushed through the panic that was still trying to suffocate me and kept my voice steady. "Yes, I under-stand the enormity of the situation, and I have no one who can vouch for everything I said to Mr. Stone. All I can say is the truth, which is that I never told him to lie under any circum-stances about anything." The judge nodded once and then turned his scowl to Malcolm.

"Mr. Charles, where are your client and co-counsel?" My eyes swung Malcolm's way and stayed there.

I didn't know what I was looking for, but I kept searching.

"Sorry, Your Honor. Right after the events, our client started complaining of chest pains, and my co-counselors took him to the hospital in a rush." Judge Lee tightened his eyes but accepted the explanation. "I'm sure you have a motion, Mr. Charles, but I will consider nothing until after I have spoken with Jack Stone properly."

"That's fair, Your Honor," he said, his tone hollow and detached. It was as if his body was in the courtroom with us, but everything else about him was a million miles away. Judge Lee assessed me and then sighed. "As of now, Ms. Vine, you're excused from this case." I couldn't tell if I was breathing too fast or too slow, but I felt lightheaded. "And pending further investigation, I may recommend possible disbarment." Definitely breathing too fast. I tried to remedy it by holding my breath for a second, but 'possible disbarment' swooshing through my brain made me let it out.

"I will notify everyone else of how we will move forward after I meet with Mr. Stone. "

Judge Lee slammed the gavel and walked out, leaving Dorian and Coleman staring at me in silent dismay. Like I was finished business, Malcolm stood with his lone file, exiting the way he came in without ever looking my way.

"Naomi, we will work this all out tomorrow. The kid was just nervous." I wanted to nod, to assure my boss that I believed him even though I didn't, but my feet were moving of their own accord and my body slammed into the semi-closed door Malcolm had just gone through.

I stopped short to not bump into Sloan, who stood right on the other side. He towered over me and watched me suspiciously, as if he were the only thing stopping me from attacking his boss. Maybe he was.

Malcolm had told me not to step down from this case. Was it so that this could happen? A fresh pain I had never experienced cracked my heart further, and I clutched my chest to stop it from ripping out. "Allow me to drive you home, Ms. Vine," Sloan offered. His softened tone was still loud and deep.

Coleman appeared at my side, touching my shoulder, and I must have let Dorian's jacket fall off me because I was freezing again. Sloan's large body blocked my view of Malcolm, but he was already so far down the hallway I would have had to run to catch him anyway.

I knew he had heard me come through the door, and he still hadn't turned around. It was as if the man I had spoken to in the dark was a different person.

I turned to Coleman, apologizing for my sudden outburst,

as Dorian was next out the door with my bag in hand. Six concerned eyes were on me, and I wanted to crawl into a ball and disappear. Instead, I took my bag from Dorian, told Coleman I was going home but would be on standby for any news, and walked down the hall until I didn't feel their eyes on me anymore. Until I felt nothing.

CHAPTER 32

MALCOLM

I walked out of the elevator on my father's floor, bypassing the eyes that widened as I zeroed in on the path that led to Langston's office. People stood to greet me, but I ignored their pleasantries, too consumed by the violence of what I wanted to do when I laid hands on the piece of shit that had the gall to call himself a lawyer.

"Malcolm!" The soft but urgent voice broke through my ire, but only enough for me to flick my eyes down at Gabby, who sped-walked to keep up with my stride. "Don't do this here. There are too many eyes."

What she said made sense, but it wouldn't stop me. Walking away from Naomi used up the last of my restraint, and the promise of pain I was going to give my father was the only thing keeping me going. The prying eyes and whispers dulled as I turned into the quiet corridor only his office occupied.

Gabby was still quick on my heels, but I ignored her as Langton's new assistant came into view. She stood as we approached, her short dark bob swaying as she moved, and I wondered if she had slept with him yet. She would be gone within three months once she did.

Langston had a high turnover rate that NDAs and cushy severance packages rescued him from confronting.

"Mr. Charles?! He's on a call!" I didn't even look in the assistant's direction as I passed, but Gabby squeezed my arm, holding on, and I slowed to a stop before I barreled through

Langton's closed door, taking her with me. I looked down at the slender woman on my arm, and she winced at my expression. "Think of the firm," Gabby whispered.

When I didn't respond, she reached up and touched my cheek. "Be smart, Malcolm."

With one last look, she turned and walked back into the sea of eyes that would train on her as soon as she rounded the corner.

The advice cooled some of the bloodthirsty thoughts that had taken over my mind, but when I turned back to my father's door, my objective came back. The assistant was saying something I didn't listen to as I considered kicking Langston's door down, but then it was open and my father was standing in the frame. Mock astonishment marred his face, as if he hadn't seen this coming.

"Malcolm! What brings you down to the lowly lower level?" I wanted to punch him right there, watch him fly further into his office and hear the crunch of his nose under my fist, but Gabby's reminder stopped me. Still, I pushed past Langston with enough force that he stumbled back and his assistant gasped. He only chuckled. "It's okay, Heather. Hold my calls, please." I heard the click of the door and the lock, but waited until my father walked back into my view, taking a seat at his desk. If I was going to get through this without public bloodshed, I needed a buffer.

"I have a press conference scheduled in thirty minutes, son. Missed the one at the courthouse to make that phony hospital visit plausible. I think the press will eat the chest pains up, though. Shows the trial is taking a toll." I ignored my father's lame attempt at a distraction. He had left the courthouse with Drayman to avoid the conversation we were about to have.

Gabby had wanted to stay with me, but I told her to go. I had a plan to demand a meeting with the judge and didn't want an audience. I took a breath and rolled my shoulders. *That didn't happen though, did it?* I brushed aside my disgust with myself and turned it on my father.

"What did I tell you would happen if you messed with Naomi again?!" I boomed, not caring who heard.

Langston considered me before speaking, his head cocked to the side like he didn't understand me. "Son, I'm worried about you." I blew air through my nose to contain the madness clawing to break free. I took a step forward, and Langston put up his hands.

"What happened in court wasn't me."

"You're not getting out of this, old man." Langston sighed. "I mean it, Malcolm." My father moved from behind his desk as he spoke. "I won't lie and say an opportunity wasn't presented to me for something like this to happen, but I discarded the idea. Too dramatic for my taste."

It was my turn to look confused as I watched him come closer. "Eugene." I grated out, not sure if I even believed what Langston was saying. "As much as I would love to see you attempt to go to war with your grandfather, he had nothing to do with this." I looked down at Langston, who stood in front of me now, assessing my rigid stance like I was a wild animal.

"Have you ever stopped to think that Naomi could have enemies you didn't put in her path?" I shook my head at his nonsense.

"Then it was Drayman." I concluded, and Langston pursed his lips. "I never told Drayman I had been approached. Sometimes it's best to keep things from your clients for their own good, son." Langston looked older as he stood in front of me, like all the years of deception had taken their toll in the last hour.

"I don't believe you," I spat out, and my father brushed his hand over the top of his graying head before glancing up at me.

"I have no reason to lie, Malcolm. The case is over, whether or not I or whoever else orchestrated this. What's done is done." I grabbed him by the front of his tailored suit and leaned down, pulling him closer to me. "What's done is Naomi's career. What's done is you breathing another breath unless you fix this." I thought back to the pictures taken outside Naomi's home.

Even if my father was telling the truth, he knew who *was* trying to hurt Naomi.

"I didn't do this, Malcolm."

"But you can undo it." We stared at each other, and I could see the wheels turning as Langston's eyes searched mine. "I suggest Jack Stone recants his accusation. Clear Naomi's name by tomorrow." I released my father, and he glared at me as he tried to wipe down the wrinkles I had made in his suit.

"As you like to remind me, I am your son. You know what I'm capable of." His mouth a grim line, I took Langston's silence as agreement and turned from him, heading for the door. "You *are* my son," Langston echoed, and I turned to see a sad smile on his face. "I'm glad you haven't forgotten."

Langston held his press conference in one of our firm's meeting rooms, and every news network had been playing it on a loop since he went live hours ago. I wanted to rip my eighty-five inch screen off the wall and throw it across the room, hoping it could erase the day as it crashed to pieces on my marble floor. Instead, I watched him speak for the tenth time about the "Triumphant day" we had in court, never giving details, but providing just enough to whet the appetite of the ravenous crowd.

I stared at my untouched glass of whiskey where it sat on my living room table. Naomi's devastated face wouldn't leave my mind, and I didn't deserve to use alcohol to make it go away. I promised I would protect her, and then immediately helped ruin her life.

I leaned back on my sofa and stared up at the needlessly extravagant chandelier that hung from my vaulted ceiling. Two things became clear the second I looked into my father's eyes as I was cross-examining Jack Stone. First, the boy was a plant, and he was on the stand to instill doubt in the prosecution after the damage of Lennard's testimony. And two, that I was going to sink my own firm by making Jack Stone tell the court who had told him to lie. I had a split second to figure out Langston's plan and come up with my own. But Jack wasn't a plant to discredit the prosecution; he was the killing blow of an insidious plot to wreck Naomi's career.

Too late. I was always too late for anyone that mattered in my life.

I didn't want to believe Langston had nothing to do with Naomi's downfall, but he was right; his tactics were more discreet than a courtroom confession. There was no point in beating him to a pulp, and no evidence to bring the deceit to Judge Lee's attention. My father's words came back to me, and I grimaced. The trial was all but over. If the court didn't immediately dismiss the case, the prosecution would have difficulty recovering from this, and Drayman would walk free, giving my firm a very public victory.

To the outside world, Charles and Charles would be bulletproof. And no one would know who we crushed to get there. I always knew I didn't deserve Naomi Vine, but the feeling I had at the prospect of my firm coming out on top from this dirty case solidified how different we were.

I was ready to risk it all for Naomi in court, but as I sat in the dark, with no one to lie to, I had to admit the truth.

I was relieved.

It was the reason I hadn't talked to the judge in his chambers and had left Naomi at the courthouse. Sure, I reasoned that without evidence, I would only upset the judge and potentially make it worse for Naomi, but deep down I knew. My firm and the vow I made when I was twenty years old mattered more to me than anything else.

I raised the amber filled glass and threw it hard against my living room wall, not caring where the pieces fell. I wasn't suited for love.

My phone dinged on my coffee table, and I ignored it, but when it chimed multiple times in succession, I swept the few specks of glass off and picked it up. News alerts stacked on top of each other, and I stood at the egregious headlines.

FEMALE PROSECUTOR ASKS WITNESS TO LIE IN DRAYMAN TRIAL

MISTRIAL FOR DRAYMAN? WITNESS PUSHED TO LIE BY PROSECUTION

NAOMI VINE ORDERED TO STEP DOWN AFTER WITNESS SCANDAL

My phone buzzed in my hands, and Naomi's name appeared with a single sentence.

> You are the worst decision I have ever made in my life.

All the air in my lungs left at once, and I stumbled to the

floor, smashing my hand into shards as I tried to keep myself upright.

My phone rang, and I dimly noticed I was still clutching it in the hand that wasn't currently bleeding. The ringing stopped and then picked up again, but Naomi was all I could think about. This was career-ending, and even if my father had nothing to do with it, I could have done something and didn't. I *was* the worst decision she ever made, and I was also the selfish asshole who made her make it.

My phone rang again, so I answered with a bark, not caring who it was. "What!"

The crying on the other end dampened my anger as I took the phone off my ear and saw that Avery was calling me. I was up in my next breath.

"What's wrong?" The crying continued, and I worked to quiet the rest of my temper to focus. "Avery, where are you?" He tried his best to talk through the sobs. "At home. You ha-have to come." I was already grabbing my keys while he struggled to get the words out. "Are you in trouble?" When he hesitated, I knew my answer. "Okay, hang up. I'll see you soon." I was out the door before the phone went dead.

CHAPTER 33

MALCOLM

I pulled into a spot a few blocks behind Avery's home. My Mercedes stuck out like a sore thumb in his neighborhood, and in case it mattered later, I didn't want anyone to know I had been on this street tonight.

I also turned off my phone to avoid being tracked or distracted by news about Naomi. I couldn't think of that right now. I came to the front of Avery's house, glancing around the small but well-kept lawn, the grass cut short with a small flower bed to one side, and listened for any noise. Hearing nothing, I slipped on leather gloves and crept slowly up the three steps to his front door and listened again.

Soft cries were muffled by the door, but otherwise the place was quiet. I knocked twice and waited.

A tall figure opened the door a crack and then wider to reveal Avery. Dry and wet streaks stained his cheeks, and it looked like more could come at any moment. He let me in without a word, and I inched past him as he closed the door back, locking every lock.

The front door led straight into the living room on one side and the kitchen on the other, everything completely dark. There was a smell, something pungent, and I couldn't see where it was coming from. Avery had stayed by the door, making no attempt to talk, so I moved closer to him.

"Tell me what happened." I placed a hand on his shoulder, and he looked up at me, his eyes filling with fresh tears.

"My mom—" a sob made him suck up a huge breath, but then he continued. "I came home, and my mom had a black eye." Carl Burris. I tightened my grip on Avery's shoulder but let go when he winced. I moved to the wall to find a light switch, but Avery reached for my hands. "No lights!" He whined.

Not listening to his pleas, I found the nearest one and flipped it on, and immediately saw the reason he was in the dark.

Avery had a large bruise at the base of the left side of his throat, and I lifted his shirt to see that it covered that side of his back and arm as well. "I'll find him," I growled and was already grabbing for the door to go outside and start making calls.

I was considering the best way to ensure he couldn't come back when a harder sob from Avery halted my train of thought.

"He Ca-came back and and and—" Avery's head fell into my chest as he cried. "My mom had given him a key." I looked around again; nothing seemed out of order, but the crying and the smell made my thoughts turn grim.

"When I to-told him to get out, he pushed me hard into my bedroom wall, and then my mom pushed him, and he he he— " Avery stopped stammering, choosing silence instead. I didn't want to spook the boy, but I was worried by his hesitation.

I carefully spun him around and looked to see if he was hurt anywhere else. When I found he wasn't, I met his red-rimmed eyes.

"Where is he now?" I asked, hoping that my conclusion wasn't correct. Slowly, Avery lifted a single finger toward the dark hall off the living room. Avery and his mother's bedrooms were down that way, as well as the single bathroom they shared. I turned in that direction, but Avery gripped my arms, stopping me from moving. "I didn't mean to! He was going to kill her!"

New tears streaked down his terrified face, and I smoothed

my expression. "I'll handle it." He took his time loosening his grip and hung his head once had completely let me go.

I left him by the door and made my way down the hall, not needing to turn on anymore lights as the metallic smell grew stronger and was enough to guide me into Avery's room. I saw Reba first. She had bunched herself up in the corner of the room, looking at the side of Avery's bed with one big, wide left eye. Even in the dark, I could see the swelling around her right, the puffy skin clasped tight.

I looked above her to see the deep indent in the wall where Avery must have gotten his bruises. Carl pushed him so hard, Reba sat in chunks of drywall.

I muted every other emotion as I turned methodical in my examination of the scene.

Avery's basketball trophies had been strewn about on the bed and floor; the bed comforter was disheveled and had a large red stain; and I could see the bottoms of work boots upside down and side by side but not moving. Reba stared at the boots' owner and didn't look my way when I stepped in further.

Avery's bed was a king that I had bought him when he grew too tall to sleep comfortably in anything else. It took up more than half the room, leaving only a walking space in front of the bed and a small gap that ran along the side wall occupied by his dresser and carl's body. I looked at his mother and snapped my fingers until her glazed look focused on me.

"Reba, get up." Avery hadn't come down the hall, but at my voice, I heard him make a sort of grunting noise. Reba stared at me without blinking. "Up, Reba. Your son needs you." Her gaze became sharper at the mention of Avery, and a single tear fell as she looked down at herself.

I reached out my hand to help her stand, avoiding Carl to keep her eyes on me. I walked backward to get her out of the tight space, pulling her all the way into the hallway before she let my hand go. Avery was now sitting on the couch in the lit living room, his head in his hands. Reba walked over to him and gingerly took her son in her arms. It wasn't until she laid her head against his that Avery fell into his mother's embrace, violent sobs tearing through him.

I looked away and walked back into the room, concentrating on the task at hand. I clicked on the light and confirmed the blood on Avery's comforter. The small pool smeared down the bed into the corner. I kept going step by step until I was standing in the corner Reba had sat and saw the body of Carl Burris, limp and twisted, on the floor.

I couldn't see his face, but the back of his head had a small gash; the blood dry in some places but still wet in others. One of Avery's basketball trophies was on top of the wound. It looked like as soon as Avery hit him; he dropped the weapon, and it found its intended target again; the blood now seeped into the marble bottom.

The thought of Avery having to go through the system and carry this memory around with him forever made my jaw tick. I understood what Avery dreaded, and as I looked at the body, bile churned in my stomach. The case was clear self-defense, but that wouldn't matter for a Black kid from the not so nice part of town.

That uppity school that I paid good money for would find a reason to "suggest" Avery got transferred elsewhere, and his basketball prospects would dwindle. Avery was talented on and off the court; he was a decent son and a good person. I had rarely encountered people like him in my life, and now he was going to be punished for protecting his mother.

Naomi's turmoil whispered in the back of my mind, but I hushed the sound. I couldn't think about her and solve this for Avery at the same time.

Sloan would know how to hide the body where no one would look. I ignored the adrenaline that made my heart speed up at the idea I was forming, and concentrated on the details. I hadn't used him for this type of service before, but I was aware of Sloan's prior history, and disappearing a body would be like a Tuesday to him. Though I'd be trusting the man more than ever, it was a necessity for Avery's benefit.

I stood over Carl's body, looking him over as best I could without touching anything. His stench was just as awful as it had been at the chop shop, and I grimaced at the poor excuse for a human.

And then Carl twitched.

His left arm, folded behind his back at a weird angle, slowly slid down, trying to right itself. My heartbeat abated watching his pained movement, and I walked to the door and closed it, just as Carl let out a whining groan. I locked the knob right before the handle jingled.

"Malcolm, is he alive?!" Avery banged on the door. "I got it, kid. Stay in the living room with your mother." Avery continued to bang, but I was already walking back to Carl, who was trying to lift himself up. I kicked his legs out of the way, eliciting another groan, and sat at the corner of the bed.

"Hello, Carl." He took his sweet time rising and groaning until he had spun himself around enough to see me. "I thought I was clear during our last conversation." He still looked confused, staring at me until he absentmindedly touched the back of his head and cursed loudly. The banging at the door had quieted, but I was sure Avery was still there listening.

Realization swept over Carl's face as he took in his surroundings before coming back to me with a sneer. "I'll kill that boy." I smiled and leaned in, making him lean back until he cursed again from bumping his injured head against the wall. "I don't think you understand your predicament, Carl." My anger laced each word, and Carl's eyes widened for a second before squinting.

"What the fuck are you doing here, rich lawyer?" Even with blood still seeping out of his skull, Carl seemed to over-exceed my expectations of being a pig.

"It's Mr. Charles, you piece of shit, and if you don't listen closely, I'm here to make that hole in the back of your head a little deeper and watch you bleed out on my Ferragamos." Carl's eyes darkened, but his mouth stayed shut.

I sat back and assessed the man as he stupidly kept trying to touch his wound only to wince and curse more under his breath. Boosting cars and the events of tonight could get him seven years. It wasn't a lot, and if I spoke to the right people, that could easily turn into ten. But he could always get out, a voice whispered, and I ground my teeth. I didn't want this hanging over Avery's head for the rest of his life.

"Ten grand and you leave the city tonight. You will forget that Avery and Reba ever existed." Carl smirked. "Don't think so. That boy could have killed me, so I'd say that's worth at least a million." Something akin to anticipation spread through my body and had me smiling at his feeble attempt at negotiation.

Carl was trying to stand, and I took his distraction as an opportunity to slip my gloved hand behind his head and clutch onto the bloody mess. He collapsed to the floor, screaming out jumbles of syllables that weren't quite words. His lids lowered, and I reluctantly released him, smacking him twice to make sure he hadn't blacked out.

"You will also sign an NDA. An associate of mine will be here soon with the details and to make sure you make it out of town safely." Tears were running down Carl's face, and he smelled of piss, but I stared at him until he nodded.

I stood and wiped my bloodied glove on the comforter before making my way to the door. I took a breath to conceal the venom that was still coursing through my veins and then turned the knob to find Avery still standing there. He didn't move forward, so I didn't close the door behind me.

"I have to make a few phone calls, and then I'll take you and your mom somewhere else to stay." He looked over my shoulder into the room, Carl's whimpers and curses spilling out into the hall. Avery walked toward me, and I thought he might try to confront the man that had almost ruined his life, but he wrapped his arms around me, squeezing hard with his head in my chest. I put my hand on his back while he cried and could feel his muscles ease.

I was aware of my own tight muscles still ready to pounce, to conquer, and felt that familiar feeling that I had worked to contain all my life but allowed free tonight. That desire not only to win but to annihilate. I had never known Eugene to be anything other than a monster, and my father had fooled me for a while, but I soon saw the truth.

I thought about what I was willing to do to make sure Avery's life didn't transform tonight, what I had been willing to cover up, and realized that I felt no remorse. That Carl Burris was still alive and had taken the deal so easily disappointed me.

I tried to fight the emotion, push it away, but it warmed the ache in my chest and whispered the truth. The only difference between me and the men in my family was that I was in denial.

CHAPTER 34

NAOMI

"You can stay with me," Myra announced, grabbing my overnight bag from my closet after I had refused to get it myself.

She was banging on my door before the first absurd headline dropped, and now they were everywhere, claiming I was a shady prosecutor who bribed a witness to lie. Myra thought news crews would be at my door at any minute and everyone in my family had called me to figure out what was going on. I had given them the details I could but held back from saying who I thought was responsible.

Langston and Malcolm. I thought of them as a team to quell the twist of my insides whenever I really thought about Malcolm doing something like this at all, let alone to me.

It hadn't stopped me from sending him a message and letting Malcolm know exactly what I thought of him. He probably didn't care, but it was the only closure I would ever get where he was concerned.

I had told Myra everything, including about my accident and the weird note I had gotten, and other than scolding me for not telling her sooner, she was the rock I knew she would be. She was adamant she could help figure out who was behind everything, but I noticed she still shied away from my idea that Malcolm had anything to do with it.

Myra moved to my dresser and started tossing a handful of underwear in the bag as I rolled my eyes. "I don't need to leave my house. I should focus on saving my career." She nodded, and we both pretended that it wasn't going to be extremely hard now that the press had the story. "I don't want to run away from this." The lie was already out there, and I didn't want to seem like I had something to be ashamed of.

"I know the press, Ni, and they will chop up whatever you say. There's no point in talking to them right now." Myra started on my work clothes, and I had to step in to stop her from crinkling them up. "Okay, fine, but maybe I should go to my parents. I know you have the Kline story to deal with." She paused from tossing socks into the bag for only a second and then started chucking them harder. "You're my best friend, Ni. You come first. Also..." Myra stopped throwing clothes and sat on my bed.

"I think I'm going to give up on the story." I stopped reorganizing everything she was packing and sat next to her. Myra concentrated hard on undoing and redoing a sock ball over and over, and I would have laughed, except she looked like she was on the verge of tears.

"My, what's going on?" She raised her eyes, forcing out a breath. "I don't know. It's complicated." I knew very well what complicated could do to the psyche, so I didn't push and grabbed one of her hands. "Hey, I love you, and I know I can be a killjoy sometimes, but if you want to tell me something, anything, you know I won't judge you, right?" Myra nodded and smiled. "You're my favorite killjoy." She squeezed my hand, and I pulled her into a hug. Then the lights went out.

We both looked around in the dark, and I stood to try the switch on the wall. "Ugh, a blackout? Traffic is going to be a nightmare if this is citywide," Myra mumbled as I walked around the house and found that she was right; the power was out. Mac barked and growled outside, and I remembered the breaker was in the backyard.

I grabbed my phone from the bed and went to the sliding

door but paused when I noticed the neighbor's back porch light was still on over my fence line. "My, come here," I whispered, and she came by my side, her phone flashlight already on. I pointed to my neighbor's light and then looked at her to confirm what I thought. Myra's eyes widen, and she hastily shined her light outside. I did the same but couldn't see Mac anywhere.

"We should call the—" 'cops' was on the tip of my tongue when something loud and hard banged at the front of the house. The alarm started blaring, and I was grateful Myra had encouraged me to set it even though we were inside as she chucked the sliding door open, and we both scrambled into the backyard. I found Mac lying too still on the ground in a corner and ran to him while Myra was dialing the cops on her phone. Between her call and the alarm dispatch, someone had to be on the way.

I touched Mac and felt him breathing and sighed as tears fell in relief. Myra tugged at me silently with the phone to her ear, and I stood.

The voice through the phone was asking for our emergency, but we went mute at the sight of a tall figure in all-black stepping through the sliding glass door, and both took off running down the side of the house, heading toward the back gate. "The cops are already coming, you asshole," Myra yelled as we slammed into the wood. I flipped the latch to open it, pushing Myra through but screamed when an arm clutched me around my throat, pulling me back.

Myra shrieked and threw her phone at what I thought was a man's head while I struggled for air. Something sharp pierced my side before withdrawing, and the pain formed white dots in my vision.

I could hear wailing and focused on where it was coming from.

I kicked and swiveled to see Myra on the ground clutching her arm as blood trickled down to the pavement. The assailant didn't say a word, but his breathing was hot and fast against my ear, and I could feel his mask scratch against my cheek. He gripped my throat harder, and the night became blacker as I fought not to lose consciousness.

I clawed at his sleeve with all I had, trying to get to some skin and cause damage, but felt weaker with each passing second. Two spots of bright white burned my vision from my driveway as my eyes fluttered, and then the arm released me, and I fell to the ground choking for air. I heard him running but didn't look to see where he was going, satisfied enough that his footsteps were growing distant.

My blurry vision slowly righted itself as I sucked in air, and Myra's body came into view on the concrete.

"Myra!" I crawled to my friend and shook her leg.

A woman appeared by my side, but I never took my eyes off Myra, trying to see where she had been hurt. "Naomi Vine?! What happened here?" I noticed the puddle that had accumulated under Myra's arm and found a long gash still seeping with blood. A sob tore through my body as I tried to shake Myra awake by her waist.

"I'm with Channel Twelve News! Can you tell me what happened here?!" More footsteps and then shouts for space as cops surrounded us and pushed out the reporter and the camera I hadn't noticed.

"Ma'am, are you hurt?" I tried to stand and get out of the way so they could see how serious Myra's wound was but tripped over my feet and fell backward, the ground swallowing me up as darkness took me.

CHAPTER 35

MALCOLM

I sat up in the waiting room seat I had occupied since dropping Avery and his mother off at a hotel. I had given him cash for anything they needed, but could think of little else after I got the call from Naomi's alarm company that her system was going off and they had sent police.

My bad timing was the dreadful thread that never failed to weave its way through my life, always there to remind me I couldn't protect the few people I cared about, no matter my intentions. I had helped Avery, but his sunken eyes told me it would take a lot more than a shower and a good night's sleep to wash away what he had been through.

As soon as I found their hospital, I had Naomi and Myra moved to VIP suites and given the best doctors the facility offered. Naomi's family had thanked me for my help and suggested I go to her room, but the thought of seeing her attached to tubes made my feet feel encased in cement, and I had to decline, settling for regular updates from the sitting area. She wouldn't have wanted me there, anyway.

Because Sloan came to me to help with Avery, Naomi was vulnerable. Her stalker had stabbed and nearly choked her to death. He had cut her friend's arm so deeply that she needed surgery. Someone could have killed them both, and all this time I had known Naomi was in danger and kept it from her for my benefit. I huffed out a bitter breath. How could I have ever thought I was anything other than a monster?

Naomi walked away with a minor puncture wound in her abdomen that only required stitches, but she still hadn't woken up. The doctors said she had passed out from shock and would wake up when she was ready, but it was a struggle not to demand they do something with each hour that ticked by.

Coleman had come by in the early hours but ignored me when he went to check on Naomi's condition. I thought he might blame my firm, so it didn't surprise me when, on his way out, he demanded my team remove the terrible video of Naomi from the internet. A reporter had come to Naomi's house to try for an exclusive and captured her tearfully cradling her hurt friend as the police arrived.

I let him throw his accusations around and leave, but the truth was I had already taken care of it. Some barely contained threats of lawsuits wiped it from public view. Wielding money and power was always easy, but as I sat alone, the hollowness in my chest expanding and constricting with each breath, none of it mattered if Naomi wasn't safe.

I had ignored dozens of calls from both my father and Gabby about the trial, and Camden had come early to drop off a change of clothes and toiletries but held his tongue when it didn't look like I was planning to leave.

I knew I wasn't acting like myself, but I couldn't give anyone an explanation even if they had asked.

What I did know was that when I could persuade myself to leave the hospital, my father had some explaining to do, and I only hoped for his sake that I was satisfied with the answers.

If he had nothing to do with this, he would tell me who did.

My phone buzzed with a text from Sloan. Carl Burris had signed the NDA. He would also make sure Carl left town and dissuade him from returning.

I looked up to see Augustine walking down the hall from

the elevators. His usual smile was reasonably absent, but he still turned his lips up slightly when we made eye contact. When he got to me, he motioned for us both to sit down.

"She's awake." He murmured, and the rapid-fire emotions that shot straight to my heart made me shut my eyes briefly. I opened them to Augustine's sigh. "She doesn't want to see you, but she called your name right before she woke up." Nodding, I tried to remain impassive to her reasonable reaction, but it sliced so deep that I took a quick inhale to temper the impact. What I wanted and what Naomi deserved warred in my mind as I tried to reject the hope that whispered we could get through this. I didn't deserve to get through this.

"I think it's best I go." I was already standing, needing to get some distance now that I knew she was going to make it through. The pain was acute, and I would put it towards finding whoever had done this to her.

Augustine stood too, stepping forward to stop me from leaving. "Malcolm, I don't know what's going on between my daughter and you, but I will not stand by if she's hurt. By anyone." Augustine stared me down, and I understood perfectly. "Me neither, sir. She'll never get hurt again." I stepped back to conceal the threat in my expression, but he had seen it, and the anger seemed to seep out of him at my conviction. "Just...take care of her the way she needs to be taken care of." I nodded because I knew exactly what he was trying to tell me, and I agreed. Naomi deserved the best.

He assessed me once more and then turned to walk back the way he had come. Before he made the corner, I was walking out of the hospital doors into the bright sunlight.

I took a step off the curb but then stepped right back up to avoid being hit by a black Lincoln that screeched to a halt in front of me. Within a second of it stopping, the back door opened, and Martin Kline stepped out onto the pavement. His long, hurried stride didn't wait for his driver, who popped up from the other side of the car, exasperated that his boss was already walking toward the entrance. "Kline, wait for the security team!" Kline either didn't hear or care to acknowledge his driver's plea. He glanced at me briefly, sizing me up how all elites could do in half a second, and then continued quickly through the doors. His driver was right on his heels, flying past me without a second glance and leaving the car parked haphazardly with both doors still open.

Why Martin Kline was at this hospital, let alone Crestwood, when he had the biggest case of his life back in New York in a couple of months, wasn't my concern. I had other things to deal with.

As if on cue, my phone rang again, and my father's name scrolled across the screen. Yes, I needed to make a few things very clear.

To his credit, Samuel didn't attempt small talk, only leading me quietly through the house to my father's study.

As I stared at Langston, his serene smile thinly veiled the cunning beneath, and I realized he had been expecting me. "Son, have a seat." He motioned to a chair in the corner of the room, but I didn't even look in its direction. Instead, I walked around his desk and waited for him to stand. The anger I had long felt toward my father was simmering under my skin, but something had shifted in the last few hours, and all I cared about was keeping Naomi safe.

It didn't stop me from hovering over the old man as he raised his eyes to look up at me. "I don't want excuses or riddles. Just a name." The corner of his lips quirked up, but the usual ire it evoked was dulled. I raised a brow to wait for my answer when the soft timbre of my mother's voice floated through the room, and the reason he was calm became clear.

"Malcolm, what's wrong?" I took a step back from my father's smiling face and cleared mine of anything ominous before facing his only saving grace. One he didn't deserve.

My mother had lost considerable weight since I had told her about my father's constant affairs all those years ago, and it was especially noticeable with her slim frame swallowed up by the flowing white dress she wore. I saw her grip tighten on the wineglass in her hand and knew she didn't want to discuss her chardonnay in the afternoon.

"Hi, Mom. No lunch with Carrie-Ann or May today?"

She stepped in further, looking between us. "Not today, dear. May isn't feeling well, and Derrick brought his new girl-friend to meet Carrie-Ann." I walked over to my mother as she spoke and leaned down to kiss her cheek. She brushed mine with her free hand and then released me.

"Did he reach out to you? Derrick and you used to be such good friends." Derrick was an asshole who only talked to me because of my grandfather's money.

Instead of voicing the truth, as always with my mother, I only smiled. "I'll reach out." She returned my smile, and I tried to ignore the glossiness of her eyes and how the sight gripped my heart. "I was thinking about going to San Marcos with Shirley, but since you're here, maybe you could take your mother out for a nice meal?" For a second, I thought she had missed the tension in the room, but the pleading in my moth-er's eyes told me she was still in there somewhere. The tightness in her shoulders begged me to listen to her, but the thought of Naomi in a hospital bed strengthened my resolve against it.

"I'll make time to take you out soon. Right now, I have a few things to discuss with Dad." The worry on my mother's face grew as she glanced at her husband. "Surely, it could wait a few hours?" She wrapped her hand carefully around my forearm, clutching gently to usher me out of the room.

As I turned to study my father, who still stood watching us, no doubt hoping my mother's pleas would work as they always did, I realized that my mind was quiet and sure—without the usual hum of rage that affected everything I did.

"It can't. Have fun with Shirley." I gave her another kiss on the cheek to distract from the shock and hurt clear in her features and turned fully to my father.

She was gone without another word; the door clicked quietly shut, signaling her absence.

My father eyed me, surprise raising his brows, but as he rounded his desk to meet me, his small smile came and disappeared in an instant.

"I have the name, but son, I want you to know I truly had nothing to do with what happened to Naomi." Though I cut my eyes at him, I remained silent. "I know you think I'm the bad guy, and I don't deny I've been ambitious in my pursuit of greatness, but I would never go this far with someone I knew you cared about."

We both knew that was a lie, but my father put up a hand at my quiet skepticism. "No matter what you believe, that's not who I am."

Something resembling hurt marred my father's expression, but it was gone with a sigh, and I let his poor attempt to convince me of his innocence hang between us. While I suspected he was telling the truth about not having a hand in Naomi's attack, the sentiment that it couldn't have easily been his idea rang hollow. Naomi was too valuable a piece against me to take off the board completely, but I wouldn't put it past him to use her in whatever other scheme to bring me to heel. He had already done it once.

"A name."

My refusal to play his game earned a chuckle as Langston walked back to his desk. He opened a drawer to reveal a thin file, extending it out to me, but kept hold of the edge when I tried to take it from him.

"All I ask is that you consider *all* of your options before you act, son." I raised a brow. "Spin whatever tale you want to my grandfather. I don't care about him right now." I jerked the folder from his grasp, but he put a hand on mine until I met his eyes.

"Not because of Eugene, but because you've worked too hard to position Charles and Charles back on top to let it all fall apart over something as fleeting as love." I held back my retort.

I didn't care what he thought about my work at the firm, and he was the last person I would listen to when it came to love. He never understood emotion beyond its use for manipulation, and I found his caution laughable until I opened the file and read the first paragraph.

One name stood out, making me grip the papers until they crinkled and my eyes blurred.

CHAPTER 36

NAOMI

I allowed my dad to steady me into the house, his arm tight around my shoulders. I had given up parroting the doctor, who said the bruising around my throat looked worse than it was and that the cut wasn't deep enough to cause any major concern.

My parents had been noticeably silent since I'd discharged myself, and I knew it was about more than them wanting me to stay in the hospital. They didn't mention his name, but Doctor Reyes told me Malcolm had been there, adamant about my and Myra's care and footing the bill for both of us. Soon after, I told them I was well enough to leave. I wanted nothing from that man. It didn't matter that he was the first person I thought of when I opened my eyes. The need for Malcolm went away once reality came crashing in.

My heart refused to believe Malcolm had a hand in last night, no matter what my brain tried to reason. It didn't change the events of the past, though. Malcolm was involved somehow, and I wouldn't let him assuage any guilt he might have by throwing money at me.

My dad released my shoulders when we were inside, but only to position me gently on the couch in the living room. I wanted to emphasize I wasn't fragile, but the truth was the pain meds were wearing off, and my side had started to throb. I hid a wince and held my tongue, adjusting myself to relax against the armrest before my mom could stuff the pillows she had ready in her hands behind me. She sighed but dropped them back on the couch before disappearing with my father, probably to talk about how to get me to open up.

A few seconds of the pressing quiet reminded me I didn't know where my phone was, and I darted my head around to see if either of them had set it down somewhere close. I probably had a thousand messages, not to mention Judge Lee's ruling and my fate as a...my thoughts trailed off when my eyes landed on a few shopping bags brimming with clothes sitting next to the large TV stand against the wall.

My mouth turned dry as I remembered Myra and me packing my clothes the night before and what she was going through. Myra didn't have any other family, but the doctors were surprisingly open with us, never once demanding a next of kin. They said the surgery on the tendons in her left arm had been successful, but that its use would be determined once she started rehabilitation. She had a long road ahead of her, and even though I knew my friend was strong and I would be there every step of the way, my heart still broke for the pain Myra would endure.

Once I got the courage to sit; I stayed with her for a long time, trying to quiet my sobs and telling her how much I loved her. I should still be there, and I planned to go back, but the mention of Malcolm covering our bills, demanding we receive the best care, made acid run through my veins, and I didn't think the negativity was what Myra needed around her. My mom returned, shaking me from my murky thoughts.

"Just got off the phone with the vet. Mac is okay. He ate some kind of sedative, so they're going to keep him overnight to make sure it all leaves his system." I exhaled loudly, relieved. I could still picture how still his was on the concrete and feared the worst when my mom didn't have an update when I asked at the hospital.

"And Annalise grabbed a few things for you to wear since you can't go home." My mom paused, and then her tone turned bitter. "Your brother went by your place to see if the cops had any leads, but there were so many camera crews he didn't stop. He's on his way here now."

The memory of the woman and her cameraman shining a light in my face while Myra lay unconscious flickered through my mind. They may very well have saved our lives, but the eagerness in her wide eyes made it hard to think of them as heroes.

My mom sat down next to me while I could hear my father tinkering around in the kitchen. I thought of food and immediately realized how hungry I was. I placed a hand on my stomach to stop it from announcing itself loudly. "A detective wants to come by and get your statement. They wanted to wait at the hospital for you to wake up, but Mal—" She cut herself off, and I felt bad that I had created such a weird situation and wouldn't explain.

No one had pushed when I said I didn't want to stay in a bed Malcolm was paying for, which means he must have at least told them we weren't on good terms, but I knew they wanted to hear what was going on from me. "I can talk to them now." I said, and my mom ran her hand up and down my arm but didn't speak as the delicious smells from the kitchen took my attention. It was past noon, but I would know the smell of grits and sausage anywhere. The aroma beckoned my mother and me to the kitchen to find my father stirring a small pot, making sure the grits didn't burn.

"Hey baby, making your favorite," my dad announced as he continued stirring with one hand and flipping a few sausages with the other. I wanted to hug him, hug all of my family for always being there, and could feel the tears trying to surface again. "Thanks, Dad," was all I could cough out before sitting on a stool next to my mom.

Her hand found my back and rubbed in a rhythmic circle, grounding me and my erratic emotions. "After this, why don't we have that Game of Thrones marathon you've been trying to get us to do?" For the past seven years, I had begged them to watch it so I could laugh at their reactions. The audible gasps from my mother every ten minutes alone would be enough to endure the long series again, but I stifled my enthusiasm.

"I know you're worried about me, but you all should get back to work." My mom's hand never stopped, but she pursed her lips as my father set hot bowls in front of us.

He cleaned his hands with the towel on his shoulder even though they didn't look dirty and gave me one of his rare stern looks. "Naomi, you were attacked. We don't care that you think you're fine; we aren't letting you out of our sight." My dad stared me down, waiting for my argument, but the fight wasn't in me.

"All I'm saying is at least we could hang out at the restaurant for a little while. Even Teddy can't handle the lunch rush like you." My dad was making his own bowl now, and my mother had already begun eating. I took my first bite and closed my eyes, savoring the heat and flavors. "Teddy will be fine." Even as my father said the words, I could hear the uncertainty he tried to hide. I gulped down another mouthful and then looked at my mom.

"I know it must have been hard to postpone your hearings today, and I can't even put into words how much it means to me for you all to be here, but I don't want to be cooped up all day. I want to feel at least a little normal." She eyed me, trying to search my face for anything that said I was just putting on a strong front.

"Augustine, maybe a few hours out would be good. I'm

sure a few people at the restaurant would love to see Naomi well, anyway." I turned to my dad to see him sharing a silent conversation with my mother. They had always been like this, connected well beyond words. Finally, my dad grunted. "Fine, after Dante gets here, we'll stop by Vine, but only long enough to give Teddy a breather, and then we'll head to a movie."

My dad put up a hand at the brightness that I'm sure was apparent in my eyes. "Nothing too scary, Ni." I grinned, knowing he would give in later.

It felt good to be surrounded by so much love and almost made the hole Malcolm had left behind less noticeable. It would be hard, but I would get over everything that happened. I had to be strong for Myra.

I let each spoonful of warmth fortify my intentions. Myra would get better; they would catch the son of a bitch who did this, and I would forget Malcolm Charles.

CHAPTER 37

NAOMI

Dante ended up having a work emergency with one of his players tearing his ACL, so it was only my mom and me at our table at the always busy Vine. Annalise called to tell us she would head our way as soon as she finished a photoshoot she couldn't cancel.

"I have so many missed calls," I groaned, but my mom seemed unaffected, her hand still outstretched to take the device that held my whole life. After discovering that she had been hiding my phone from me to make sure I relaxed, I coaxed her to hand it over just so I could check for any important work stuff.

Even when I sighed loudly as I shifted through the several texts I found—mostly well wishes, and a couple of texts from Detective Cruz asking me to call him; she didn't take the bait and would only let me check in with Coleman when I threatened to get on my hands and knees. I thanked my boss for the flowers he had brought to the hospital and silently prayed he hadn't crossed paths with Malcolm while visiting. I wasn't sure if I was ready to explain if he had.

"The court held Langston in contempt when he couldn't account for the breach about you to the press." I sputtered when Coleman told me about the five thousand dollar fine, and I wished I had been there to see the look on Langston's face. The thought soured when I remembered it was a drop in the bucket for him.

"Judge Lee almost charged him more for his son not showing up, but Ms. Scott was adamant Malcolm had a life or death emergency." The silence that followed made it clear Coleman knew where Malcolm had been.

I glossed over the awkwardness and asked what I was most afraid to hear the answer to. "What about Jack?"

Coleman sighed. "The boy recanted his statement. He said he was just scared to testify and didn't know what else to say to get out of it." I held my breath, waiting for the rest. "And... under the circumstances, Judge Lee thought it best you still sit out the rest of the trial and recover." I knew the judge didn't want a news circus bigger than the one he already had, so I swallowed the painful verdict with the relief that at least Jack had told the truth. The story would die out in the press on its own.

After Coleman passed along Dorian's well wishes, I thanked him, and my mother once again took possession of my phone, turning it off so I couldn't hear the soft vibrations whenever I got a new notification. "Thank you for at least charging it, Mom." Her pursed lips told me my sweet talk would not get my phone back, so I gave up.

My dad had retreated almost immediately into the kitchen, and while the restaurant was still bustling, the crowd had died down to a manageable capacity since we'd arrived. We were still full from the sausage and grits at home, so my mother and I opted for a couple of strawberry lemonades, people watching, and chatting about my dad's vision for the additional space. Staff had come by periodically to check on us, and Jeffrey had almost cried when he saw me, even though I had covered up my bruising with a thick scarf I had borrowed from my mom.

"Naomi Vine?" I looked up at an eager face, and a phone pointed at me. "It is you! Damn, you look kinda fine without blood all over you!" I heard gasps and snickers around us, but

couldn't look away from the scrawny teenager whose gleeful face didn't match what he was saying.

"Nuh uh, get! You and your family are out of here!" The kid couldn't have been older than fifteen and was already rushing away before Jeffrey came barreling down the walkway after him to a small table on the other side of the restaurant. I ducked my head down and closed my eyes, but my mother's cleared throat made me straighten up. "Head high, Naomi."

I wanted to believe everything could go back to normal, and I tried my best not to squirm under the constant eyes. People were taking second and third glances at our table, and the TV above the bar that usually played whatever game was on or the news was noticeably off.

Was my attack bigger news than I had considered? Sure, it would be interesting to people because I was part of such a high-profile case, but I didn't think anyone would care enough for it to be a trending topic. I glanced at my mother, who was trying to appear calm, but I could see how rigid she had become. I had been an idiot not to worry about how all of this might affect my family. The questions from colleagues my mom would get or the gossip my dad could hear in his restaurant. What if players shied away from Dante's firm, not wanting to be associated with the bad publicity?

I wanted to glare at everyone surrounding us, judging my family on lies and scandal, but my mom leaned in and distracted me from my mission. "Naomi, the important thing is that the boy cleared your name with the judge. Everything else will work itself out." I shook my head at the optimism, though I didn't feel the same.

Glimpsing all the staring faces, it was clear my reputation was damaged, and the least I could do was stay out of the limelight so my family didn't get caught in the crossfire. I could spend the rest of the day by Myra's side. She was receiving the best care, so for now, I wouldn't untangle Malcolm's influence at the hospital, but I could at least be there when she woke up.

I needed to figure out how to sell going on my own, but I lost my train of thought when Teddy appeared out of nowhere, walking through the tables straight toward us.

He looked worn out, with various stains on his open chef's button-up, and his brow was so bunched together I looked behind me to see what problem he was charging to. He stopped in front of our table and, without a word, lifted me up, gingerly taking me in his arms and exhaling with a heavy rush. "I'm so glad you're alright!" My body tensed up at the contact and didn't loosen until after Teddy released me. "Sorry, I was just so scared! Your father practically flew out of here when he got the call that you were in the hospital, so I didn't know how bad it was for the first few hours, and we were so slammed I couldn't come out sooner."

Teddy looked like he wanted to hug me again, but settled for scanning me up and down over and over. It wasn't until my mother sniffed that I realized we had just been staring at each other. "I'm going outside to check in with my clerk. Be back in a few." She stood and dashed through the crowd, and I looked back up at Teddy to see that same goofy smile that used to make my legs wobbly. I noted how sturdy my limbs currently felt.

He motioned for me to take my seat before taking up my mom's old one. When he still didn't speak, nervous energy bubbled up to the surface, making my lips move. "So, um... sorry you were worried." I wasn't sure if what I said made sense, but Teddy laughed, so I relaxed a little further. "Same old Ni. Surprised someone would care about you." He frowned at his own statement before I could comment.

"Sorry. I didn't mean... I *was* worried about you. Still am." He slid his hand across the table and opened it for mine, and I remembered this was how it always was; us both saying the wrong things and then trying to ease the pain with a quiet contact that fixed nothing but felt good anyway. I eyed his hand and then looked up at him. "I hope the kitchen didn't get too crazy while my dad was gone." Teddy looked down at his palm before sliding it back to sit in his lap. "It was chaos, actually," he chuckled. "But we have a good team and got through." I met his smile with my own, and the silence stretched between us until Teddy leaned in, all humor gone.

"The thought of you hurt Naomi...." Pain tightened his face, and my heart pulled. "I already knew I wanted you in my life again, but now I feel like I can't let another second go by without telling you how important you still are to me." He laid his hand on the table again, and I bit my bottom lip, trying to assess what I wanted.

We had so much history. So many questions from the past and present, and I wasn't sure if I wanted the answers to any of them. Still, I found my hand creeping up into his warmth and could feel his sigh as he closed his on mine. "I know this isn't the time, but I really want to have that catch-up. There's a lot I want to tell you, and I hope you'll be open to listening, but most importantly, I'm not seeing anyone." Teddy eyed me earnestly, and I told myself I didn't care about his dating life, even as more questions formed on my tongue.

As I stared into his hazel eyes, I noted that even though my heart raced; I didn't feel the raw need I felt with Malcolm. I had never felt the same electric-crazed energy with Teddy, but maybe that was a good thing. My eyes slid from our connected hands to Teddy's waiting gaze, and then caught sight of my mother making her way back to the table, and panic made me wiggle my hand free with a quick smile.

Teddy noticed my distraction and stood to meet my mom just as she made it to us. She didn't speak but smiled as she sat, and I knew she would have an opinion later. My cheeks heated, but when I looked up at Teddy to shoo him away in the politest way, he silenced me with a piercing gaze. The look was nowhere near polite and hinted at a hunger that made my mouth dry.

Slowly, Teddy leaned down, stopping when his lips grazed my ear. "We'll talk." His lips barely brushed my cheek before he stood, and then he was gone back through the crowd to the kitchen.

"I wonder how his little boy is doing." My eyes snapped to my mom, who was pretending to look over a menu she knew by heart. "I, uh, I'm sure he's fine." I stammered, not knowing what else to say. She met my eyes, and I could only shrug at her questioning gaze.

I glanced around the room to stop a conversation I didn't want to have, and another stranger's stare brought me back to my plan. "Dad should be out soon. Could I please have my phone? I just want to check in on Myra. No work, promise." My mom's mouth thinned into a suspicious scowl. She would be upset when I called a car to take me to the hospital, but I would send a text, so at least they wouldn't worry.

She sighed and retrieved it from her purse. "Five minutes, Ni." I tried not to squeal when it was in my hands as I made my way through the restaurant to the hot sidewalk outside. I wanted to take the scarf off, but knew the looks would be significantly worse than the mild overheating. Once my phone came to life, alerting me to a missed call from Cruz and three texts, all from Malcolm. I immediately cleared them without reading a word, clicking through his contact and blocking him completely. "Cold turkey," I mumbled and switched to Detective Cruz's number, deciding that I should make that call so it wouldn't distract me when I was with Myra.

It rang a few times before going to voicemail, and I left a message and a text to let him know I was taking a break but would check my phone periodically if he wanted to get ahold of me. Messaging him reminded me I still needed to talk to the detectives about last night and added the police station to my list of stops when my phone buzzed in my hands. This time it was Coleman.

> Something has come up in the Drayman case, and I need your help. It's time-sensitive.

I stared at the message, confused. Coleman liked me, but he was by the book, even more than I usually was, so asking me for help on a case I'd been dismissed from didn't seem right. I hovered over his number to call when I got a second message from him.

> Can't give details over the phone. Meet me at 1245 Roland Ave. as soon as you can.

I paused, trying to make sense of the situation. Our case was in shambles, so if Coleman had found something, of course, I wanted to help. I turned to the closed glass door of Vine and tried to make out my mom through the sea of heads. Jeffrey and I caught eyes, and I smiled, going for nonchalant as I turned back around.

I shouldn't go. Sneaking off to the hospital or police station was one thing, but I had worried my family enough, and while helping outside of the courtroom was really a gray area, the judge might take offense. I tapped my foot on the pavement, staring at Coleman's messages as adrenaline began coursing through my body.

A quick stop on the way to the hospital wasn't so bad, right?

I texted my mom I was heading to see Myra as I slid into the waiting car and then sent a message to Coleman, letting him know I was on the way.

CHAPTER 38

MALCOLM

Keep Naomi Safe. As I sped down the highway toward her parent's home, the words circled my mind. Naomi wasn't responding to my texts or calls, and I growled as I chucked my phone onto the passenger seat and punched the gas, barely making it through an intersection before the light turned red. Car horns sounded in my wake, but I ignored them, trying to think of who else I could reach out to if Naomi wasn't with her mother and father.

"Naomi! Are you in there?! Open the door!" I jiggled the lock and considered kicking it down when I heard my phone blaring from the car. I raced back to it and answered as soon as I saw Dante's name.

"Hey, what's wrong with Naomi?!" He sounded as panicked as I felt, and I tried not to bark at him. "Where is she right now?" Before he spoke, I could hear a voice in the background on his end. It sounded like it was coming from an intercom saying something about a doctor, and I gripped my door.

Why would they all have gone back there? The hospital informed me as soon as Naomi had discharged herself. My heart fell into my stomach at the thought that something else had happened. "I'm with a client right now, but Naomi and my parents should still be at Vine." The relief made me see stars, and a second later, I was back in the car. "Call them and make sure Naomi doesn't leave."

Dante was quiet for a moment. "You know something about the attack?" I calculated what I knew and decided that Naomi's safety was more important. "Just tell her to stay away from Dorian Keates." I ended the call before Dante could ask more questions I wasn't prepared to answer, and then concentrated on avoiding a collision as I drove to Vine.

I noticed that the usual glances I got were more like blatant stares as I entered the packed restaurant. The news had been non-stop with coverage of Naomi and her attack, coupled with the witness testimony. I had seen nothing about her innocence yet, but the added scrutiny of the trial had me and my father's faces in the press more than usual.

I bypassed the empty host stand and walked through the mingling of voices until I saw them all huddled together at a table. Augustine and Frances were both on their phones while a tall man in all black stood over them.

He periodically looked up at different tables, signaling wait-staff, so I assumed he was a manager. Dante's fiancée sat across from them, one hand comforting Frances and the other on the phone at her ear.

I caught eyes with a man haphazardly dressed in a half-buttoned chef's uniform, but my phone rang and I turned to answer Sloan.

"Did you find him?"

"No. His phone isn't on, and he's not at the office or his home." I cursed under my breath, and my building rage threatened to cloud out rational thoughts.

"Find him. And try tracking Naomi again. Now!" I hung

up and turned back to Naomi's family, seeing their shocked faces. The chef walked forward, taking my attention.

"I'll go to the hospital and check on her. Augustine, maybe you should call the police." I flexed my jaw at the pretend hero. "I have someone out searching for her. He's faster than the police."

I stepped forward to make it clear I was talking only to him. "And I will check on her at the hospital." I turned to walk out because I really didn't have time for this, but I would circle back to this chef later.

"Then I'll head to her office. I know how hard it is for her not to work. She probably didn't want you guys to think she was stressing herself out." That comment stopped me in my tracks. Who was he to believe he knew a goddamn thing about Naomi? I turned to see Augustine grip the man's shoulder. "That's a good idea, Teddy. I just don't know why she wouldn't at least answer the phone."

Augustine glanced over at me. "Let us know if she's at the hospital or if you hear anything else. I'm calling the cops soon; I don't care if I have to make them do something. Someone's finding my baby girl." I extinguished the fire that blazed at Teddy's familiarity with an exhale.

"I'll find her. You have my word." Augustine nodded to me once, and then I was gone, a million thoughts racing through my head, but those same three words rang the loudest.

CHAPTER 39

NAOMI

The driver glanced at me silently through the rearview mirror as we pulled through a narrow path. We had driven close to the San Harper docks and then veered off down the black makeshift roads between the large storage facilities.

After texting my mom where I was going, I turned my phone back off to conserve battery. I could ask the hospital staff if they had a charging station when I got there.

As we slowed in front of an old, nondescript building that was supposed to be my destination, I decided that maybe having my phone on would be a good idea.

I pressed the power button, waiting for it to boot up as I glanced at the driver. He was an older man with neatly trimmed dark hair that he wore slicked back and a graying goatee. He looked just as nervous as I felt, but said nothing.

When he came to a complete stop, and I didn't reach for the door, his fingers drummed on the wheel. As my phone lit up, he twisted in his seat to face me. "Are you sure this is where you want to get dropped off?" He had a slight accent that I couldn't place, and his voice was soft and steady, but I could hear the concern.

I'd seen the photo on his dash; him and who I assumed was his family, all smiles.

"This is the address?" I muttered, looking out again at our quiet and isolated surroundings. He turned to check his phone. "Yes, the one you put in the app." I opened the app myself and confirmed it was the right place after checking my driver's profile to make sure I hadn't missed any red flags.

His name was Jakub Nowak, and he had a five-star rating with hundreds of reviews. Multiple dings with several messages from my family started pouring in, and it only made the pit in my stomach worse.

"Are you supposed to be meeting someone?" Jakub asked, and I absentmindedly nodded as the messages kept coming in. They were from everyone, even some from Teddy and Jeffrey, and were varying degrees of "call now," except my brother's.

> Malcolm says to stay away from Dorian
> Keates. CALL BACK!

"Maybe...we should just drive out of here," I said to Jakub, who nodded. He put his hand on the clutch to push into drive when a tap on my window made us both jump.

Dorian blocked the view, kicking my frazzled nerves into high gear and making me fall back as far as my seat belt would allow. "Hey, Naomi! Coleman's inside!" He stepped back, giving me room to open the door, and I looked at it to see that the lock was up. The next second it was down. Jakub shot a glance over his shoulder at me.

"Ni, come on." Dorian returned to the door and reached for it, jingling when it didn't open right away. He brought his face back down to the window to stare at me, confused.

"I forgot I have a police interview about last night. They're expecting me. Tell Coleman I'll call him later." Jakub was already rolling forward by the time I finished speaking, and I gripped my phone, ready to call my brother to see what the hell was going on.

Dorian shouted my name, but we kept driving until we

turned a corner, making him disappear from view. Jakub and I kept making eye contact through the rearview as we drove, and he gave me a small smile that I easily returned. "Thank you," I breathed, and he dipped his head before focusing back on the road. I was definitely giving this man the biggest tip in the world.

My erratic heart slowed, and I tapped Dante's contact to call him but looked back up at Jakub's grunt.

We had hit a dead end.

I searched around for another road we could take, but with all the buildings and narrow passageways, the only way out was the way we had come. Back toward Dorian. Jakub slowly reversed the car and then swerved it so that we pointed toward the open street but didn't go any further, instead putting the car in park and turning in his seat to face me. "Is this man dangerous to you?" If it weren't for Dante's weird message from Malcolm, I would have said no, but now I nodded. "I'm sorry. I'm not sure what's going on. I'll call my brother—"

A loud bang ruptured the quiet, piercing my ears. I felt the shards of glass cutting me before I saw them and realized I had my eyes snapped shut with my hands wrapped around my ears. Someone was shouting, but as it came into focus, so did the pain.

I looked down to see the blood on my right shoulder, and then it seemed to flow even faster. "Are you alright?!" Jakub was still shouting, but the heat and pain only intensified until I couldn't concentrate on anything else. Another bang rang out, and then Jakub was shouting in another language before I lurched forward hard.

I cupped my gushing wound, trying to ease the bleeding, and looked up to see Dorian and the large silver metal shining in his hand as he stood in the road. Even with the engine revving, I could hear his brash, jagged laughter as he pulled the trigger again. We skidded to the side, but Jakub gripped the wheel tighter, keeping us from spinning out of control as the tire Dorian busted flew off its axle, sending sparks everywhere.

I didn't know where my phone had gone, but I could hear the ringtone continuously and looked around on the floor, but didn't see it amongst the random things scattered all over. I released my grip on my injury, knowing I wasn't doing much to contain it anyway, and latched onto the seat in front of me as Jakub got closer and closer to Dorian, who didn't seem at all worried about us crashing into him.

"We're going to get out of here, even if we have to go through him," Jakub shouted, and I braced myself for impact, but then another shot rang out and the car jerked.

I saw the loll of Jakub's limp body for only a second before we flipped. My seatbelt dug into my chest hard, pushing the air from my lungs and stopping the scream from roaring out of me as we slammed into a building.

Creaks and moans echoed all around, and the throbbing of my already injured side brought tears to my eyes. The butt of the seat belt dug hard into my reopened wound, and my shoulder leaked against the strap, sending shooting pains up and down my arm. Air wouldn't stay in my body long enough, and I couldn't stop panting as I squinted up at the sky through the window that now pointed upward.

I dropped my head down to see Jakub dangling in the driver's seat, held in place by his seatbelt. His body wedged between the two front seats, blocking the entire front of the car and making it impossible to see out the windshield. His one intact eye was wide and frightened, as if he were still alive with me, but the other was obliterated along with the rest of that side of his face. The sight made my stomach roll, and I coughed hard, spit falling from my mouth as I dry-heaved.

Between retching, I took breaths through my mouth to stop smelling the carnage that surrounded me so I could concentrate.

All I could hear was the car hissing and ticking as parts still tried to adjust to the crash, the spilled gasoline and burnt rubber making me cough harder. With my eyes watering, I reached for my belt buckle and clicked the button to release myself, falling down into what used to be the driver-side back-seat window. Glass and debris scraped my body, and I let out a long snarl as tears continued to cascade down my face. The ceiling pushed into the car at weird angles from the impact of the wall, and I had to stay as upright as possible not to be pierced by jagged metal.

Through my blurred vision I stared up at the window above me, wishing I hadn't unhooked myself. The pain shooting through my shoulder told me I wouldn't be able to crawl back up there, let alone lift myself out.

With a grunt, I leaned up to see over the backseats and saw the shattered rear window and battered trunk near a white building. I held my breath and slid closer to Jakub to get a better angle and saw a narrow pathway between the car bumper and the building wall I could squeeze through.

We were so close to Dorian before we crashed; I wasn't sure if we had hit him or not, but even if we hadn't, I couldn't stay in a wrecked car that could blow up at any minute. I looked down at my shoulder, but all I saw was blood. I loosened the scarf around my neck and wrapped it around my arm, tying it as best I could with one hand. My side was also bleeding, but that would have to wait. I gritted my teeth and sat up fully, readying myself for the burst of pain when footsteps made me freeze.

"You alive in there?"

Dorian's voice floated through the air, and my whole body

trembled as I looked around frantically for anything I could use as a weapon. I shrieked and fell back when Dorian's head suddenly peeked through the back.

Dorian peered down at me, his eyes wild and smile bright. "Well, of course, you are. You're just won't die, Naomi Vine."

CHAPTER 40

NAOMI

Dorian stared down at me over the back seat and watched as I scrambled to grip onto anything that I could use against him without taking my eyes off his face.

"Jesus, Ni. You don't look too good." His hand came into view, and I stopped moving at the sight of the enormous gun. I wasn't an expert, but it looked much bigger than any regular handgun, with a wide barrel large enough to cause even more damage up close than it already had. "Alright, counselor, out of the car." Dorian waved the gun as if to summon me, and I backed as far into the corner as I could.

He could kill me right here, but I knew if I got out of the car now, it would only be worse. He chuckled at my hesitation, and I sneered up at him, positioning my body to hide my good arm still searching. I stretched it as far back under the sideways seat as I could, debris scraping at my hand until I felt the tip of my phone brush my fingers. It was too far to reach without turning around, and Dorian's smile was dropping as his eyes turned to slits.

"Out, Naomi." He tried to step in further but cursed when he couldn't slide into the small opening. He turned to maneuver himself better, and I took the precious second to swivel and shoot my hand under the passenger seat, holding my breath through the sharp stab of pain that assaulted both of my injuries.

My fingers gripped the tip of my phone and tried to bring

it closer to me, but screamed when I felt a hand on my leg. "Come here!" Dorian grabbed at my legs, and I kicked as hard as I could, abandoning my phone and turning to my side to get a better angle. A strangled scream tore from my throat as I watched Dorian force himself laterally between the wall and car, his long arm getting closer. His gun sat precariously in his jeans waistband, swaying back and forth as he moved forward.

"I should've killed you a long time ago!" he shouted, and I screamed back, too exhausted and terrified to say anything coherent to the man who I thought was my colleague.

A loud clang halted my cries, and I ducked to avoid the gun that dropped through the shattered window from Dorian's pants and onto the trunk floor, hitting a headrest. When I tipped my head up, I could see the large black hole of the muzzle pointed at me, and I lunged for it at the same time Dorian did, both of us wrapping a hand on a part of the warm silver before he let go only to snatch my hair. I lost my grip, but kept reaching, blocking out the fire scorching my scalp with each strand Dorian was yanking out.

Dorian didn't sound human as he howled and groaned, slamming my head against the seat again and again. Each time I could rear my body back up to go for the gun, I would stretch my fingers as far as they could, but was getting no closer. Everything hurt, and I was barely holding on to consciousness, with every muscle wanting to give out and let go.

"Just die!" Dorian repeated between guttural noises, and I knew I wouldn't last long. With the last bit of strength I had, I thrust myself back and wrapped my hands around his arm, using the downward momentum to pull him further into the car. When his body slammed into the back seat, I didn't hesitate, sliding myself over his crumpled body and kicking as I made it through the broken glass. Our limbs collided and tangled as Dorian groaned from his fall, but I didn't look back, forcing my body through the small passage, scraping my side against the jagged wall. My legs wouldn't move as fast as I wanted them to, but I pushed through, ignoring the bellow from Dorian, and headed for the nearest building. I made it into a small alleyway and braced myself against a wall for just a second to stop from falling over.

Panic clawed at my throat, but I pushed it down and made myself move, searching for anyone who could help me. Large, white vacant buildings lined the deserted, makeshift streets.

The dark gravel-paved road made it harder to walk as I staggered toward the nearest door and turned the knob as hard as I could, slamming my hands on the hardwood when it didn't budge.

"Hello! Help!!" I took off, leaving bloody handprints in my wake, continuing down the side of the building, not wanting to stay in one place for too long.

I begged my legs to corporate as I came to a smooth cement wall at the end of the path, at least seven feet high, running for a mile in each direction. I didn't risk trying to climb it and instead started sprinting along the barrier, screaming with everything I had. "Please!! Someone, Help!!" I turned another corner to find myself at the same dead end that Jakub and I had navigated.

"Niiiaommiii?"

Dorian's singsong voice made me spin around the way I came, but he sounded like he was still far away. Frantic, I looked around and saw a large rock sitting at the base of the never-ending wall. It wasn't big enough to use as a stepping stool, but bigger than the rest of the small gravel pieces around me, and I grabbed it as a weapon before running again.

Gaps between the buildings led out onto the main road where the car had crashed, and if I kept running down that way, I could make it to the entrance. It left me in the open, but Dorian's running steps were getting closer, so he would see me soon no matter what I did.

My lungs burned, but I continued down the isolated road, glancing sparingly at each opening to track Dorian. Turning from an empty gap, I wasn't ready for the hard and warm smack across my face, making me stammer backward and stumble onto the hot ground.

"Breathing pretty hard, Ni. You made it too easy." I cradled my pulsing jaw and swallowed the blood that covered my tongue as Dorian crouched down to meet me. Deep scrapes covered his face and throat, signs of the difficulty he had getting free of the car.

I gripped the rock, ready to throw it, but my limbs felt numb and heavy as the adrenaline slowly faded without my permission.

"Stay away from me!"

I swung the rock with my bad arm, catching Dorian off guard. The edge smashed against his temple, making a cracking sound, and he screamed out, clutching his eye. I tried to stand, but he was on me the next second, gripping on the same side he had stabbed me last night.

I cried out, and he tightened his grip, raising and turning me so he could see my face. A rotten, blood-soaked smile overtook Dorian's features as blood ran down the side of his forehead where I hit him.

"You're gonna beg to die when I'm through with you," he snarled, raising the butt of the gun above his head.

I struggled weakly and screamed my throat raw, but the gun still came down.

CHAPTER 41

MALCOLM

Traffic had backed up on the freeway, and the streets weren't much better. I yelled every profanity in the book, but it wasn't getting me to the hospital any faster, and no one else had heard from her yet.

Dante called to let me know Teddy hadn't found Naomi at work and that the family had reached out to the cops, who were predictably unhelpful, saying they would "check around." Fucking useless.

I gripped the steering wheel as the car in front of me inched forward at a glacial pace, using the time to think of any other place Dorian or Naomi might be. From what I had found out about the ingrate, he loved cars and money, but left no paper trail.

My dash screen lit up with a call from Sloan. "Boss, her phone was back on, but not long enough to track her." He continued quickly, knowing I was on the verge of going nuclear. "But I got into her Uber account and found the last address she paid for this afternoon. It's at the docks in San Harper. Just texted it to you."

I revved my engine and cut in front of the car next to me to take the exit, only to be stuck behind twenty other vehicles trying to do the same thing.

"Fuck!"

"I can be at the docks in thirty, and I'll alert the cops as well." I swallowed, letting Sloan's words sink in to calm me down. "Fine. I'll be there as soon as I can."

He grunted his agreement, and I knew he was already driving.

"And call when you have her. I don't care what you have to do."

I hung up and looked out my windshield at the setting sun. The docks were remote and easy to hide in. There were so many abandoned buildings that no one bothered to secure anymore, and the thought of Naomi being found in one of them made me yell so loud I felt the eyes of people in the surrounding cars. Someone needed to get there now, and I knew who was closer than anyone.

I texted Dante for his number and then called Teddy. After leaving the restaurant, I recognized his name from the dossier Sloan made on Naomi.

"Hello?"

"My guy is headed to the docks in San Harper, where Naomi's phone last pinged. I'll send you the address. I'm stuck in traffic, so get there now and find her."

He sounded like he was running, and traffic had finally started moving enough that I could get all the way off the freeway and onto a side street.

"Okay, I'm on the way. GPS says fifteen minutes. Why do you think—" I didn't wait to hear what Teddy had to say, hanging up as I sped beneath the highway, trying to get to the other side of the city before it was too late.

CHAPTER 42

NAOMI

A burst of cold made my eyelids fly open. Acrid fumes hit my nose while a tall, dark figure loomed in my dim view.

"There she is! I thought I might've hit you too hard." Dorian split in two before becoming solid as my fuzzy eyes adjusted to the dark. It was too dim to see anything further than him, but he held a large, dirty bucket that swayed at his side.

The terrible smelling liquid he threw on me dripped down my hair and face as I shook. Every part of my body throbbed, but as I twitched my hands and feet, I realized I wasn't bound.

My brain demanded I stand, but my legs felt like lead and couldn't follow orders. Another violent shiver ran through me as I tried to look around, but I always came back to Dorian's wild eyes as he watched me silently with an amused, twisted smirk.

I didn't know how long I had been out, but it stunk of a stable more than the docks. Gripping what felt like straw between my fingers, I also felt cold dirt beneath me, and my stomach turned. I could be anywhere.

"Are the accommodations not up to your standards? This isn't where I wanted our night to end, but we had a few uninvited guests." I wanted to close my eyes and focus on any sounds that could signal where I was or at least calm my frazzled nerves, but I couldn't risk taking my eyes off Dorian for more than a second. As if to remind me of the fact, he suddenly advanced, chucking the bucket with a loud clang, and squatted down right in front of me.

I instinctively moved back but could only push up against what felt like a wooden fence.

Dorian gripped my chin, bringing our faces so close together that his nose almost grazed mine before I jerked out of his grasp. "Don't fucking touch me," I rasped, my voice low and labored. It had been a struggle to move so fast, but I tried not to show it as I turned back to Dorian, disgust clear on my face. He smiled, scanning my features, but slowly stood and stepped back.

"I have to say, this isn't how I imagined this going." I discreetly glanced around for an exit or weapon, but it was so dark that I could only see straw and dirt.

"This is all Coleman's fault, really. He told me I needed to 'take a step back'" Dorian's air quotes were rigid as he stared down at me. "I always knew he didn't think I was good enough to work beside him. Not the right school, not the right family, no silver spoon to bond over. Not like the perfect Ms. Vine."

I kept my eyes on him as he paced but touched around the ground and along the wood behind me, feeling for a weapon. I didn't see the gun on Dorian, and that bucket was somewhere nearby, but I would have to get past him to get to it. "I wasn't even off the case a day before he brought you on, did you know that?" he asked, but seemed engrossed in his own thoughts as he walked back and forth.

"Coleman never thought I was smart enough. Funny, because I was clever enough to convince him I wasn't selling information to the defense." Dorian glanced at me briefly with a smirk.

"That's right, Ni, the intelligent John Coleman has been giving out plea deals and not guilty verdicts because of me.

Right under his nose." I grew angrier as I thought of the victims that Dorian's actions robbed of justice.

"Why?" I whispered it, but Dorian's response was a booming cackle, giving me a sinking awareness that we were somewhere no one could hear. "Money, of course." He stopped pacing, cocking his head to the side as he watched me.

"But you wouldn't know anything about struggling, would you?" His face contorted into something hateful. "Even when you fuck the opposing counsel, you still manage to stay in Coleman's good graces." My stiff fingers froze at his words. "I told him the night before he let you introduce that rich asshole, Lennard Curtis, to the jury. You know what our honorable boss said?" We both stared at each other, but I found it difficult to listen as the realization that Coleman knew about me and Malcolm ricocheted through me.

"'Naomi would never do anything to jeopardize our case. I trust her.' Just. Like. that." Dorian's face went blank, but he was so rigid, as if he could pounce on me at any moment.

I couldn't afford for him to stop talking, so I tried my best not to flinch and stared at him dead on. "How did you get Jack to lie?" Something flickered over Dorian's features, but then a smile appeared. "That was good, wasn't it?" He turned to pace again just as my fingers grazed what felt like a gap in the wooden wall. It didn't make it all the way down into the dirt and instead cut off, leaving a space I could barely fit my index finger through. I wiggled it down as far as I could until I felt cold metal.

The actual wall dipped slightly like a small wave and then came back up to dip again. I was in a storage container.

"My whole plan had just been to scare you a little. Some light stalking, the note, and that fun car chase. Jack was going to be a dud from the beginning, but he wasn't meant to smear you." Dorian's laugh rang out as he paced. "But every day you came in with that look on your face that said you thought you were better than me, and well...." I got a hand completely underneath a piece of wood but stopped pulling when Dorian turned back to me.

"The Charles firm has paid me for plenty of information in the past, so it was the perfect situation for me. Bringing forward an eyewitness got me back in Coleman's good graces; Jack tarnished your reputation, and the defense got a win." He paused for a moment, letting his words sink in. If that were true, then it meant my suspicions were right all along. Malcolm had played me.

Dorian stepped closer, and I gripped the wood harder, but it wouldn't give. "Jack's parents owe Drayman a lot of money. Which is why when Jack saw the fight in the elevator and heard Drayman in the stairwell later, he was told to shut his mouth."

Jack had been telling the truth? I had suspected that maybe his entire story had been a lie, but the earnest way he told it to me in the office again and again made it hard to discard. The poor kid was a pawn used by terrible people to get their way. His own family.

I positioned my other hand under the board and tugged slowly. I could feel the wood give, but feared it would creak if I pulled anymore. "I simply had to adjust the approach. A quick payoff from Drayman and the Stone's were on board to ruin your life."

Dorian paused when he was only a step away, making me angle my head up to see his shadowed face. "But you almost ruined it. One night with you and Jack was ready to throw in the towel and confess all. Told us he wouldn't take the stand unless he could recant the next day. Save you somehow." Sirens sounded in the distance, and Dorian glanced around the dark but came back to me. "The glorious Naomi Vine had struck again. After that, I couldn't let you go. It's clear you'll remain in places you don't deserve to be."

Dorian was in front of me before I could throw my hands up to deflect his from wrapping around my throat.

He squeezed so hard, so fast, my limbs flailed wildly without conscious effort. "Just die," he breathed, his eyes wild and lips tightly gripped by his teeth. My hands found his face, and I scratched at his eyes, but he shook me like a rag doll, making my hold slip. My legs kicked furiously against his body, and he loosened his grip when my foot flung into his abdomen. Using the distraction, I kicked at him harder and heard his groan as he held himself, his body thumping on the dirt and metal.

I was up in the next second, gulping in air, my head light and swimming while I kicked him all over his body.

"Fuck you!" I screamed, but Dorian's swift movement cut my voice short as he took my legs out from under me. I hit the ground hard, the impact echoing in the container, and I scrambled to get out of his grasp before he could get the upper hand again. Dorian tried to crawl up my body, but I kicked and screamed, hoping the sirens that were now quiet meant cops were nearby. "Your luck has run out!" Dorian roared as he held me down by my thigh. I frantically grasped around me, but there was nothing to hold on to. I wrenched my head up to see more wooden fence along the container and zeroed in on a broken piece just out of reach. It was still attached to the fence, but the jagged, pointed bottom jutted out enough that I could wrap a hand around it.

Dorian was snaking his way onto my butt, but I snatched up as much dirt as I could and threw it into his eyes, making him stagger off me. His snarl was fierce, but I blocked him out as I quickly closed the distance between me and my intended weapon.

I got up on my knees and pulled until the wood creaked with the force. When it still wouldn't give, I stretched my torso back, my arms burning as it resisted.

It snapped just as pain ripped through my scalp from Dorian's harsh grip on my hair. He snatched hard, forcing my head up to see the crazed look in his bloodshot eyes. "Fucking die!" His other hand came down hard, but he got my wounded shoulder instead of my face as I pivoted, plunging the broken piece of wood into his stomach. Dorian staggered back, taking me with him, his tight fist still tangled in my hair, and loud screeches in my ears as I fought to disconnect us.

I felt my hair ripping at the roots, but didn't care as I tugged away from him until I fell backward from the force. I hit the ground hard, but I was up in the next second, ignoring Dorian's wails as I ran through the darkness.

"I deserved it! I deserved it all!!" Dorian shouted, his repeated rant ricocheting against the container walls as I raced to get as far away from him as possible.

He quieted as I sprinted, but I couldn't tell if I had been running for a long time or if he had just stopped screaming. Still, I didn't stop until I slammed into a wall.

I barely felt the impact and immediately started feeling for a door, concentrating only on getting away.

My hand hit against a large padlock that I feared meant I was trapped, but I twisted the joints to find it unfastened. I pushed the heavy door open to the cold night air and the smell of the sea invading my lungs.

Mile-long shipping containers stacked on top of each other surrounded me, making the path look like an intricate metal maze. I looked back at the blue and white one that I had just come out of and saw three more bright orange ones on top of it. The cold air hurt with each breath, and I found it harder and harder to stay upright. My movements were becoming erratic, so I leaned against the nearest container and moved along the path, listening for the sirens or the flash of red lights.

Harsh coughs jostled me as I walked, and when I touched my mouth, my hand came away with splatters of blood. I could feel my body shutting down, my eyes losing focus with every other blink, but I had to keep going.

"Naomi?! Naomi?!" Teddy's shouts woke my senses, and I took a few more painful steps until his voice was so close a sob of relief escaped me. I rounded a corner and saw him; the worry on his face turned to horror before the bright flashlight in his hand took my vision.

I welcomed it as a beacon, a sign that I could stop. "Oh shit, baby," Teddy's voice cracked as his arms wrapped around me, but I heard nothing else as the warmth of his skin and the beating of his heart lulled me unconscious.

CHAPTER 43

MALCOLM

Hospital again. Arguing with doctors and making sure she was taken care of. Trying not to destroy expensive equipment when the physicians had no excuse for Naomi not opening her eyes. The only difference was that this time I couldn't leave her side.

Naomi was so battered and bruised that she was barely recognizable, and it had taken a talk from both of her parents for me to give anyone the space to be near her.

I didn't deserve to be in the room, but it didn't stop me from pulling up a chair, daring Teddy to say something when I did. He had been there at the docks and found her wandering around half-dead. I'd made it just in time to see her lifted into an ambulance, and that brutal sight would stay with me for the rest of my life. I yelled out her name before the doors shut, and even with two swollen eyes, I felt it when hers met mine.

"Blue and white," she whispered, and then the doors closed on whatever she was trying to tell me, and the ambulance sped off before I could bang on the door to demand to know what she meant.

Blue and white, blue and white. I paced, knowing I should head to the hospital, but her words hit me hard in the chest as if they were the most important thing and she had given them to me. I glanced around at the brightly lit cop cars that were parked all around and walked up to a uniformed officer who guarded the wreckage of the Uber Naomi had taken.

Sloan had filled me in when he arrived fifteen minutes

prior, and I gave him one last shot at finding Dorian. The cop noticed me before I approached but turned to the side to stop me from asking him questions. I cleared my throat, so it was clear that wouldn't work, and he reluctantly turned back and assessed me. "Have you found Dorian Keates?" He looked me up and down before resting his hands on his holster.

"Sir, if you could please step aside. This is a crime scene." My blood boiled as my eyes moved to the officer's name tag. "Officer Grant, I'm not a reporter, nor am I a looky-loo. I am representing the victim and would like to know what you have." This time he sighed. "Then go to the hospital. We'll handle it from here." I stepped away from Grant, or he would be the next one carried off in an ambulance.

I moved further away from where the officers believed the crime scene was, knowing Dorian must have taken her somewhere else because the cops didn't find them when they got here. The air was thick with sea and cold, but I ignored the dampness as I walked further past the storage units and into an area across the road filled with shipping containers.

The enormous tins looked worn and discarded, like they had been there for years with no oversight, and I wondered when the last time anyone had set foot on this side of the docks. I moved through the makeshift rows; racking my brain for anything that could help find the scumbag. Sloan's background check confirmed that Dorian was a mediocre loner who crept through life with no real purpose. All the money my father and other defense attorneys supplied him seemed to go to fixing old rare cars that he kept at a rented garage just outside of town, but I wouldn't have put it past him to have a safety net of cash tucked away to escape.

When searching for Dorian this morning, Sloan had torn his shabby apartment apart looking for anything to locate him. Not knowing his intentions, we had even flagged Dorian's passport to ping if he tried to go overseas, but I knew better than most how money could make circumventing most systems easy. He could be on a private jet right now, while Naomi sat in the hospital fighting for her life.

With only an estranged father to call family, Dorian was a useless human being who no one would miss if he disappeared off the face of the earth. An unfamiliar sense of helplessness made me curse into the wind.

Dorian should pray the cops find him before I do.

I pulled out my phone to check Sloan's progress when my eyes caught on a shipping container.

It was blue and white with linear holes dotting the sides, along with a huge label for an animal facility. The large door was dead-bolted shut, but when I looked around, I noticed others. Some sandwiched between different colored containers and some on the ground level. All locked. I put my phone back in my pocket and began jogging down different paths, looking for more blue and white containers.

"Mr. Charles, she's been through a lot. I assure you she's receiving the best care possible. I'll have a nurse come in and check her vitals every fifteen minutes." Dr. Reyes' impatient tone brought me back to the present, and I raised a brow at the physician. The doctor appeared exhausted by my demands, but I didn't care. Naomi looked as if a freight train had hit her, and I would not stand by if she were suffering somehow. "Every ten minutes."

Naomi's family had gotten used to my bossy tone in the last few hours and focused on Naomi, but every once in a while, Teddy would glance my way before turning back to her side, caressing her hand.

Knowing I'd be the last person she wanted to see when she woke up, I didn't sit too close, but I couldn't leave the room entirely. I had to see her open her eyes. I needed proof that she would really be okay. It was greedy, but if the night had taught me anything, it was that I would do anything for Naomi Vine, so I'd permit a little selfishness.

Staring down at the floor to control the rage and sadness that threatened to consume me every few minutes, I noticed a single red dot on my once white shirt cuff. It was a neat, small spot, but it told stories of events that no one could ever find out about, especially Naomi.

I tugged my suit jacket sleeve down and looked up to watch Naomi's chest rise and fall. Camden would bring me another set of clothes by morning.

"Um, Mr. Charles?" I glanced over to see a petite nurse leaning into the doorway from the hall. "There are some people in the lobby to see you. Police."

Everyone in the room glanced between the young nurse and me until I stood. "I'll be back soon," I murmured to no one in particular and then headed past the nurse, who stared up at me like I was a superstar she wanted an autograph from. I rode the elevator down, my chest tightening with each floor that separated me and Naomi. Before the doors opened, I slid my mask into place and hid the effect the night had on me.

Two uniformed cops and a seasoned looking detective stood waiting at the bank of elevators, walking the few steps it took to meet me as I stepped out of mine. "Mr. Charles, thank you for meeting us." The detective stretched out his hand, and I took it, hoping it would speed up whatever bullshit he wanted to discuss. When I remained silent, he continued. "I'm Detective Henry Dobson, and I wanted to ask a couple of questions about today's events—" I slipped my hands into my pockets to stop myself from grabbing the man by his worn lapels. "I'm Naomi Vine's attorney. She's not even conscious. And when she is, the last thing she will want to do is talk to the cops, who still haven't caught the scum who did this to her."

Dobson took my snide comment in stride, but his brows perked up at my statement. "How do you know we haven't caught Dorian Keates?" I contained a sigh and assessed the man who thought he was smarter than me. "Have you?" The corner of Dobson's mouth ticked up as he shook his head. "Not yet, but that's why I'm here. I understand Ms. Vine isn't up for talking to me just yet, but I was hoping you could account for your whereabouts from this morning until you got to the hospital this evening."

I watched the way Dobson's eyes crinkled at the sides as he smiled at me, like he was a sweet old man just out for a chat. The disheveled hair, dirty fingernails, and slight whiff of alcohol emanating from him didn't match the illusion.

"Worry about finding that monster, detective, or shall I add your name to the gross incompetence suit I plan to bring against your worthless department?" Dobson nodded with feigned amusement. "Alright, Mr. Charles, there's no need to file any suits. We are doing everything in our power to find Dorian Keates." The way the detective eyed me made it obvious he was waiting for me to ask more, but I had other ways of finding out updates on the case.

"I would like to offer the help of one of ours to sit by Naomi's door until Dorian is found." One of the two uniformed cops who had been pretending not to listen in on our conversation stepped up but I was already turning back to the elevators.

"No need, I have it handled. Do your jobs."

I walked into the elevator without another glance back, but heard the tired sigh Dobson released before the doors closed.

CHAPTER 44

NAOMI

I heard the beeping first, and for a second, thought I had never left the hospital.

The smells were the same, and so was the feel of the cold, stiff sheets against my skin. But when I opened my eyes, I realized this was a very different situation. "My baby's awake!" My father's voice sounded so close, but all I could see was the man sitting in the corner, staring daggers at me. The pain penetrated whatever drugs they had me on, and I winced and closed my eyes again, wondering why I would wake up. Someone wrapped their hand around mine and called my name, but sleep felt so much more alluring.

"Naomi." That damn voice. As always, my body came to attention at his call, and I opened my eyes to see that Malcolm was now at the foot of my bed. Doctor Reyes entered a second later, and I noticed Teddy for the first time as she scooted past him to get to me. "Teddy?" My voice sounded hoarse and weak, and for some reason, Malcolm hearing it made me want to cry.

"I'm here, Ni. I'm so glad you're awake." Teddy's voice broke with his own tears welling up, and I attempted a deep breath to stop mine, but that only made me cough. "Enough talking." Malcolm's harsh tone blanketed the room, and everyone fell silent. I wanted to tell Malcolm to leave, to stay, to hold me and tell me that everything that happened was a bad dream, but I only watched him as I felt rogue tears fall down my face.

"It's okay, Naomi. You've been through a lot, but you're going to be okay."

Doctor Reyes' soothing voice turned from me to look at everyone else, but Malcolm kept my gaze. "I understand you're all worried, but you need to leave now. I'm going to run some tests, and then Naomi needs to rest." My parents both gripped my limp hand, and I pulled my gaze from Malcolm to smile at them. I hated the tired expressions everyone had.

"We'll all be right outside," Dante whispered, and Annalise nodded in agreement before they moved toward the door. Teddy leaned over and kissed my forehead lightly while caressing my face, and I wanted to tell him I would be okay, but I couldn't make my mouth work again. "I'll see you soon." He murmured but made no motion to leave. Malcolm cleared his throat, and Teddy's features changed from loving to murderous before he turned from me.

"You both need to go now." The doctor's authoritative tone got through to Teddy, and he made his way out of the room, but when I turned back to Malcolm, he hadn't budged, his eyes still on me. I wondered if he would walk closer, but he remained at the foot of the bed, staring me down as if he could single-handedly heal me with his glare. The more he stared, the more I wanted him to stay, and the desire scared me. His always immaculate facial hair had gone well beyond the five o'clock shadow, and his eyes were red-rimmed and so black I feared for whoever had made him that angry.

The rhythmic beep from the machine beside me sped up, screeching much faster than I'm sure was healthy, and I found that embarrassment was still possible even in the shape I was in as I felt the heat tinge my cheeks.

Doctor Reyes leaned over me, concern on her face as she felt my chest and then directed her ire at the cause. "Mr. Charles, she needs rest!" The doctor looked seconds away from trying to push Malcolm out herself. "I still want her checked on every ten minutes." Reyes sighed, nodding, and Malcolm finally listened, walking out of the room without another word.

He didn't come back after that. Days had gone by, and while my parents had admitted he was still footing the bill, Malcolm was nowhere to be seen. His gigantic bodyguard was everywhere, however. When the doctor finally said that I could get out of bed, I was shocked to see Sloan stationed at my door. I didn't know how long he had been there, but his solemn nod greeted me whenever I peeked out into the hall, regardless of the time of day. Never sleeping and always standing. He had to be a robot.

I had given up trying to convince Sloan he could leave his post, and now only returned his silent greeting whenever I left my room.

I lay in bed staring up at the ceiling, wondering when I could go home, and ignoring the fear that prickled at the base of my spine whenever I thought about leaving the hospital. My pain had lessened, but I still had bruises everywhere, and the stab wound in my side had gotten infected, making me hospital-bound until they could get it under control.

Doctor Reyes said the gunshot wound to my shoulder was just a graze, explaining that it had sliced through a piece of my muscle but hadn't hit anything significant, so I wouldn't need surgery. I swallowed my thoughts about what the doctor thought was significant. I lost a lot of blood, but after the first few touch and go hours filled with transfusions; she was sure I would make a full recovery. Dr. Reyes seemed just as relieved as my family.

I was glad everyone was happy, but I couldn't feel the same. Myra's injury and Jakub's death were both my fault. My carelessness and bravado had ruined people's lives, and I would have to live with that for the rest of mine. After two weeks, I had persuaded my family to go back to work, but I was only alone during the day, with them visiting in shifts in the evenings. Teddy had come a few times as well, but he kept our chats short and stuck to small talk, which I was grateful for because I couldn't handle much else.

The moments alone in my room gave me time to think about everything that had happened and the choices I had made. The trial, the attacks, and Malcolm were a constant loop. I knew I couldn't have a future with a man who lied and cheated to win cases, but the need to see him hadn't gone away, and I didn't know what to do with the useless feeling.

A soft knock at my door roused me from my contemplation, and I smiled at Detective Cruz as he walked toward my bed. "Hey, Ni," he murmured, taking me in and doing his best to curtain his reaction to my black and blue face.

Everyone tried to interact with me like I was my usual self, but I saw my reflection every time I went to the bathroom and knew how much worse it could have been.

"Hi, Cruz." I sat up in bed as he took a seat, and it occurred to me then that I still hadn't spoken to a cop about anything that had happened. The anxiety and fear that rolled around in my stomach made me ask myself if I ever would be ready.

"How are you feeling?" I took a deep breath and nodded. "Better every day. How's the family?" Cruz gave me a smile and, to my surprise, an eye roll. "The oldest is giving me trouble. Wants to be a cop like her old man." I laughed and pretended it didn't hurt.

Veronica Cruz was always giving her father something to worry about. She refused to go to college when she graduated and instead spent a couple of years traveling the world. She had only come back a few months ago. "Well, with you in her corner, I know she'll be in good hands." Cruz shrugged, and his smile slowly turned into a straight line. "So, this isn't just a social call." Cruz eyed me to gauge my response, and I nodded for him to continue. "The detectives on your case have been trying to get in here to talk to you, but they've been running into some interference." I was sure that "interference" was a 6'3 pushy defense attorney.

"So, we agreed I would come in, see how you were doing, and get your account if you were up for it." Cruz looked down at my hands as he spoke, his head tilting.

I released my grip on the sheets with a smile.

"Sure."

He stopped a second, assessing, and then sighed. "If it's too much, let me know. I'll tell the guys to fuck off until you're ready." The urge to hug Cruz came back, and I shook my head. "No, go ahead." Cruz eyed me a second longer and then pulled out a small notepad and pen.

"We can get into the events of the day in a moment, but to finally catch that prick, what they need to know are the details of your escape. Do you know where he took you?" The strong animal smell hit my nose as if I were still there. "It was a storage container. There was a weird smell to it, like it housed horses or pigs."

Cruz scribbled something quickly and then looked back up at me. "Do you remember the color of the outside?" A flash of me staring at Malcolm as the ambulance doors closed conjured up in my mind. I didn't think I had seen him before waking up in the hospital, but I must have.

He looked terrible in his expensive but rumpled suit, and the tears on his face made my heart stutter. The memory replayed, and his pain became clearer each time. "Naomi?" I blinked, and it was gone. Cruz gently tapped my wrist, and I looked back at him but couldn't muster a smile. "Blue and white." He tapped my wrist again before writing the new information and then took out his phone, presumably to relay what I said to the detectives on my case.

When he was done typing, Cruz put his phone away and readied his pen again. "Okay, better plan: let's start with what we know and work our way out from there. I found better footage of the car from the night of your car accident. While the vehicle's windows were heavily tinted, I zoomed in enough to see the top of the windshield wasn't as dark as the rest of the car. The driver was wearing a mask, but the initials GW were scrawled all over the passenger seat, and luckily, the seat cover was gaudy enough that after some research, I found a custom place that remembered making them. I tracked the former owner, George Wilson, who sold the car to a repair shop when it wasn't worth fixing."

Cruz's face turned grim. "I called you a few times on my way up to Fresno to talk to the owner of the shop. I didn't know about the attack at your house until afterward." I tapped his hand resting on the bed. "I'm okay." Cruz grunted but kept going.

"The shop was owned by Craig Keates, Dorian's father. He knew nothing about what his son was up to, but that's how Dorian got the car. I called it in to arrest Keates, but you both were already missing." My hands grew clammy at Dorian's name, but I kept my face neutral. Cruz was watching me closely for any sign that I wanted to stop, and I needed to hear everything.

"Did you notice your phone dying quickly throughout the day?" The question caught me off guard, but I nodded. "Once the police got to the docks, they recovered it from the wreckage. We don't know for how long, but at some point Dorian put spyware on the device." The sharp intake of breath I took made my ribs ache. "He could intercept and listen to your phone calls, read your text messages, and track your location." All the moments I spent with Dorian flew through my mind as bile crept up my throat.

How long had he been listening to my conversations? Was he watching while I texted my family? Did he listen to me telling Myra about what happened in Malcolm's office? My tongue tingled, and I swallowed hard to avoid heaving.

When had he done this? Had it been one of the late nights we spent in the office together? At Coleman's home? Had he stolen it from my bag at some point? Questions I might never get the answers to swirled, making my head throb.

"You answered a text from Coleman to meet at the dock, but we've confirmed that Dorian actually sent that message. From the evidence at the scene, we know that Dorian shot and killed Jakub Nowak with a 500 Smith & Wesson, but we haven't been able to recover him or the gun yet. Since the night he went missing, we've had round the clock patrols on his house and his father's shop, but Dorian hasn't returned to either place, or tried to leave the country. It's like he's vanished off the face of the earth." Cruz cleared his throat and rubbed down his beard, leaning in slightly.

"And that's why we need you to fill in the blanks. So, we can catch that asshole." I was having a hard time comprehending Cruz's words as my heart thrummed hard in my chest and my body trembled. Dorian was still out there, and he had gotten close to me so many times before. Could he come to the hospital? My eyes went to the door where I knew Sloan stood just on the other side.

He would keep me safe, *right*? Suddenly, Sloan's massive frame seemed minuscule compared to Dorian's cunning. He had gotten me twice, and he could do it again.

"I'll come back later." Cruz stood, but my shaky hands shot out, grabbing his arm to stop him. We stared at each other, Cruz doubting my mental state while I tried to get ahold of myself. He sat down when I didn't let go, and only then did I release him, tucking my hands under the cover, trying to warm them even though the chill I felt hadn't come from the temperature.

The last thing I wanted to do was talk about that day, but Jakub deserved to be celebrated as a hero, Myra deserved justice, and Dorian would only benefit from my silence and fear.

"I'll tell you everything."

CHAPTER 45

NAOMI

It had been a few days since Cruz had stopped by, but there was still no news on Dorian. On the outside, I was healing slowly every day, but inside it felt like I had never left that shipping container.

Had he really disappeared, or was Dorian hiding out in my dreams, relishing each night that he got to torment me in my sleep? He appeared in the now constant nightmares I had, laughing at how broken he made me and promising that he would see me soon. Dr. Reyes had given me a card for a therapist, and I understood I would need to talk to someone eventually, but I wanted it all to be over first. I needed Dorian in custody.

The memory of stabbing him in the stomach was never far from my mind, and the thought that I should have stabbed him again to make sure he was dead worried me, but not enough to stop wishing I had.

Even in the most heinous cases, the worst I hoped for was life in prison. I used to consider it the ultimate consequence—a person forced to stare at four walls and remember what put them there forever.

The usual decency I had for human life was absent where Dorian was concerned.

.   .   .

The days passed, and my family visited less frequently as work obligations got in the way, and it was nice not having to put on a brave face as much. Since the accident, my emotions had taken on a life of their own, and I found I was either on the verge of tears or they were already falling without my permission.

My stab wound infection had improved enough that Doctor Reyes said I could start walking outside some days, but I went no further than the quick strolls around my floor. The nurses were kind and greeted me by name when they saw me, but didn't chat beyond that, and Sloan was still at my door being his same stoic self.

They all must have been told not to let me use their phones because they would hurriedly stuff them in their scrub pockets when they saw me, like I was a kleptomaniac feining for my next fix.

Sloan was no better, giving his somehow gentle but very blank stare whenever I asked to check the news.

My family all agreed that I didn't need the distraction and going so far as to leave their phones in the car when they came to visit. I resigned myself to eavesdropping on random conversations as I meandered through the halls, hoping that someone cared enough about the Drayman trial to gossip about it within earshot. I usually only overheard speculation about Sloan's relationship status, though.

I had almost talked Teddy into letting me see his phone during one of his visits, but he had changed his mind at the last second, telling me he didn't want to be the reason I got worse, and while I could respect his choice, I politely threw him out.

It was all so ridiculous, but I understood I had scared them all half to death the last time I used my phone.

I settled for the large window in my room that gave me an amazing view of the very boring front parking lot to pass most of the time. I avoided the distinct burgundy Mercedes that sat in the same spot night and day, convincing myself that I was mistaken. It made no sense that Malcolm's car was always there. He had an active case and a life that didn't involve me, and I hadn't seen him once since the night I opened my eyes.

I wanted to ask Sloan about his stubborn boss, but refrained. If Malcolm was at the hospital, he had his reasons for not coming to my room, and I didn't care what they were.

"Hey friend."

I spun around too fast at the sound of Myra's voice and almost tripped over air. She ran to me, her light blue hospital gown wrapping around her legs, but stopped short of trying to keep me upright, remembering about her cast. "Shit, sorry! Are you okay?" I recovered before falling on my face and stood only long enough to fall into Myra's arms.

My best friend was recovering a floor below me, but I hadn't gone to see her.

What happened to Myra had been my fault, and the thought of her placing the blame at my feet where it belonged kept me from venturing to her room even after my parents announced she had woken up a week ago.

I embraced her tightly, tears already falling, and she did the same. "I missed you," I whispered, and she responded with a head nod against my shoulder and a tighter hug with her one good arm. After refusing to let go for way too long, I finally relented and loosened my grip to get a good look at her. The deep circles under Myra's eyes worried me, but I smiled through the concern so she wouldn't catch on.

Hiding the effort it took, I pulled two visiting chairs close together so that we could sit, and coughed through the unease as Myra scooted hers farther away before getting comfortable. "Are you okay?" I asked, and Myra nodded, her smile fake and stiff. "Well, the doctors say that I'm healing faster than expected, but there's still a long way to go to diagnose permanent damage." She shrugged as if the vague prognosis didn't bother her.

"Anyway, I'm fine. How are you?" I sighed but let her change the subject. "I'm... I don't know." I had been saying I was getting better to every person who asked, but the truth was I wasn't, and this was Myra. I didn't want to lie to her. She nodded again, but this time looked right into my eyes like she understood me completely.

"They'll find him, Ni." Her cast was nearest, but she extended out her right hand for me to take, and I quickly did; happy to break through even a little of the stone wall Myra seemed to have built since she woke up. She had been this way when we first met in college too, but I had torn that wall down, and I could do the same to this one.

After a moment, she dropped my hand, but I could still feel the connection. "Have you seen anything in the news?" I ventured hoping I didn't sound too eager. Myra shrugged again, and I frowned. "Sorry, Ni. I've been embargoed." I pursed my lips, but she only shook her head. "I love you, and in any other circumstance, I would give you all the tea, but it's not my news to tell." I wanted to pry and demand who had told her not to speak with me, but I didn't want to ruin the time we had.

"So, did they say when you could go home?" Myra chuckled at my question, but then she threw her head back, closed her eyes, and loudly exhaled. I furrowed my brow but said nothing, waiting to hear whatever was bothering her so much.

"The thing is...well, the thing is, Martin Kline has offered me three weeks on his all-inclusive resort island while I recover." Myra peeked at me and then grinned at my shocked expression.

I sputtered, trying to think of what to ask first. "Are you going? When would you leave? Will he be there too? Are you guys...together?" I decided to ask them all.

"I like him, Ni. I shouldn't because I'm pretty sure he's a terrible person, but I like him, and I don't know what to do." I considered my next words, knowing what it meant to have feelings you couldn't understand for someone you never thought you would want.

"I guess just like him, then."

It was Myra's turn to be shocked. "Seriously? The perfect Naomi Vine thinks I should go for it?" I wrinkled my nose at her description of me. Dorian had called me that. I felt the panic that clawed at my insides whenever I thought of him, but I pushed it away. "I'm not perfect. Incredibly far from it. All I'm saying is that I know firsthand how tangled up feelings can get, and sometimes the best way to handle them is to just let them play out."

Myra's wide gaze turned melancholy. "But what if Martin is just as bad as I think he is? I don't know if I could live with myself if I ignored something because of an attraction." The answer I was ready to give got stuck in my throat. It was a sensible response that Myra should walk away if she wasn't sure, cut ties and move on before the feelings got too strong, but something kept it from having a voice. Instead, I cleared my throat and let the truth slip through.

"Myra, you're a strong, capable woman, and you know what you can handle. If Martin Kline is what you want, then have him. Just make sure he's worth the trouble of having." Myra's eyes glistened as she stared at me, taking in everything I had said. I held back my own tears, not wanting to reveal how hard the words had hit me as well.

A single tear fell before Myra wiped it away with a laugh. "Okay, enough talk about my billionaire, let's talk about yours!" A laugh bubbled out of me as I glanced at the closed door. "Oh, you're not denying it anymore?! Now, we're getting somewhere!" Myra slid our chairs back together and waited for me to talk.

My eyes shot between the door and Myra to convey the importance of inside voices, but she only huffed. "Yes, I saw the incredibly large hunk of a man standing outside your door. What's his name, by the way? He only nodded when I tried to speak to him." I felt the redness of my cheeks reach the tips of my ears and lowered my own voice since my friend refused to do anything with hers.

"His name is Sloan, and I thought you were head over heels for Martin?!" I hissed, and she smiled.

"Infatuated, yes. Blind, no." I held back my laughter but couldn't help the smile I returned. "Back to your man! Where is he?" I sighed, all humor gone at the question I had fought not to wonder myself every day.

"Unlike you, I know Malcolm has done terrible things." Myra narrowed her eyes, and I knew she wanted to give me the same speech I had just given her, but I put up a hand. "And I think I like him anyway. It's terrifying." My best friend's jaw dropped, but the sober admission made me want to curl into a ball.

"There is so much about Malcolm I don't know, but when we're together, it's like the world stops." I grimaced as the tears I was holding back fell. "And when I'm in his arms or even when our eyes meet from across the room, he stops being this rich asshole defense attorney and turns into a man that I could..." I stopped short of revealing a truth I wasn't sure I could accept, let alone talk about.

Myra wiped a tear from my face with her good hand and caught another on her finger. I leaned into my friend's hand, happy to have her by my side again. "That's enough to give him the benefit of the doubt, isn't it? To let him prove he's the man for you?" Myra meant well, but her questions stoked a fire I didn't know existed inside me. I wanted to scream that my man would never lie and cheat people, keep things from me, or not show up when I needed him. My man would have been at my bedside every day, begging for forgiveness and giving me an explanation as to his involvement in my near disbarment and his weird relationship with his father.

He would have earned the relentless desire that coursed through my veins during every waking moment.

Malcolm's absence left me with emotions that he didn't deserve but that I couldn't shake, and the only way I was going to get the answers I needed was to demand them. "You're right." I stood as I spoke and headed toward the door. "I usually am," Myra purred. Before I lost my nerve, I pulled the door open and stuck my head out in the direction I knew Sloan would be.

"Please tell Mr. Charles that I would like to see him today." He gave me his signature nod and swiftly pulled out his phone, deftly typing out a message as if he had been waiting for me to ask, and I closed the door back and stared at my friend, unsure of what I had just done.

CHAPTER 46

MALCOLM

> She wants to see you.

I stared at the text message Sloan had sent me an hour ago, trying to understand what kept me from going to the woman I wanted to see more than anyone else in the world.

I had spent countless hours in this hospital room two floors down from Naomi, never leaving and barely sleeping while she recovered. After a sizable donation, the hospital stopped questioning my sequestered room, and Camden had arranged for some necessities to be brought in when it was clear I wasn't coming to the office anytime soon.

I hadn't laid eyes on Naomi since the night she had woken up and stared at me like she couldn't decide if I was her savior or her undoing, and now she wanted to see me.

Perhaps she had finally decided.

My phone had been buzzing nonstop with interview requests since I went public with everything three days ago. Camden had been fielding calls and questions at the office from the media and our staff, reminding me frequently about his end of the year bonus expectations.

The incessant attention was a necessary nuisance, and I would soon explain it all to our board of directors, who seemed to be in a contest with the press to see who could call me the most.

I had expected push back from Eugene and Langston as

well, but both had been quiet since Naomi's abduction, and Camden confirmed my father hadn't visited the office in weeks, emailing the go ahead for Gabby and the other upper-level associates to handle our high-profile case load.

It wasn't like Langston to stay on the sidelines, especially when he was in a position to win, and coupled with Eugene's silence, trying to predict their motives put me on edge.

The information my father had given me about Dorian was vital to saving Naomi's life, but I wasn't naïve enough to believe it was out of the goodness of his heart. It was a test to see if I cared enough about Naomi to outweigh my hatred of him. I needed to figure out what his next move was now that he had his answer.

I tapped the reject button on another reporter call and stared past the paperwork Camden had just dropped off, not comprehending a thing. Naomi was well enough to bargain with anyone who would listen for phone access, and Sloan kept eyes on her movements, but she made it easy for him by not venturing far from her suite.

The doctors said Naomi was getting better, but what she went through was horrific, and I had told myself many times that if she wanted me out of her life, I would still protect her from afar, vowing that she would never have to deal with anything like this again.

The thought of Naomi's potential rejection did nothing to help uproot my feet from the sterile white floor.

I raised my head at the knock at my door and grimaced when it opened. The staff knew not to come into this room, and I readied to remind whoever it was, but paused when Martin Kline poked his head in like he was lost. My scowl deepened when our eyes met, and instead of leaving, he glided in like he owned the place. His bespoke suit shared the same dark gray that sprinkled his fresh cut fade.

With all the press coverage he was getting, I knew he was five years older than me, and I saw the age in the slight slope of his shoulders and the shallow laugh lines that etched his face as he smiled as if we were old friends. I didn't bother getting up from my desk chair but turned to meet his cordial gaze, waiting to see the point of his intrusion.

He took me in, looking for something as he sized me up, and I returned a bored stare, wondering if he meant to surprise me. If he did, he would be disappointed. I had visited Myra a few times since she had woken up, and she was tight-lipped about the gun strapped security that searched me at her door, but I had Sloan do some digging.

It had taken him considerably longer than usual, but he found out it was Kline who financed the protection but didn't see a connection between him and Naomi's friend other than a recent interview in New York.

Kline didn't advance close enough to tower over me, a smart move, instead stopping close to the lumpy couch I had been calling a bed. He gave it a once over and then turned his full attention back on me. "Malcolm Charles, I'm glad to finally meet you." The small grin on his light brown face didn't reach his eyes, which were busy cataloguing me as if I were an exhibit in a museum. When he was done, he slid his hands into his pockets and met my now irritated stare. "Mr. Kline, I don't believe we have an appointment." I said, not disguising my impatience. He nodded once but didn't heed my thinly veiled dismissal.

"As I'm sure your fixer has told you by now, I have a... special interest in Myra Moore." Kline's gaze was probing, but I didn't break eye contact or give him the satisfaction of an expression. He smiled anyway, like we were having a conversation I wasn't a part of.

"The name sounds fake, don't you think? *Kris Sloan?*

Charles Harrington, his real name, suits him better. Distinguished." My jaw tightened, but I didn't move from my seat. "Are you sure you have the time to be digging around on someone who has nothing to do with you? I heard they're trying for fifty to life in New York." Kline sighed dramatically. "Come on now, you had him looking into me. He had to dig through nine different shell companies to get my name, you know. You've got an eye for talent."

Kline was far more animated in person than he had been on television, and it made it hard to take him seriously. If it weren't for the hard glint in his eyes, I would have found it easy to dismiss him. "Anyway, that's not what I came here for. First, Myra is getting discharged and will travel with me while she heals. I believe I have your woman to thank for that." I raised a brow at the mention of Naomi, the question apparent in my expression. "She spoke to Myra today, and whatever she said changed her no into a yes, so I figured I should speak to her and say thank you in person."

My patience gone, I stood slowly, coming to my full height while taking the time to button my suit jacket. Kline didn't move, but his fake smile got brighter, showing sharp teeth that were too white. "Oh, scary." Kline quipped, giving me a wink and then turning his back, dismissing me like I wasn't a threat as he took in the nearly bare room. "I thought it was only fair since you found yourself in Myra's room more than once since she's woken up." His tone never changed its affable tilt, but I felt the chill in his words.

"I did," was all I responded, annoyed with the frivolous conversation. Kline turned slightly, giving me only the side of his face as he spoke. "Friendly."

The angle was jarring, with only his right eye and half of his mouth visible, and my muscles tightened, my body aware of a danger my mind didn't see. I knew Kline had a reputation for being ruthless. He had risen through the ranks of his adoptive father's finance firm, a man who plucked him out of poverty at ten years old, only to usurp him and sell the company for parts. There were also the many alleged financial crimes pending, where Kline supposedly swindled thousands of rich and blue-collar investors alike out of their money, but all I saw before me was a bored, rich suit who was wasting my time.

"I guess she would be the right person to go to for media advice." For a split second, the one eye he had on me sharpened, all pretense gone, but then he swiveled away from me again, nodding to himself like I had replied. There were a few ways he could have known what Myra and I had spoken about, but the look he gave was a clear message. He had eyes everywhere. "I have somewhere to be." Kline kept roaming like I had said nothing.

"You know, it surprised me to hear you were staying in a separate room from Naomi. From what I've seen in the news, you're obsessed with that woman." He walked around lazily, taking in but never stopping at the reproduced artwork on the walls, or the wardrobe cabinet Camden had demanded for my suits. There was nothing about him that should have signaled my wariness, but as Kline moved, I sensed the ominous current that had steadily filled the room, and I wasn't taking him out of my sight. "I heard you had another bed brought into Myra's room...until she woke up and kicked you out." He should know he's not the only one who could get information.

Kline huffed out a short laugh. "Yes, well, the love of my life is a feisty one. I guess you can relate." The ache in my chest agreed. "But Myra's been an interest of mine for some time. Longer than even she knows, and I don't give up that easy." I frowned at Kline's back. Even if Sloan couldn't find a connection, it was clear Myra and Kline had something that went beyond a simple interview. "You're a little curious, right?" He murmured, his back still to me as he stopped at the large window across the small space.

"Not at all. All *you* need to know is that they'll be hell to pay if Naomi becomes upset because of something you did to Myra." Kline chuckled. "I like you." It was easy to underestimate him. Kline had an impressive mask, but it was slipping, and I had a feeling that was intentional.

"Second, I came to confirm a hunch." Kline turned abruptly, facing me dead on, and awareness sharpened my senses. My expression remained impassive, even as I was beginning to understand why he had really come.

"My people can't find a trace of him anywhere. And they are truly fantastic at what they do, similar to your Kris Sloan." I cocked my head to the side, feigning ignorance as Kline's genial demeanor melted off of him. I watched as he morphed into a different person, his shoulders falling back to a more upright posture, and even the small lines on his face smoothing out.

"No one who touches Myra like that gets to roam free."

The menace in his tone spoke to the darkness inside of me, and while he was crazy if he thought I would tell him a damn thing, I could respect the urge to find Dorian.

"You should speak with the police if you have questions about the investigation." Kline sighed and took a step toward me, and I slid my hands into my pockets to match his stance as we stared each other down. He was at least an inch shorter when he walked into the room, but now that he wasn't pretending, he somehow matched my height.

"As you well know, I'm currently going to trial for crimes I didn't commit, so I lack faith in the judicial system. Anyhow, I was hoping you could give me some better news." I gave him the same fake smile he had given me.

"What news would that be?"

"That he's dead."

Kline searched my face for a reaction to his monotone assertion, but I didn't give him one. "Mr. Kline, as I said, I have an important appointment to get to, and I'm already late." I spoke the next words slowly to ensure he understood. "And stay away from Naomi. She doesn't need your thanks." Kline's smile returned, but his eyes never crinkled. "Yes, I really like you."

With a blink, all his menace disappeared, as if Kline had flipped a switch back to the easygoing billionaire. "Don't worry; thanks to Naomi, I have a plane to catch, so we won't get to meet. But she will receive a dozen bouquets of roses. The least I could do."

With a click of his tongue, he dismissed himself, walking toward the door. "See you at the next family get together, brother."

Martin Kline waved without looking back, leaving the door open and me standing alone, wondering what the hell that man was. Human didn't seem to fit.

CHAPTER 47

MALCOLM

I walked down the hall leading to Naomi's room, noticing the roses that decorated the nursing stations as I passed. Sloan had blocked Kline's delivery as instructed, and the staff looked happy for the floral surprise.

I looked down at my own flowers I had gotten for her and thought again if I should have bought more. Naomi loved to bring up how rich I was, but hadn't yet seen the full extent of my wealth. I knew my tax bracket bothered her, and if she gave me another chance I wouldn't hold back, but for now I would play it safe.

Sloan nodded when I made it to him, a hint of a smile on his usually unreadable face. "You can take a break. But we need to speak later." He left without a word, leaving me standing at Naomi's closed door. Sloan wouldn't be thrilled that Kline found his real name, but the finance mogul didn't seem inclined to use the information, and I knew we would handle it if it became an issue.

The nurses pretended to be working, but I felt their eyes as they whispered at the closest station. I could barely hear them past the blood rushing through my ears.

I knocked on the door once and clutched the deep red roses too hard as I waited for her to tell me to come in. Stepping forward at her soft reply, I shut the door behind me, allowing myself a few more seconds before I met her eyes.

I hadn't heard Naomi's voice in weeks, and even that tiny sound made my head spin. This woman was my addiction, and I was still amazed that her mere presence made life worth living again.

When it got too weird not to, I turned to see Naomi standing by her bed, her hospital robe tied tight around her waist. The swelling had faded significantly around her face, allowing her perfect brown eyes to show all the emotion she tried to hide.

She glanced from me to the roses, and only then did I remember I had brought the damned things. I closed the distance between us and extended them out to her, and she grasped the paper wrapped stems without a word, leaning in slightly to smell them.

"Did you get these from outside?" She asked, her eyes still strategically on the flowers. I was going to kill Kline. "No," was all I could muster through clenched teeth. Naomi's small smile, which she was trying to hide in the petals, hinted that she was teasing me, and undeserved hope sprang in my chest.

"You look better." Naomi side-eyed me as if I were lying, turning away and going to her bedside table where other flowers sat from her family's previous visits. She scooted them over to make room for mine, and I watched her in silence and tried to be patient, knowing she used them as an excuse to put some space between us.

Finally, she turned back to me but stayed where she was. "I want the truth. All of it. You lie to me, you leave, got it?" Naomi looked ready for a fight, like we were in a courtroom and not a hospital, and I couldn't help my smirk.

"Got it." She looked at my mouth for a split second and then frowned before meeting my eyes again.

"Has your firm ever been involved in illegal dealings concerning cases?"

"Yes."

Naomi sucked in a sharp breath.

"In the past, before I took over, yes." She let the breath go, but still eyed me suspiciously.

"The past? You weren't involved in the witness tampering for the Drayman case?"

"Me? No."

Naomi's eyes flicked to the side as if she had already finished talking to me. "But my father, in a way, yes. And Drayman, definitely." Her apparent interest made me keep going. "Evidently, my father had been paying for information from Dorian for years, but since Coleman had taken him off the case, Langston had no need for him anymore." I noticed the tiny twitch in Naomi's shoulders at hearing Dorian's name, and I was glad I had savored my time with him.

"That asshole took it upon himself to find the Stone family and talked to Drayman. My father knew afterward and did nothing about it, but he didn't initiate it." Naomi seemed to weigh my explanation against something in her mind, but she didn't tell me to leave, so I took it as a win.

"And you knew nothing about it at all? Not even after Jack lied?" I wanted so badly to say I didn't, but she had made her terms abundantly clear, and I was hiding enough already. I took a step toward her as I spoke, not above using our connection to keep her from throwing me out.

"You would never coerce a witness, so as soon as Jack said you did, I knew something was wrong." It was an omission, and by the look on Naomi's face, she would not let me get away with it. "And?" I took another step. "And after the trial, Langston told me you were being set up." Naomi folded her arms in front of her, and the natural movement made my dick leap to attention.

How on earth did I ever think I could walk away from her?

"So, you knew what the reporters were saying was false, how the accusations could be the end of my career, but you didn't stop it? Or even come and check on me?" Her hurt expression took all the arousal from me.

"I was ashamed. Langston didn't know about the press release. It was all that asshole's idea, but once it broke, I *felt* like the worst decision you ever made, and I didn't know how to fix it."

"Without hurting your firm, you mean?"

The venom in her words hit the intended target, and I had to look away. Seconds of silence ticked by, and when I looked back at Naomi, there were tears in her eyes.

"You're right. I couldn't see beyond my need to keep my father under control and put Charles and Charles back on top where it belongs." I didn't need to tell her where I was the night she was attacked. Another omission.

Naomi looked up at the ceiling to stop the tears from falling, but they didn't listen, so she quickly wiped them away before staring back at me. "What is going on between you and your father?" The plea in her eyes loosened my clenched jaw, and I realized that this was what had stopped me from coming sooner. I didn't want to talk about my family, but Naomi was too clever not to have sensed the divide between my father and me. Still, if she was truly considering me, I didn't want her to know how fucked up I was.

At my silence, Naomi's tone turned stern. "I mean it, Malcolm. Answer or go." My mind raced to come up with an excuse; a reason to keep her in the dark but still mine. The look in Naomi's eyes told me I had less than a second, and my lips were moving before I could come up with one.

"When I was in the sixth grade, I found Langston cheating on my mom in our home." Naomi's eyes widened, but I kept going before the pity could solidify in them. "Until that moment, I idolized him and believed it when he said he'd made a mistake. He begged me not to tell my mother, and I listened." Naomi's arms went to her sides, and I thought about stopping there, but the words wouldn't stop. "Until I found him on three other occasions, all with the same woman. Our head housekeeper. After that, I became a problem child. I didn't want to hurt my mother, but the secret was eating me from the inside, and I got into fights at the prep school I was attending."

It was the same school Avery now attended. "One night, after two years of pompous therapists, tension filled family dinners and several large donations to the school board so I wouldn't get expelled, my grandfather sat me down and demanded an explanation." I was avoiding Naomi's sad eyes, instead focusing on the wall behind her to get through what I needed to say before my emotions got the better of me.

"I told him the truth, that Langston was cheating on his beloved only daughter, and his response was to ship me off to boarding school." My bitter laugh didn't help the rage that was building, but I couldn't stop. "Being away from my father helped, and I got into the routine of taking trips over summer break so I wouldn't have to see him. It wasn't until after my sophomore year of college, when my mom begged me to come home, that I did." The memory of my mother's tight hug and elated face when I saw her for the first time in years made my stomach turn. I had taken that happiness from her.

"I thought I could handle being around my father again, but I was wrong. We got into one of our usual fights, but this time I was stronger. It almost got physical until my mother broke down crying." I closed my eyes and took a deep breath, trying not to succumb to the pain the memory always brought up. "Malcolm." When my eyes focused back on the room, I realized Naomi was much closer now, within arm's reach, but she didn't touch me.

"I couldn't take it anymore, so before I left for my junior year I told her the truth." Anger burned inside me as the rest of the story stayed on the tip of my tongue.

It held dangerous truths that ensured I never forgave my father, but it also wasn't something Naomi would take well. Her sympathy was apparent in her features, but she still seemed guarded. When I didn't continue, she sighed.

"What you went through was terrible, and I'm so sorry that you grew up like that." I could hear the but she was trying to soften and waited. "But why would you join his firm if you hate Langston so much?" I withheld the urge to smile at this intelligent woman who wasn't going to let me off the hook because I told her about my fucked up childhood and thought back to what Kline had said. Feisty was definitely my type.

"I wanted to ruin the one thing he loved. Take his firm out from under him and watch Langston Charles fade into obscurity." I watched carefully as Naomi took in my explanation, understanding how it sounded. "That's..." she trailed off, walking backward as she held my gaze.

The long stretch of silence as we stared at each other worried me, but I covered it with a smile. "It's true that I hate my father, but my revenge, the firm, all of that means nothing if I have to sacrifice you." Naomi's brow knitted, and I knew she was overthinking. I slid my hand into my pocket and retrieved the other gift I had brought for her, hoping the device would confirm my intentions and serve as a necessary distraction.

Naomi's eyes widened at the brand-new phone I held, but hesitated when I extended it out for her to take. "Aren't you wondering what's been going on with the Drayman case?" That got her to grab it and hastily turn it on, and I was glad I had already set everything up because she instantly went to the news app, not having to go further than the front page to see what I had done.

The heat in her twinkling eyes when she looked up at me made every decision I had made in the last two weeks worth it. I was happy to die right then and there because Naomi looked proud of me.

CHAPTER 48

NAOMI

I looked back down at the headline, bewildered even as hope sped up my heart.

WITNESS TAMPERING ON THE SIDE OF THE DEFENSE, NOT PROSECUTION IN DRAYMAN CASE

I skimmed the article, too excited to slow down, but quickly gathered that Jack had come forward to give a revised statement, saying not only had I never told him to lie, but that Drayman had paid his family to blame me during the trial.

There was also a tiny blurb about Dorian being involved, but it was vague and skipped quickly to his attacking me over apparent jealously. I stopped reading after I saw that the court remanded Drayman to prison without bail and that the Charles and Charles firm had dropped him as a client.

I looked up at Malcolm again, and the smile he gave me took my breath away.

"You did this?" I pushed out the words in a whispered rush and then had to look back down again because I still couldn't believe it.

"The story has been running in every news outlet for a few days now." He said, and I clicked off that article and went to the search engine to see that he was right. Different variations of the same headline were everywhere, but I slowed my enthusiasm as I realized each one mentioned the defense.

"What about your reputation?" I asked, and Malcolm only shrugged. It almost looked genuine, but I caught the tension in his clenched fists. "This was the only way to completely clear your name. The firm will be fine in time." I didn't know what to say to that, so I went back to scrolling through the articles until I came to one that made my stomach turn.

DORIAN KEATES STILL MISSING AFTER THE BRUTAL MURDER OF UBER DRIVER AND KIDNAPPING ASSAULT OF PROSECUTOR NAOMI VINE. COPS STILL HAVE NO LEADS.

The way they had dismissed Jakub as only an Uber driver and hadn't mentioned Myra was infuriating. Just me and worthless speculation about Dorian and my relationship. My family wasn't wrong; the news was sickening.

I felt Malcolm close the small space between us, and I glanced up to see him too close, his body heat doing a much better job of warming me than the hospital robe. He glanced at the article I was reading, his mouth turning into a grim line. "Don't worry, a piece featuring Jakub's family will come out soon." The sharp intake of breath I took made my head spin, but I didn't care as I stared up at the man I thought I had figured out.

"Myra didn't want to be in the news if she could help it but gave me a few friendly reporters' names." A million questions formed on my tongue, but Malcolm was still talking. "I got a look at the police report, so I know you would want to talk about him. If you would like to make a statement for the article, we can arrange a short meeting."

Malcolm's dark brown eyes fastened on mine, and I couldn't look away. "Jakub's story will be told, Naomi. I promise." The man I had tried so hard not to want appeared to have transformed overnight. He was saying all the right things, and I wanted to believe that I had been wrong about him the whole time.

But what about his father and Malcolm's need for revenge? When he spoke about Langston, his eyes had turned dark and distant, and the hurt from his past was clear on his face. I wanted to tell him it wasn't healthy to hold on to so much anger and pain, but who was I to talk when I spent hours imagining the deadly things I wished I could've done to Dorian so he wouldn't be out there somewhere possibly plotting his return?

Malcolm's eyes narrowed on me, and I realized I had zoned out of the conversation. My knees wobbled as I tried to move too fast to get away from his observant gaze, but his hand was around my waist in the next second, holding me flush to his chest.

The rhythm of his steady breathing soothed my rapid heart, and I gave up trying to wiggle free, instead savoring his dark, spicy scent and allowing my nerves to calm. It felt good to be in Malcolm's arms, and I wasn't sure I wanted to deny that anymore.

"I want to be with you," he whispered, and I rested my chin on his chest and saw the question in his eyes.

I thought my mind would go blank as it had done in the many other situations when I found myself cornered by Malcolm Charles, but this time it showed me every memory with him, making them crystal clear.

He wasn't perfect, but neither was I, and if I was going into this situation knowing who he was, I could handle whatever came next.

Before I let the words tumble from my lips, a question popped into my head.

"That's it? There's nothing else you should tell me?" Malcolm tilted his head just slightly, but didn't speak. I lifted off of him, but he kept me in place with both of his arms around me. "Because if there is, tell me now, Malcolm. If you lie or keep something from me again, I'll be done. Forever."

I caught the clench of his jaw, but then he released it just as fast. Doubt, cold and sharp, swirled in my stomach for a few harrowing seconds, but then he placed a finger under my chin and came down, bringing our lips a whisper apart.

"No more secrets."

As I searched his eyes, the doubt fell away, and my heart wanted to burst out of my chest with the words I was scared to say. "I want to be with—" Malcolm's lips were on mine before I could finish my sentence, and my arms went around his lowered neck at the welcome interruption.

He held me close to him, gentle but firm, as if he didn't want to hurt me but didn't want me to escape either. I smiled into our kiss, and Malcolm only deepened it, making the world and all our troubles melt away.

And when it was just us, here together after all we had been through, I could finally admit the truth to myself.

Like wasn't a big enough word for what I felt for Malcolm Charles.

∾

Thank you for reading!

Reasonable Doubt is book one in the Doubt Trilogy. Book two out in 2026!

. . .

Malcolm and Naomi have more story to tell, but if you're enjoying their chaotic journey so far, consider leaving a review!

ABOUT THE AUTHOR

Jasmine Cassidy is an emerging author of Black romance. This is Jasmine's first published novel, and the first book in the Doubt Trilogy. The second book, Benefit of the Doubt is out in 2026!

You can keep up with all things Jasmine on her website jasminecassidy.com where you will find the latest updates on releases, cover reveals, and snippets of new chapters. Follow her on socials as well!

 instagram.com/authorjasminecassidy
tiktok.com/authorjasminecassidy